Praise for the novels of Kimberly Belle

"Absolutely superb. Kimberly Belle is the queen of domestic suspense, and *Stranger in the Lake* is her darkest, most hypnotic work to date."

—Cristina Alger, *New York Times* **bestselling author of** *Girls Like Us*

"*Stranger in the Lake* is a spellbinding tale of lies and deceit that unfolds piece by devastating piece. Another outstanding novel by Kimberly Belle, masterfully written to lure you in and never let go."

—Samantha Downing, *USA TODAY* **bestselling author of** *My Lovely Wife* **and** *He Started It*

"Clear your calendar because once you've started Kimberly Belle's utterly engrossing *Stranger in the Lake*, you won't be able to tear yourself away! Old and new secrets abound in this tense and atmospheric thriller that will make you question how well we can really know anyone, and how much we might be willing to forgive for those we consider family."

—Kathleen Barber, author of *Follow Me*

"Belle's latest is another riveting, superbly written, didn't-see-that-coming thriller that will keep you up way past your bedtime.... Tension build[s] on every page."

—Kate White, *New York Times* **bestselling author of** *Have You Seen Me?*

"Belle explores the shocking depths people will go to keep their secrets buried in her latest slow-burn thriller *Stranger in the Lake* before building to an explosive and unexpected finale. A must-read!"

—Mary Kubica, *New York Times* **bestselling author of** *The Other Mrs.*

T0043034

Also by Kimberly Belle

MY DARLING HUSBAND

KIMBERLY BELLE

PARK ROW
BOOKS

PARK
ROW ™
BOOKS ™

Recycling programs
for this product may
not exist in your area.

ISBN-13: 978-0-7783-1156-0

My Darling Husband

This edition published by arrangement with Harlequin Books S.A.

Park Row Books
22 Adelaide St. West, 41st Floor
Toronto, Ontario M5H 4E3, Canada
ParkRowBooks.com
BookClubbish.com

Printed in Italy by Grafica Veneta

To Frans and Saskia, with love.

Hopefully one day soon you'll be reading this book in Dutch.

MY
DARLING
HUSBAND

THE INTERVIEW

Juanita Moore: Mr. Lasky, thank you for speaking with me today, and sharing your story with *Channel 7 Action News*. I know rehashing what happened to your family can't be easy for you to talk about.

Cam Lasky: [squinting] Do you mind turning those lights down?

Juanita: Those lights are necessary for our viewers to see your face, and people are clamoring to see you. You haven't spoken to the media for months now, and for those of us who have been following your story, we are eager to hear it from your own lips, a firsthand account of what happened and how you've survived the months since. You've become quite the celebrity, though—

Cam: I believe the proper term going around socials these days is *celebrity asshole*. Can I say that on TV—asshole? We're not live, are we?

Juanita: No, we're not live. My editors will cut that one out, but if you wouldn't mind keeping your answers PG, it will save them a lot of work later.

Cam: [doesn't respond]

Juanita: As I was saying, the narratives that have come out since the home invasion haven't exactly painted you as a hero of this story. You are the aggressor, the fraudster, the money-hungry villain.

Cam: Too bad I don't have a mustache or I'd twirl it.

Juanita: Here are just a few of the stories circulating about you: that you're involved in the mob, the head of a satanic cult, that your kitchens served as clandestine meeting spots for a ring of international child traffickers—

Cam: Now, that last one's just ridiculous. And absolutely un-true. They all are.

Juanita: But still. Having all these unfavorable stories written about you must feel…

Cam: Invasive. Intrusive. Annoying. People love to make stuff up, don't they?

Juanita: I meant the criticism.

Cam: [shrugging] I'm used to it by now.

Juanita: The BBC did a series on America's biggest grifters and cited you as a classic example of an American businessman who will stop at nothing to succeed. Netflix is currently in talks to resurrect the show *American Greed*, with your story dominating their first three episodes. And a poll floating around Facebook last month declared you the most hated man in America behind Pharma Bro, Martin Shkreli.

Cam: Well, since Facebook says it, it must be true.

Juanita: And yet for months now, you have refused to talk to the media. Our many phone calls and emails and texts were left unanswered. You threatened legal action if my producer or I didn't leave you alone.

Cam: All true.

Juanita: Until yesterday, when out of the blue you contacted me to request an interview. You were quite insistent, in fact. Why is that?

Cam: Well, I guess I figured it was time to set the record straight.

JADE

2:51 p.m.

I'm pulling into the Westmore Music Academy lot when I spot him, the man leaning against the building's brick and carved concrete sign. Pocked skin. Black-rimmed glasses. Skinny shoulders hunched against the rain. Atlanta is getting plowed with the tail of a tropical storm stalled over the gulf, blasting soupy heat all the way up to Tennessee, and he's wearing that same cracked leather coat like it's January and not early August, his hands shoved deep in the pockets as if for warmth.

I gun it up the hill hard enough to make my tires squeal, tapping a button on the steering wheel. "Call Cam."

While the call connects, I glance in my side mirror, trying to pick him out of the trees and shrubs.

The grocery store. The nail salon and yoga studio. Yesterday at Starbucks, he passed me a stevia packet before I could ask for one, which makes me wonder how many times he's seen me there, stirring sweetener into my coconut latte.

Cam's deep voice booms through the car speakers. "I'm in the middle of something. Can I call you in thirty?"

My husband always answers, even when he's busy. *Especially* then. This is our steadfast rule ever since our oldest, Beatrix, took a spill on the playground when she was four, knocking herself out and breaking her arm in three places. Cam was in the middle of a renovation at the Inman Park restaurant at the time, covered in construction dust and arguing with contractors whose every other word was *over*. Overdue, overworked, over budget. Thirty times I called him that day, frantic and bouncing in the back of an ambulance while comforting a scared child and trying to keep a fussy toddler on my lap. Cam didn't feel his phone buzzing in his back pocket, didn't notice the screen lighting up with a long line of increasingly desperate messages from me.

The last one I left as they were wheeling Beatrix into Children's Healthcare.

"Your daughter is in the hospital, Cam. Maybe pick up your phone and call us sometime."

Mean and petty, I know, but I've never been so furious. Or so stressed. Or so downright petrified.

Beatrix was fine. Cam and I, however, lost five years of our lives that day.

Now I say to Cam, "He's here."

"Who's where?"

"That guy. The skeevy one I told you about, with the glasses and the comb-over man bun. He's here at Westmore."

"Well, maybe he has a musically gifted kid."

I roll my eyes, lift my hands from the steering wheel. "Right. And he just happens to go to the same gym as me and shops in the canned goods aisle at Whole Foods whenever I walk through their door."

In the back seat, Baxter leans as far forward as his booster seat will allow. "Hi, Daddy!"

"Hey, buddy. You keeping your mom company?"

Except for his fine mousy waves, our son is a spitting image of Cam. Baxter gives an enthusiastic nod. "She took me to Bruster's, and then she made me get the frozen banana."

And he's still salty about it, too, no matter how many times I explain that food coloring is bad for his six-year-old body, and the scoop of Purple Dinosaur he's constantly begging for is more dye than ice cream. The banana dipped in dark chocolate is our hard-won compromise.

I twist around on my seat and hold a finger to my lips, my next words for Cam: "Of course he doesn't have a musically gifted kid. I'm telling you, Cam. This guy is following me. He *is*."

"Who is?" Baxter says, looking out the back window. "Who, Mommy?"

I ignore him and check my mirrors, all of them, but the man is gone. The line of parked cars, the hill between here and the busy, he's nowhere. Even if I could see the sign from where I'm sitting, there are dozens of people on this stretch of street, pedestrians and runners, employees popping out for fresh air or to the nearby sandwich shops, people socializing on the covered benches. If he's still down there, it would be easy to conceal himself in the crowd.

And yet he made sure I saw him when I was turning into the lot, didn't he? The way he was dressed in all black like some kind of daytime cat burglar, how his shoulders straightened and his head popped up when he spotted my car, how he stared at me through the windshield like he was daring me to see him. Like he *wanted* me to see him and be scared. Maybe *that's* why he's been following me for days.

I gasp as something occurs to me. "Omigod, Cam. What

if it's not me he's after, but the *K-I-D-S*? What if that's why he's been following me all over creation, because he's trying to get to them?"

"Why would he be after the kids?"

I cringe at the way he said the word, already dreading the conversation I'm going to have to have with Baxter later. "I don't know. For ransom. For creepy shadiness I don't want to say out loud because you're on speakerphone. Plus, I don't want to give it energy."

"Saying the words…" Something clangs in the background, metal on heavy metal. Cam waits until the noise dies down. "Saying them out loud doesn't bring something into existence, you know that as well as I do. And why would he be after the kids when there are a thousand other families in this city with fancier cars and bigger houses than ours? I mean, one look at our street and it's clear there are plenty of bigger fish."

"Yeah, but it's your face on the cover of *Atlanta Magazine*." When Cam walks into a place, everything tilts. Heads turn, bodies shift, gazes stick. Going to a restaurant with Atlanta's Steak King is like dining out with a rock star. The waitstaff, the chef, the other patrons in the restaurant—they all come over to bask in Cam's glow.

And Cam knows he's visible, even without his chef's gear. Thick black hair, a square jaw, straight white teeth he flashes often. My husband is handsome, but it's the combination with his height that gets him noticed. Six and a half feet of big, Mediterranean man.

"Go talk to the building's security guard. That's what he's there for."

"And say what? That there was a strange man standing on the sidewalk? The road is public property."

"True, but I'm sure the guard would want to know if one

MY DARLING HUSBAND

of their clients is being stalked. At least give him a description of the creep."

I shiver, the reality of this conversation inching up the back of my neck. Maybe I'm wrong. Atlanta is a big city that can feel like a really small town. I run into people I know everywhere. Maybe this is all some strange coincidence.

I rewind back to the first time I noticed him, a few days ago through the plate-glass window at Kale Me Crazy. There I was, seated alone at the bar with my phone and a smoothie I didn't want, killing an empty hour between playdates and pickup times by scrolling through Pinterest. I was feeling sad and nostalgic for the offices and boutiques I used to design, back before I met Cam. This was before his name became synonymous with Atlanta's high-end dining, before I came up with the sleek stone and metal look that would become a recognizable part of his brand, before I pushed out two babies in three years and closed up shop. But that day, I looked up and he was there, squinting into the sunshine and watching me.

A weirdo, but a random one, I assumed—until I spotted him later at the dry cleaner, at the deli across from my yoga studio, at the Starbucks and the canned goods aisle of the grocery store.

And now here he is again, today.

At my child's music school.

My skin prickles with alarm.

"I'm sure it's nothing, but next time you see this guy, point your phone at his face and tell him you're streaming live to Twitter. If it doesn't scare him off, you'll at least have a visual to show the guard."

His voice gets sucked up into more clanging, followed by a heavy crash and multiple voices, all of them shouting. I realize it's been like this since the start, his voice pushing through loud and chaotic background noise.

"Babe, why does it sound like you're at fight club?"

"I'm at the shop on Bolling Way. There was a fire."

My stomach drops at his words. Bolling Way is Cam's signature restaurant, a booming scene surrounded by Buckhead's finest stores, a place that's packed from noon until midnight.

"How bad was it?"

"On a scale of one to ten? Four hundred and fifty-seven." He sighs, and it occurs to me that the concern I thought I heard in his voice wasn't for me and the kids, but disaster at his most profitable restaurant. A torched Buckhead kitchen means a big, giant hole in our income. "I'm here with Flavio. We're talking through our options."

Flavio is the location's general manager, and Cam's highest paid employee.

I'm opening my mouth to respond when I spot the clock on the dash: 3:01. A whole minute late, and to pick up a child who loses her shit at the tiniest adjustment to her daily schedule. "Oh crap, gotta go. Call me later."

I hang up, swipe my bag from the floor and Bax from the back seat, and race to the double glass doors of the building, looking over my shoulder the entire way.

I look for him after. Instead of turning left for home, I point my car right, steering past the spot where I saw him last, leaning against the sign. Four times I hold up traffic to search him out of the crowd, twice headed in the wrong direction, then two more times on the drive back past the building. I press my iPhone to the window and ride the brake the entire time, creeping by the entrance to the lot so slowly that more than one impatient driver honks.

But he's not there. The patch of trampled grass by the sign is empty. The man-bunned man is gone.

Baxter pushes up in his booster seat, straining to see out the window. "Mommy, where are we going?"

"We're going home." I'm headed in the right direction, but my hunt took too long. Now we're stuck in traffic.

"Then why do you keep turning around?"

"And why are you going so slow?" Beatrix adds before I can explain. She swipes a wet finger down the back window, pointing at two women speed walking past us. "Are you sure we're not going backward?"

Beatrix knows we're not going backward, but she enjoys being a smart-ass. Too clever for her nine years. Too sassy and energetic, too, and as tightly wound as the composite core strings on her DZ Strad violin—at least that's according to her teachers.

And as much as I love my daughter, they're not wrong. Beatrix has been a handful since the second she came into this world, bloodred and hopping mad. Colic. Sleeping issues. Sinewy muscles that hated to be swaddled. My pediatrician called her a high-needs baby, patted me on the shoulder and promised me most grow into normal, well-adjusted kids.

Something that for Beatrix will never happen.

My daughter is a musical genius, something I accidentally discovered when she was four, when after a quick dash through Fresh Market she hummed a perfectly pitched concerto all the way home. A few weeks later at Target, she picked out the melody with two chubby fingers on a keyboard, but it was the pink toy violin she begged to take home. Within a few months, I managed to find a teacher willing to give formal lessons to such a young student. The woman, a stern grandmotherly type, emerged from their first session pink-cheeked and throwing around the word *prodigy*.

My Beatrix is special. Thanks to an accident of fate and chance and random genes, she will never grow into that normal child the pediatrician promised. She has this astonishing, one-in-a-million gift, but one that comes with an ear that hears her every mistake. A perfectionist with mile-high standards for herself, quick to become frustrated and anxious when her fingers don't cooperate.

But when they do, it is magical.

I grab two packets of Goldfish from the glove compartment, then pass them to the back seat. We're only a few miles from home, but I have learned to always come prepared. Juice boxes, snacks, iPads with every movie known to man. I'm not above parenting by distraction.

"Help Bax open his, will you?" I say to Beatrix, but I'm too late. They're already playing tug-of-war with the bag.

"Give it to me. I can open it on my own." Baxter kicks the back of my seat in protest.

"You can't do it by yourself," Beatrix says, her voice matter-of-fact. "You're too little."

"I'm not little! Give it here." Baxter swipes at the bag, but his big sister is too strong. He can't pry the packet from Beatrix's fingers. "Mommy, Beatrix won't give me my Goldfish. Make her give me my Goldfish!"

This happens hundreds of times a day, relentless bickering over anything, everything, nothing.

I take a deep, deep breath and try not to death-grip the steering wheel. How does this happen? How can it be that I spend every second my kids are out of sight missing them terribly, picturing their adorable little faces all day long, seeing their sweet smiles, imagining the feel of their bony arms around me, then I have them for ten minutes in the car and I'm counting the seconds until bedtime.

"Miss Juliet says you worked on a new piece." I stuff my words with enthusiasm and smile into the rearview mirror, trying to catch Beatrix's eye under those tousled white-blond curls, a cloud of a million tiny ringlets she wishes would lie flat like her brother's.

The distraction works. Beatrix sighs and lets go of the crackers. "Yeah."

"That's great. Which one?"

"*Fantaisie Impromptu*. But I think I want to play the piano."

I can't help myself; I laugh. School starts in two weeks, and thanks to Miss Juliet's nonnegotiable requirement for a minimum of three hours of daily practice, our schedules are already packed. With Beatrix's ear, she could probably pick up a new instrument quickly, but still. "When on earth would you find time to practice the piano, too?"

"Not 'too.' I want to play the piano *instead* of the violin."

I roll to a stop at the intersection, and my foot punches the brake a little too hard. I lurch against the seat belt and twist around on my seat. "Don't be ridiculous. You can't quit the violin."

Beatrix hears the horror in my voice. We all do. Even Baxter stops tugging on his Goldfish wrapper and waits for his sister's answer.

"Why not?"

"You know why." It's something we talk about often, how this spectacular gift comes hand in hand with a spectacular responsibility. "You can't throw away all the work you've done. You just can't."

"Says who?"

"Says me. Says your father and Miss Juliet. You're a violin prodigy."

She frowns and drags her gaze to the window. "I hate that word. I wish people would stop saying it."

I stare at my daughter's profile, trying to puzzle out if there's anything fueling this sudden change of heart, or if her announcement is for shock value only. Ever since that day in the toy aisle at Target, Beatrix's musicality has felt equal parts exhilarating and consequential, an all-encompassing talent that means my daughter's most important relationship is with an inanimate object. I've tried very hard to make sure she doesn't miss out on friends and school and normal, nine-year-old life, fighting traffic to squeeze in playdates and birthday parties when really she should be practicing, but quit? Put down the violin and let all that talent and hard work go to waste?

Like hell. Not going to happen.

The car behind me honks, and I turn back to the road.

"Mommy, what happens when a kangaroo jumps on a trampoline?" Baxter says apropos of nothing, his voice light and carefree. The pureness of him melts my heart.

"I don't know, baby. He jumps even higher, I guess."

But Beatrix is still feeling combative. "No, he doesn't."

"Yes, he does."

"No, he *doesn't*. Mo-om."

I'm still debating how to handle Beatrix's little bombshell when I slow to a stop in front of the house, an ivy-covered brick-and-stone high atop a hill, to grab the mail. I keep pestering Cam to put a lock on the mailbox, something to stop strangers from digging through our post, but he hasn't made the time.

Why bother? he said last I mentioned it. *All the important things are digital these days.*

I flip through the stack, junk mail and flyers folded around a lone bank statement. Not that there's much in this one; it's for the debit account, which we run down every month. But the point is, not everything is digital. If anyone wanted to know how much money we have in any of our accounts, all they'd have to do is rifle through our mail.

I drop the papers in my bag, steer the car up the driveway and press the button for the gate while behind me on the back seat, things are escalating. Baxter punches Beatrix. Beatrix pulls Baxter's hair in retaliation. Both kids scream and cry.

I pull into the detached garage on the back side of the house, slam the car into Park and hit the remote for the garage door.

Later, this is the moment I will keep coming back to, in our windowless garage with only one flickering lightbulb on the mechanical box above my car, the darkness descending as the big door rumbled to a close. To the smell of dirt and oil and something foreign, something that didn't quite belong but that I dismissed as carried in on the wind. To the chaos of holding my shit together while dragging two squirming children out of the car, of gathering up juice boxes and crackers and empty wrappers, of strapping backpacks and instrument cases to little shoulders because they're big kids now and Mommy shouldn't have to carry everything herself.

To how I was too busy, and far too distracted to see the body in the far corner.

How I didn't hear his rubber soles hitting the concrete floor, or notice the dark smudge of the man stepping out of the shadows.

How I didn't register any of it, not until it was too late.

JADE

3:18 p.m.

I see the black figure in the shadows, and my first thought is of the kids, an immediate, full-throttle alarm that comes on like a freight train. This is parenthood in a nutshell: utter terror for your children's welfare, always. It's something Cam and I never thought about back when we were trying to get pregnant—the overwhelming insecurity when the doctor settled our babies into our arms, the unrelenting worry whenever they're not near. I spot movement and I reach for them at the same time—instant and instinctual. My brain identifies a person, a male-sized form that does not belong here, and I shove their little bodies behind mine.

A man, looming in my garage. Breathing the same air.

I don't move. I can't. No fight. No flight. I just stand here, transfixed, dumbstruck, stock-still.

I think of my phone, buried under the mail and trash in my bag. I think of the panic button on the alarm pad in the house, on the other end of a breezeway and tucked safely behind a locked door. I think of my keys, next to my phone. Even if I managed to get us out of this garage, where would we go? I'd never make it inside the house, and the backyard is fenced, the gates either electronic or secured with a complicated, child-safe latch. There's nowhere to escape.

"Don't move. Stay quiet and I won't hurt you."

The voice is so frighteningly close. Hoarse, rattling in air hot with my sticky fear, and I don't believe a single word. Especially not when he steps closer, and I get a better look. The man is wearing a mask. He's holding a gun, a stubby black thing in a fist. Head-to-toe black, every bit of him covered, even his hands. His fingertips.

Run. I scream the word in my head, urging myself on. *Grab the children and run.*

Now.

A chill races down my spine. The hairs soldier on my skin. This man is here to hurt me. To hurt *us.*

And still I can't move.

So this is it, then. This is how my body responds when faced with sudden fright, with this hot, sluggish horror— like when your fingers brush over a strange lump under your armpit and you realize your life has veered sideways. Some people run. Others scream. Me, I just stand here, paralyzed by the mounting terror.

The kids, too. They stare at him with big, frightened eyes. A little hand grabs my pants leg.

"Please," I somehow manage to squeak, but I can't finish. *Please don't touch the children. Please don't shoot us.* The words are too horrifying to say out loud.

He moves closer, his gait smooth, but there's something sinister in the way he's walking across the concrete floor. He's like an animal on the hunt, joints loose, ready to pounce. All dangerous, coiled energy lurking just below the surface.

"Take my car." I hold out my bag, a stupidly expensive designer thing from a couple years ago. "The keys are in here somewhere, and so's my wallet. I—"

"I don't want your purse. Don't want your car, either." His voice is deep and scratchy, the kind that sounds filled with cigarette smoke.

My stomach spirals, and I search his face for more, but the parts of him I can see—his lips, his eyes—are closed off. I search for something recognizable, something human I can appeal to, but there's nothing. It's like searching for meaning on a covered canvas.

Still, I take in every detail I can see and commit it to memory. Just under six foot, medium build, broad shouldered. Caucasian. I know this from his eyes, olive green and flecked with amber, the pink patch of skin around his mouth. His teeth are white and straight, the kind of straight that comes from braces.

"Do you want money? I don't have cash, but take my card. My pin is 4-3-0-8."

"Jade. Shh."

My name on his tongue tightens a knot of panic in my gut, and I scurry—*finally*—backward, putting some distance between me and this man, pushing the kids behind me and toward the door.

Stay calm.

Don't panic.

Whatever happens, do *not* let the gunman in the house. That's how people get killed. That's how entire families end up in a pool of blood. As soon as you let the gunman into the house, you're already dead.

I hold out my left hand, offering up my wedding band and

an old, battered Rolex. "I have jewelry. Some money in the safe. Loads of electronics. Go inside and take whatever—"

"*Quiet.* This is how it's going to go. The four of us are going to walk outside and move slowly and calmly to the back door, where we will stand like silent little statues while you dig your keys out of your bag and let us in. No running or trying to get away. No flailing and hollering for the neighbors. And once we're inside, I'd think real long and hard before you tap some secret code that's going to call in the cavalry." His gaze flits to the kids, and one of them—Baxter, I think—squeaks. "It'd be a shame if the cops showed up, wouldn't it, Mom?"

The secret code! A silent alarm that lets the control room know someone has forced his way into the house. The technician who installed it entered a code straight down the middle of the keypad, but Cam and I were supposed to change it because *every criminal on the planet knows the 2-5-8-0 trick.* But did we change it? And if so, to what? My thoughts are too tangled up with terror to remember.

"What do you want?"

"I already told you. I want us all to go inside, quietly. I want you to turn off the alarm without me having to use this thing." He lifts the gun by his head, jiggles it in the air. "I don't want to hurt you or the kids, Jade, but I will. What happens next is up to you."

My mind flips through my options, at gunpoint and with two small children. Fight, one of us gets shot. Run, we get shot in the back. I consider lunging for the gun, sacrificing myself for my babies, but what will happen to Beatrix and Baxter then? I don't know anything about guns. I have no clue how many bullets this one holds. Enough to kill all three of us multiple times, I'm guessing.

"Whatever you want, I'll give it to you. Just please, *please* let the kids go." My voice cracks on the words. Behind me, Baxter starts to cry.

The man puffs a breath, a put-out kind of sigh. "Already you're making this harder than it has to be. I'll tell you everything you need to know as soon as we're inside."

Another wave of his gun urges me onward, but it's hard to move with the kids hanging on my legs like monkeys. I shuffle backward, my heels sliding across the concrete so I don't step on their toes. I don't turn around. I don't dare to. I keep my eyes on the weapon and move back, back, back until there's nowhere left for us to go. The kids and I are pressed up against the door, no air between us.

The man's brow quirks. "You're going to have to actually open it, you know."

And then what—scream? Our neighbors on either side work big jobs, managing big departments at Fortune 500 companies. The Home Depot, Coca-Cola, Delta. They leave before dawn and come home well after dark, but this is a family-friendly neighborhood. It's filled with kids and nannies and stay-at-home moms. If I scream loud enough, surely, *surely* someone will hear.

But first I have to get outside.

I reach behind me with a hand, fumbling for the handle stabbing me in the hip. I have to nudge the kids out of the way first, pushing them toward the patch of wall farthest from the man, between the door and Baxter's tricycle, its front wheel flush against a giant blue bucket filled with sports equipment. It's a tight squeeze, and I kick the bike to move it out of the way, but it doesn't budge. The bucket is too heavy. The space is too tight for all three of us. With my other hand, the one still holding my bag, I shuffle Beatrix to the other side. Her violin case bonks against the wall, an angry sound that makes her flinch.

The flickering lightbulb on the door opener times out, plunging the garage into blackness. Both kids let out a frightened wail. I let go of Beatrix just long enough to feel along the wall for the light switch, and there's movement all around. The kids flailing. The soft breeze of bodies lurching in the darkness. My bag dragging on an arm.

My fingers find the switch, and the lights pop on, a row of ceiling mounts that fills the space with bright, white light. I blink into the sudden light and—

My lungs fill with a scream.

The man has Beatrix. He squeezes her to his chest with one beefy arm. Beatrix hangs there like a rag doll, her little Converse dangling two feet off the ground. She's lost her case in the shuffle. A shoe has come untied, the laces long and dirty and frayed on one end, but all of that bleeds away because there's a gun, the stubby black barrel shoved into a fluffy cloud of Beatrix's hair. Pressed against her temple.

I hold up both shaking hands, reaching for her until the man's glare stops me. He shakes his head and my feet stick to the floor. "Please. I'll do anything. Just...*please*."

Beatrix stares at me in shock, in horror, her silent tears quivering with reflected light.

The man tips his head at the door. "Get us inside without screaming or making a run for it, and—" he glances down at Beatrix "—what's your name, little lady?"

Beatrix gives me a pleading look that pierces me straight through the heart.

"It's Beatrix," I say. "Her name is Beatrix."

"Okay, Beatrix. It's up to your mama now. Tell her to be good, and I'll put you back down as soon as she lets us inside."

His implicit threat, my daughter in a strange man's arms, a gun against her temple—it lights a fire under me. I dig my keys out of my bag, heave it onto a shoulder and Baxter onto a hip, and hurry out the door.

The breezeway is short, nine or ten yards at the most, and I don't bother with so much as a furtive glance at the neighbors' backyards. When we moved in a year ago, Cam overplanted for privacy. The hedges are thick and evergreen and, according to our lawn service, more fit for a forest than a backyard. Even if there were a neighbor home on the other side of all that greenery, which there's probably not, they wouldn't be able to see me, scampering down the concrete sidewalk to the back door with a masked man at my back, and I don't dare call out to whoever's within hearing distance—not with a gun pressed to my daughter's head. There goes that plan.

Baxter clings to me, burying his face in my shoulder. His weight and my shaking hands are making things difficult. I fumble with the key, stabbing the doorknob multiple times before the thing slides into the lock. I twist my wrist and press the knob down with a hip, and the latch releases. The door swings open.

He rushes us into the mudroom and shuts the door.

From the alarm pad on the wall comes a long, shrill beep. I slide Baxter down a leg, and he darts behind me while I tap in the code—the real one, the only one I know for certain will disarm the system. I'm rewarded with three short beeps, the light on the pad switches from red to green, and then…silence.

The man flips the lock on the back door and points to the pad. "Good girl. Now arm it to Stay."

"What?" I hear the man's words, I acknowledge them, but all I can think of is Beatrix, crying silent tears against his chest. I hold out a hand to her, and the man sets her on the ground. She darts around my legs to her brother, both of them using me as a human shield.

"Set the alarm to Stay," he says again. "That way, I'll know if anybody tries to escape."

Shit. If I reset the alarm, that means only two exits, the front door and this mudroom door, that don't immediately trip the alarm. Forget sneaking out the side door or climbing out a window. Either would result in the alarm wailing and bullets flying. *Shit.*

I drop my bag onto the built-in seat above the shoe cubbies, wiping one eye and then the other, buying myself some time, trying to remember if Cam and I ever got around to changing the duress code. I know we talked about it. I know I asked him to. He said he needed a manual, and I asked him if I looked like Google. He laughed and said I was the sexiest Google he ever did see, but did he ever do it? Did he change the damn duress code?

I don't fucking know.

"I wouldn't try it if I were you," the man says, reading my mind. His gaze flicks between me and the pad. "Same as you did just now, 2-9-2-1. If the cops show up in the next five to seven minutes, the kids are first, then you."

I swallow down a sob and tick in the code with quaking fingers, then tap 3 to arm the system to Stay. The tiny light flips back to red, and a cold numbness blooms in my chest and spreads across my skin.

We are locked in the house with a gunman.

CAM

3:21 p.m.

"Everything okay?" I look at Flavio, the best general manager I've got and GM of the charred remains of the steak shop we're currently standing in. He's asked a loaded question if I've ever heard one.

I take in the ruins of my flagship restaurant and remind myself to breathe. Faulty wiring, according to the lead firefighter, and in the worst possible spot, next to a giant tub of cooking oil. One tiny spark in a corner of the kitchen that quickly grew into a fireball, licking up the walls and into the empty space above. The flames crawled across the ceiling into the dining room, where noise absorption panels were spread like a nighttime constellation, custom-made sheets of foam and fabric that rained down sparks and fire. By the time the fire trucks got here, the place was completely engulfed.

"No, I'm not okay. It's like a bomb went off in here. I'm about as far from okay as you can get."

The tables, the chairs, the custom booths and polished cherry bar, the cut crystal glasses, the trio of art deco chandeliers by the entrance that cost $17,500 a pop. Whatever didn't go up in flames was hosed with what must have been fifteen hundred gallons of water. It's like standing in a flooded ashtray.

"I meant with Jade," Flavio says, swiping a hand down his dark beard. Like most men in the restaurant business, he gives his facial hair free rein—the bushier, the better. I used to complain, but these days hell if I care. "That's who you were talking to earlier, right?"

"Oh. Yeah, some creep's been following her around town, but let's tackle one disaster at a time. What the hell happened here? How did it get this bad?"

"Apparently, the noise panels were highly flammable." He points to a spot high on the wall to the kitchen, where the first in a web of panels is now a black, smoky blur. "The flames hit that one and poof. The whole ceiling was gone in a matter of minutes."

I stare at the maze of tangled wires and smoke-blackened insulation that runs along the spine of the building, most of it burned away. The stench, a combination of charred wood and melted plastic, sears like acid in the back of my throat, the inside of my nose, my lungs.

My best moneymaker gone. One hundred and thirteen employees out of a job. Millions of dollars turned to ash.

Flavio kicks a chunk of something aside, burnt wood scraping over glass and stone, a sound I feel in my bones. This place was his main source of income, too.

My chest tightens with a familiar weight. What kind of cocky idiot opens a fifth restaurant when the other four aren't paid off? What was I thinking, taking on responsibility for all those people? Flavio watches me, waiting for a response, and I have no clue what to say. That I never should have given him a job? That only a fool would trust me with their livelihood? I swallow and turn away.

At the front of the shop, two women with blowouts and shocked expressions peer through what's left of the plate-glass window. Thanks to the location in the middle of Buckhead's swankiest shopping district, these ladies are our typical day-time diners. They order hundred-dollar bottles of wine and steak salads they barely touch, and they come in such droves there's a two-week wait for a 12:30 table.

Scratch that—*was* a two-week wait.

I yank my eyes away from their disappointed faces, focusing instead on the markings on a far wall. Two giant sooty wings that swoop up and into the blackened ceiling. The pastry prep station. The stainless steel worktops that once stood there have been shoved to the side, a heap of metal and ash. I flip on the flashlight on my phone and move deeper into the darkness. My footsteps are loud in the hushed space, the broken glass and debris crunching under my shoes.

Flavio doesn't ask what I'm looking at, because he sees it, too.

Ground zero. The source of the blaze.

I take in the ruined chunk of wall, the melted remains of what was once an outlet. Whatever was plugged in there has been burned and melted away. An electrical fire, and in the worst possible place.

"What happened to the alarm?" I say, and I can hear the break in my voice, feel the slow swirl of dread prickling my neck.

The system I paid an obscene amount for, one the salesman guaranteed would protect this place from not just theft but also sudden temperature spikes. And a multiple-alarm fire like this one—the kind that blows out the glass partition between the kitchen and the dining area and pumps a column of black smoke high enough into the early morning sky that some lady walking her dog five blocks away was alarmed enough to call 9-1-1—would come with one hell of a temperature spike.

"How come it didn't go off?"

Flavio steps up next to me, sniffing. "I asked the alarm company the same question. They said they're looking into things and will call me back as soon as they know more. Between you and me, it sounded like they were scrambling."

"Well, keep on them. Get in your car and drive up there for answers if you have to. Threaten to sue their pants off if they don't hurry the hell up. We don't need anything holding up that insurance money."

Flavio shoves his hands in the pockets of his tan fleece, watching me in that quiet way of his. The best thing about Flavio is that he never loses his cool. The worst thing about Flavio is that he never loses his cool.

"Okay, so worst-case scenario," I say. "How long to get this place back up and running—four months? Five?"

"Probably more like seven or eight."

I do the math in my head. The average weekly revenue times thirty-two weeks, and—

"That's more than four million dollars!"

"Four point three, but yeah. I get it. It's a lot."

Flavio *doesn't* get it. He has no idea how, without the income this place generates, I will have to do triage the next time payroll comes around. How thinking about the invoices in my inbox makes my lungs lock up and my heart pound and my vision go dark around the edges. He doesn't know about last week's trip to the emergency room because I thought I was having a heart attack. I haven't told anyone about that, not even Jade. Especially not her.

At the thought of Jade, my heart double taps, and I suddenly can't catch a breath. "What time is the insurance guy coming?"

"I'm waiting on him to provide an ETA. When I talked to him earlier, he was more concerned about the short in the wiring. He called it peculiar for a building this new. That's the word he used, *peculiar.*"

I stand perfectly still despite the emotion cramping my gut. *Peculiar* means the inspector suspects foul play. *Peculiar* means attorneys and legal battles and months-long delays before I get my hands on that money.

I think about the second mortgage I just took out on the house, the price tag for Mom's condo fees, Westmore Music Academy and the kids' private school that costs as much as tuition for an out-of-state college, the new SUV we've spent the past two weekends shopping for because Jade's out-of-warranty BMW is too expensive to keep. With my best revenue source going up in literal smoke, I am going to need the insurance money fast, or the next few months are going to be a master class in money juggling.

"Kitchen and waitstaff are going to jump ship, you know," Flavio says. "Hostesses, too. There are a couple of folks we may want to move over to another shop so as not to lose them, but we're going to have to replace most of the staff."

Anybody who's paid by the hour, which is 98 percent of my employees. They'll leave, and hell, who can blame them? They've got bills to pay, too, and Lasky employees are the best trained in town. Another area restaurant will snap them up before the end of the week.

"Let 'em go. It's probably a win-win anyway."

Flavio frowns. "How so?"

"Come on, Flavio. This place is a disaster, and you said it yourself. We won't be filling tables anytime soon. Better to tell the staff to find another job. And as much as I hate to say it, you might want to make a few calls yourself."

"That seems awfully extreme. I can hang on a week or two until the insurance money bridges the gap. And Abernathy's already called. They said they'll work with us on the lease."

Abernathy is the landlord, the owner of the sixty-five shops spread across the six Buckhead blocks that fan out in all directions around us. A few years ago, in an effort to boost their business, Abernathy made us an offer we couldn't refuse: free rein on a building in the center of the development and the first thirty-six months rent-free. Three years in one of the city's most desirable locations where we haven't paid a cent, not one single penny, of rent. It's the only reason I'm still standing, because this place makes a killing.

Shit—*made* a killing.

"They're going to *have* to work with us. No way I'm paying rent on this dump, and honestly, I have real doubts about reinvesting in a shop where I don't own the building."

Flavio frowns. "What are you saying exactly?"

"I'm saying maybe I should just take the insurance money and run."

It's the first time I've said the words out loud, and releasing them loosens the noose around my neck. I inhale and think them again. *Close up shop. Wave the white flag.* The air is fresh and cool and it tingles the bottom of my lungs. What if this fire is the universe telling me it's time? Walking away from this place, from Lasky Steak, it feels like the opposite of defeat.

I don't miss the flash of distress on Flavio's face. "Are you serious right now? You're actually considering shuttering your best shop?"

"Well, yeah. Because sorry, man, but do the math. If we're lucky, insurance will pay enough for a kitchen reno, to fix up the ceiling and install fire-retardant noise absorption panels like I should have done the first time, to slap on some paint and buy some new tables and chairs. It'll be months before you and I are drawing a salary again."

Flavio's expression is an elbow to the gut, and it floods me with guilt. He and his wife have one kid in college and another starting next year. He needs the income this place generates as much as I do. I'm an asshole for ever hiring him.

A muffled ring sounds from deep in his pocket. He digs his cell out and waves the screen my way—the insurance company— and I gesture for him to answer.

He wanders off to the front of the shop, phone pressed to his ear, and I turn back to the burn pattern on the wall. I stare at the markings, sooty footprints from the flames that curled up and over the edge into the dining room.

Footsteps crunch on the glass behind me. "He says he's on his way, here in about an hour. He also said if somebody wanted Bolling Way to go up in flames, then shorting out an outlet next to a vat of flammable cooking grease would be the way to do it, which really made me wonder..." Flavio pauses, an empty silence that roars in my ears. "When's the last time you talked to George?"

I whirl around, frowning. George, the sous-chef Flavio fired back in the spring. The one who lost his shit on Flavio in front of a kitchen full of staff. "Not since that night. When was that, late March?"

The night George trashed the place and stormed out, but not before threatening to burn it to the ground.

Flavio slips his phone back in his pocket. "I asked Abernathy to change the locks, but they never did. Which means George still has a working key."

I can't believe I didn't think of him earlier.

My limbs prickle with nervous energy, and I check the time on my cell, already plotting out the route to George's town house in my head. If traffic isn't awful, a twenty-minute drive. There and back in time to meet with the insurance inspector, but only if I haul ass.

"Hold down the fort," I say, jogging across the toasted floor. "I'll be back as soon as I can."

THE INTERVIEW

Juanita: Why don't you start by walking us through your version of August 6.

Cam: 'My' version?

Juanita: I just mean walk us through your day. What you did that morning, where you were when you got the call from Jade. That kind of stuff.

Cam: Okay. Well, I didn't roll out of bed until the early afternoon—fairly typical since I worked nights. I usually started my days by making lunch for Jade and me, but not that day. She had swapped schedules with somebody at Baxter's day camp, took over their shift for craft time. Anyway, I didn't see her at all that morning, or that afternoon. I didn't even hear her and the kids leave. I was completely zonked.

Juanita: What time did you leave the house?

Cam: Two or so.

Juanita: And your truck, I'm assuming it was parked in the detached garage?

Cam: Yes, in the space next to Jade's.

Juanita: And you didn't notice anything out of the ordinary.

Cam: No. But this was a good hour, maybe more, before he got there.

Juanita: How did he get into the garage?

Cam: Through the door by the breezeway, I'm assuming. There's a lock on that door but we never use it.

Juanita: Or maybe you left it open so he could get in the garage.

Cam: I already told you, we never used that lock. And why would you accuse me of such a thing? Are you insinuating I had something to do with the kidnapping of my own family?

Juanita: I wouldn't be the first to suggest it. In the months since the home invasion, there's been a great deal of misinformation floating around about you, both online and in print. Most of the stories accuse you of some kind of wrongdoing.

Cam: Oh, is that what we're calling it now—misinformation?

Juanita: Rumors of hidden money in offshore accounts, accusations of tax evasion and conspiracy, a former pastry chef who claimed you had an affair with her roommate.

Cam: Fake news, all of it. Especially that last one, though she sure tried hard enough. Whenever she'd show up at one of the shops, the bartenders would text me a warning so I could sneak out through the kitchen. Ask any of them, they'll tell you she was a pit bull.

Juanita: I did ask them.

Cam: And?

Juanita: They said you loved Jade. That you would never cheat on her.

Cam: [spreads hands]

Juanita: But the point I'm trying to make is all the information, much of it false, that is circulating about your part in what happened to your family. Many say you're to blame, that your silence created a space for rumors and conspiracy theories.

Cam: That may be true, but this is my life we're talking about. I mean, I know the restaurants put me in the spotlight before the home invasion, but that was nothing compared to you people camped out in front of the house day and night, ambushing me in the gym and the grocery store. Nobody wants that kind of attention. I certainly don't.

Juanita: Because the public is fascinated by what happened. For most of us, a home invasion is just about the most terrifying thing we can imagine. The thought of a stranger ambushing you as you're coming in the door and forcing their way into your house, threatening you and your children. It's everyone's worst nightmare.

Cam: Then just imagine it happening to the people you love most in this world. That's so much worse than experiencing it yourself.

Juanita: Except this wasn't just any old home invasion, was it? The masked man wasn't a stranger. None of this was random.

Cam: [sighs] Not even a little bit.

JADE

3:27 p.m.

"Not bad."

The man pokes his head around the corner, checking out the space where the mudroom spills into the house. He takes in the sleek chef's kitchen that was featured in *Bon Appétit*, the keeping room with a giant sectional facing a fireplace topped with a flat screen, the more formal living room that made the cover of *Atlanta Homes & Lifestyles*, every piece lovingly designed and selected by me. Hours and hours of my very best work.

"Nice place you got here." He turns back with an appreciative nod, and I swallow down a sour tremor.

His words are pleasant enough but not his tone, so hostile that my nerves stir with fright. I can hear the thoughts tripping through his brain. That we have too much. That he has too little. It's such an about-face from his demeanor in the garage, calm and matter-of-fact even when waving around his gun, it makes my legs go mushy.

I push my words through clenched teeth: "What now?"

If the man hears me, he doesn't respond. He's too busy exploring, moving through the back part of the house, taking in the furnishings. The custom rug in the keeping room, the portrait of the kids that covers a whole wall, the Marcel Wanders chandelier with more than three hundred twinkling lights. He takes it all in with greedy, observant eyes.

The room is spinning, and I need to sit down, but I'm too afraid to move. I stand in the doorway of the mudroom, Baxter clinging to me. Beatrix stands on my other side, her back ramrod straight, her feet shoulder-width apart like Miss Juliet is always coaching. I wrap a hand around each of my children, pressing them close until there's no air between us.

He's almost to the living room now. Only a few more steps and he'll be in full view of anyone who happens to be outside. Runners. Bikers. Neighbors out walking their dog. We live on the edge of a golf course, and this is an active, busy neighborhood.

Suddenly, he lurches to a stop, parking his soles at the edge of the keeping room. One more step and he'll be in full view of whoever's out on the street. If I were closer, I could plant both hands on his chest and shove him there, screaming loud enough to get their attention.

But I can't see from where I'm standing. I can't tell if there's anyone out there. Probably, but I only get one chance. I can't waste it until I know for sure.

Behind the dark fabric of his mask, his lips stretch into a thin line. "I heard you say something about a snack."

"You..." I shake my head. Is he *playing* with me? "You want a snack?"

"No, the kids want one. Don't you, kids?" He peers into the

footed white fruit bowl perched on the edge of the breakfast bar and fishes out a red apple, holding it up like the evil step-mother. "Beatrix and—what's the little guy's name?"

The bony arm wrapped around my thigh tightens. I don't want to say my son's name out loud. I don't want his name on this monster's tongue.

The man waits. His smile disappears. He cocks his head with faux curiosity, and his eye sockets look bruised in the bright lights of the kitchen. I wonder if he's tired, or maybe sick. I wonder if his health has anything to do with why he's here, if this is about money or something else.

He points to Baxter with the gun, a silent threat. "Jade, I just asked you a question."

"Baxter." I push my son behind me, but I'm not exactly the best cover. I'm five foot four on the best of days, and I'm in yoga gear, skintight leggings over legs that have always fallen on the wrong side of skinny. "Please. He's only six."

The man steps closer, his footsteps magnified on the hard-wood. We scurry backward into the mudroom until there's nowhere left for us to go, until we're pressed between the shoe cubbies and a wall.

He squats, putting him eye to eye with the kids. "Bax-ter. Beatrix. That's some nice names you two got there. Real fancy. Are y'all hungry?"

The y'all is genuine, as is his slight Southern twang. A de-tail I file away in my brain for later.

Both kids shake their heads.

The man pushes to a stand, gesturing for them to follow. "Come on. Let's get you something to eat."

He ambles into the kitchen like it's his own, stepping to the opposite side of the breakfast bar, heading for the glass-front cabinet with the plates and glasses. He pulls out four plates, then spreads them across the marble-topped island. "How about you, Jade? You look like you could use a sandwich or something."

I don't respond. The kids and I don't move. We stare at him from the mudroom, our soles superglued to the floor.

I eye the distance, a good forty feet and a long stretch of marble between us, then glance at the door we just came through, calculating how far I could get with a kid on each hip. Or maybe Beatrix could run on her own. She'd probably be faster than I would be anyway, plodding across the terrace in these flip-flops, Baxter flailing under an arm. We'd never make it to the gate before he chased us down, dragged us back inside and put a bullet in one or all of our brains. And even if I threw the door open and took off, it wouldn't trip the alarm and alert the cops, not immediately anyway. He'd have a full sixty seconds to tick in the code he just watched me use twice now.

Better to wait for a chance to escape out one of the other doors—the steel-and-glass ones that lead to the covered patio, or one of the French sets at the front of the house. That way, as soon as our feet hit the outside ground, the alarm will already be wailing.

The man's voice pulls me back. "Jade. Not a good idea."

I look over to where he's standing, a plate in one hand and his gun in the other, watching me like he can read my mind. Like he knows exactly what I'm thinking. Acid bubbles up in a fiery wave, like heartburn.

He leans over the sink and taps the bar, three clacks against the marble with the butt of his gun. He nods at the chairs, four leather-covered stools lined up like sentries on the opposite side. "Don't just stand there. Make yourselves at home."

A joke. A stupid, lame joke. He grins with demented cheer.

I stare back at him, trying to appear fearless or at least courageous, defiant even though what I really want to do is cry.

Big, shuddering sobs are threatening to burst up my throat, and I struggle to swallow them down. Maybe if I shove the kids out the door, I can hold him off long enough for them to get away. Maybe if I grab on to the doorway and plant my feet hard enough, I can turn myself into a human bottleneck. This man may be armed, he may be bigger and so much stronger than me, but I won't think twice. I would gladly sacrifice myself for my kids.

He shoots a pointed glance at the stools, nodding harder. "I said, sit. While the kids are eating, you and I can have a little talk."

With a shaky breath, I take Beatrix and Baxter by the hands, sweat-slick and sticky, and lead them to the kitchen. Frozen with fright, they just stand there, so I heave them onto the bar stools, first Beatrix, then Bax, and push the chairs flush to the marble so they don't fall out. I sink onto the one in the middle and fight to control my breathing, to keep my little sips of air from turning into panicked gulps. I grab on to the kids' armrests and scoot their chairs in close, until the pads of their seats are flush with mine.

Wait him out.

At some point he'll make a mistake, and then I'll have my chance. The trick is to be ready.

"So what are y'all in the mood for? Fruit? Carrot sticks dipped in ranch sauce?"

Beatrix stares at the counter. Baxter buries his face in my bicep, and I wrap my arm around him and press him to my side. The last thing any of us is thinking about is food.

"Okay, then," the man says, shrugging. "How 'bout I just surprise you, then?"

As he moves around my kitchen, opening drawers and poking through cabinets, I note all the details I was too traumatized to take in before. His basic T-shirt, plain and black with no identifying logos or tags, the fabric stretched tight across a big barreled chest. Compared to his torso his arms are thin, the long sleeves loose all the way down to cuffs that bump up against tight-fitting gloves, the kind with rubber fingertips that work on a cellphone screen. His black sneakers are unscuffed, new and fresh out of the box. He pulls a knife from the block by the stove, and I catch a glint of something at his neckline, a flash of a flat golden chain, but it slides back under his shirt before I can see more.

And most chilling, the back of his head is smooth. No lump of wadded hair under the mask, no pockmarks on his skin by his lips.

I'm certain now: this is not the same man who was at Beatrix's music lesson, the same man who's been following me all over town. The realization slithers through me like an eel, ice-cold and slippery. This is someone different.

He digs a box from a cabinet and jiggles it in the air. "Cheez-Its. Pretty sure every kid on earth likes these things."

He dumps some onto one of the plates and steps around to the other side of the island, choosing a strategic spot between the counter and the fridge. Holding his gun trained on us, he tugs on the handle with his other hand, taking in the contents of the fully stocked fridge with an impressed hum. The labeled shelves and bins, the outward facing jars, the neat stacks of plastic containers filled with sliced vegetables and fruits. A chef's fridge is a beautiful thing.

I watch him and I notice everything, committing every detail to memory so that I can recite it later—to the cops, in a courtroom.

Assuming we survive.

Either way, this will be all over the news. An armed and masked man, forcing his way into a celebrity chef's home in a country-club neighborhood. What happens here will go far beyond Atlanta's nightly newscasts. Reporters all over the country will spend hours reporting on today's timeline, nit-picking the second-to-second details, amplifying my every move and mistake. My picture and those of the kids will be flashed on every LCD screen across the country. Even if we don't survive—*especially* then—people will know our names. They will recognize our faces. The kind of fame no one wishes for.

He pulls out a packet of string cheese and studies the nu-tritional information. "If you're going to eat this crap, you should probably go for the full-fat version. Because this just tastes like salty plastic, but hey. Eight grams of protein, so I guess it's not all bad."

He rips off three portions and tosses them across the kitchen to me. The throw falls short, and they bounce off the edge of the bar and land in the sink with a slap. I leave them there while he washes a bag of green grapes at the far sink.

Under the marble of the bar overhang, Beatrix's hand crawls across my lap.

No, not her hand. Something smooth and cool and hard, and I don't have to look down to know it's my iPhone.

Clever, clever girl.

I pat her leg in silent praise, then lift the phone from my leg, feeling around on the sides to figure out which way is up.

"So." The man shakes the water from the bag of grapes and carries it around the island. "Let's talk about your secu-rity system."

Three feet between us at most, separated by a stretch of marble counter. I slide the cell phone down my leg, balanc-ing it on a knee, trying to remember how to call 9-1-1 with-out using the keypad. Three clicks to one of the side buttons? Four? I try it, three rapid-fire clicks, but I don't dare to look down because now he's staring right at me. His squinty eyes pinned on mine, waiting for me to answer. I remind myself to breathe.

"Hello, earth to Jade. Your security system?"

I clear my throat. "What about it?"

"Your pad has a panic button."

I nod. The technician, a potbellied man who told me to call him Big Jim, said if I ever pressed it, I had better make sure I meant business because the police would show up with guns blazing. He also said I had to press it for a minimum of three full seconds in order for the silent alarm to activate, and I remember thinking three seconds seemed like an eternity when there's someone coming at you with a gun.

Now I'm wishing I'd asked him to install a couple of strategically placed hidden ones—right here under this breakfast bar, for example.

I duck my head, tucking a hank of hair behind an ear, using the motion to chance a glance at my iPhone screen.

The screen is completely black. *Shit.* I waited too long.

"Where are the other pads? By the front door, I'm guessing, but anywhere else? How many do you have?"

My head jerks up. "What?"

He pulls three paper towels from the roll and spreads them across the bar top, dropping on them clusters of grapes, distributing the snacks. When he gets to the cheese sticks, he needs both hands to peel back the plastic, so he places his gun on the island behind him. I stare at the weapon and wonder—could I leap across the marble and get there first? Could I grab the gun with one hand and a knife from the block with another? Cam's sharpest Nesmuk with the carbon steel blade and handle of petrified bog oak. Could I use it to stab him in the throat?

The moment passes, and when he finishes, he reaches for the gun. "Come on, Jade, I really need you to focus here. Where in the house are the other alarm pads? And before you answer,

I'd advise you to think really long and hard, because if you're lying, if you accidentally on purpose forget to mention one of the alarm pads, I'm going to find out. And then this little problem will suddenly become a big one."

"There's one in the master bedroom," I say, my heart sinking. "It's on this level, down the hallway by the stairs. That's the pad we use when we come through the front door. It's the only other one."

On Big Jim's advice, the second pad was installed on the bedroom wall instead of next to the front door, in case we ever needed the panic button in the middle of the night. From here, though, an impossible distance. Across the living room, around a corner, down a hallway, inside the door. A literal obstacle course where I'd have to dodge furniture, swerve around walls. Even if I left my kids here, which I never would, I'd have to hold the panic button down for three eternal seconds. I'd never make it there fast enough.

"And cameras?"

My heart gives a hard kick. "What about them?"

He puffs a put-upon sigh, rolls his eyes. "Stop making this so hard. How many are there? Where are they located?"

With shaking fingers I try my phone again. Three rapid clicks of a side button while looking this man in the eye. I make sure to look him *straight* in the eye.

"We have six, all outside. Two on the front, one on each side and two on the back."

"You sure about that?"

I nod. My heart is booming so hard I'm surprised he can't hear.

He frowns, watching me through squinted eyes. "No indoor cameras in a fancy place like this? I find that a little hard to believe. You sure you don't have a secret camera somewhere, keeping an eye on the jewelry box in your closet maybe, or tucked behind a plant on a shelf upstairs?"

My gut muscles clench. My ears ring with building pressure. "I'm sure."

He cocks his head, his lips pursing in thought. "Then prove it." He stretches a long arm across the bar. "Show me the footage."

Dread throbs and expands in my veins. It's like those last, breathless seconds right before your car slams into a tree. The squeal of locked-down tires, the tug of momentum, the sickening flash of understanding that there's no stopping disaster.

He snaps his fingers, a muffled slap of gloved skin hitting fabric on his outstretched hand. "Come on, Jade. A system like yours will have an app on your phone. Show it to me."

Beatrix jerks on the chair next to me, a quiet seizure of fear.

And this is where I know I'm in trouble. Beyond the gun and the alarm and the unreachable panic buttons, there's something deeply unsettling about the way this man is constantly one step ahead of me. This whole time we've been inside, while he was pointing us to our chairs and gathering up our snacks, his eyes have been alert. His mouth and hands were moving while his eyes watched. Scanning the room and our faces, coolly assessing our every move.

This is what I'm up against.

"Give me the phone, Jade, and no one gets hurt."

JADE

3:34 p.m.

Deny or admit defeat?

I stare across the counter at the man, and I want all of this to be over already. Did he see Beatrix dig the phone out of my purse? Did my body jerk when she slid it onto my lap? My nerves are so sizzled I can't be certain. The only thing I know for sure is that he saw.

And it's not like I have much of a choice here. With a shaking hand, I pass the man my phone.

Baxter is still squashed into my side, his face buried in my sweater and his body trying to wriggle closer, but there's nowhere for him to go. Despite the armrests between us, he's already more on my chair than his own, his bones pressing into my skin. I haul him onto my lap, and he crumples into my chest with a whimper. My other arm I wrap across Beatrix, a laughably ineffectual shield.

"You're scaring the children."

The man offers up a wry smile. "I should hope so. Because this should be a lesson to both of them, that trying to sneak something over on me is not wise. It will get you caught. Better yet, it will get you punished."

He lets the last word linger while he stares at the back of Baxter's head, then shifts his attention to Beatrix. The guilty one. Every muscle in my body hardens into concrete. My lungs swell with breath and hold there. If he goes for my family, if he so much as lifts a finger toward either of my children, I will take the blame. I will defend them or die trying. I am ready.

The man taps a rubber-tipped finger to my phone, waking the screen. "What's the passcode for this thing? And before you ask, yes this is a test. I want to make sure what you told me about your security system is on the up-and-up."

My back locks up, my mind racing with panicked thoughts. There are all sorts of apps on that phone, and it never occurred to me to disguise the ones I don't want people to see. That's what passwords and face recognition are for, to keep what's on the phone private.

And I'm too damn organized. If I give him the passcode, all he would have to do is flip through the pages to find every app that services this house. The pool controls, outdoor and indoor lighting, Sonos, the thermostats.

The cameras I told him about.

The ones I didn't.

He sighs and looks at me. "Jade. The password."

I could lie, but what then? I don't see any other option than to give it to him. "It's 2-9-2-1-9-2."

He ticks it in, and the lock screen dissolves.

My one saving grace—the only one—is that the app for the security system isn't anywhere near the others. *You never know when you might need to get to it lickety-split*, Big Jim told me, *and this way you won't have to go huntin'*. At his advice, I saved it to my phone's dock instead.

The man finds the security app in one go, tapping it without asking the name or for me to point out the logo. It is password protected, of course, and he flips the screen around and holds it up to my face. The lock screen dissolves into a bold, red block—armed Stay—with below it, five camera feeds.

"I thought you said there were six."

"There are."

He holds up the phone, wags it by his temple so I can see the five tiny squares. A birds-eye view of the front yard, multiple shots of the driveway and terrace, the stepping-stones on the right side flanked with trees shifting in the wind. "Then why're there only five on this app?"

"Because the Ring is a separate app."

The only problem—and it's a big one—is that the Ring app is saved on the third page. If I direct him there, he'll spot all the other apps, including the one stupidly labeled "iSpy." Footage from three hidden nanny cams, providing full-color, high-definition, 110-degree views of the playroom upstairs. Undeniable, irrefutable proof that I looked this man in the eyes just now and lied.

"If you swipe down on the screen, you can search for it."

"I know how to work an iPhone, Jade."

His sarcasm gets zero reaction from me. I hold my breath and sit stock-still as he drags a finger down the screen, the movement slow and obstinate, like Baxter when I remind him to wash behind his ears. But the man doesn't go flipping around the pages, doesn't go searching for the app himself. When he ticks in those four little letters in the search bar, my lungs release in a soft whoosh.

"Why are there so many people on your street? One, two, three, four, five, six—no, seven bodies that I can see. And what the heck are your neighbors doing? How many kids do they have?"

Five, but they live part-time with their dad. I always know when it's Tanya's turn because she lets them run off steam in the yard.

I stare at the countertop, silent.

Except for an occasional burst of angry breath, Beatrix is silent, too, the sounds much like the ones she makes whenever Cam or I discipline her. Beatrix's quick mind rarely needs me to explain things. She understands, as I do, that silence is a weapon of control—our only one in this horror show.

Baxter twists on my lap, blinking his big blue eyes at mine. "But, Mommy, what about the Santa cams?"

Sweet, sweet Baxter. This is why he will never know about the nanny cams, and why we hid them in places neither child would ever think to look: in the speaker hanging from a wall, behind a fake clock on the shelf, in a dummy fire alarm anchored to the ceiling. Because Baxter is the sweetest, most trusting, blabbermouth on the planet.

Behind the black knit of the mask, the man's eyes go small and squinty. "What Santa cams?"

I gesture to a square, white device in the keeping room behind me, wedged in the corner of the ceiling. It picks up on my movement, and a red light winks. "The motion sensors have a direct line to Santa's workshop, but there's no app on my phone. Santa is the only one who can see."

The man's lips spread in a smile so wide, the corners disappear behind the fabric. "That's… I have to give it to you, Jade, that's pretty near genius. No joke. So dang clever I wish I'd thought of it myself. Not that my house is anywhere near as fancy as this one is, but that's some real smart parenting right there. Really, really good job."

What am I supposed to say—thank you? Please don't tell my kids there's no Santa?

But I also don't miss the information he slipped in there, maybe on purpose, maybe by accident. That his house is not as nice as mine. The implication that he's a parent. The kids might not have noticed, but I did, and it thrills me. It tells me if I'm patient enough, he might just blurt out more.

"But I guess that's bad news for me, though, huh? Means I'm on the naughty list."

Baxter gasps. Beatrix doesn't respond.

The man wriggles a grape off the stem and pops it in his mouth. "But okay, kids, this is another teachable moment, so listen up. Let's talk about the lesson here. When I asked your mom about the sixth camera, what did she do?" He surveys the kids while chewing another grape.

No one responds.

Baxter wriggles around to face him. The talk of Santa has perked him up some.

The man cups a palm around the lump that is his right ear. "What's that, Beatrix? You said she didn't lie?" He leans back and grins some more. "Smart girl. Your mom didn't make up some story or try to trick me with the Ring. She passed the test. When I confronted her with the discrepancy, she told me the truth. And do you know why she did that?"

The mask is making him hard to read. Animated eyes, smiling mouth chomping away at a mouthful of grapes—but none of it's real. This man is a performer, shrugging in and out of character faster than I can keep up, switching up his demeanor like a summer storm, light to dark then back again. I have zero idea what he's thinking.

Baxter, though, is warming up to him. This man's tone, his campy grin—Baxter only sees what he sees: a smiling adult in our house, cracking jokes and eating our food. So what if he's wearing a mask? Spider-Man wears a mask. Batman and the Ninja Turtles wear masks. In all our talks about stranger danger, we've never covered what happens if the stranger comes into the house. He only knows that home is a safe place, where the adults are both authorities and protectors. In his six-year-old brain, none of this makes any sense.

He sits up straighter on my lap. "No. How come?"

It's like he didn't speak. The man stares at Beatrix, who is not fooled like her little brother. She glares across the counter at the masked man, and the air around her charges.

"Leave her alone," I say, on high alert. "This has nothing to do with Beatrix."

The man's showman smile vanishes. "Yes, it does. This has everything to do with her. If the four of us are going to get through this afternoon in one piece, I need all of you to understand that you have to be truthful. I need to know that she's not going to be constantly trying to slip something by me. Something like...oh, I don't know, sneaking a cell phone from her mama's bag when she thinks I'm not looking."

First of all, *get through the afternoon*...what does that even mean? Cam doesn't get home until well past midnight. This situation can't possibly sustain itself until then.

I straighten up. Level my gaze at him. Wrap my arm around my daughter like a seat belt.

"She understands, okay? She gets it." My voice is loud and strong, surprisingly fierce in the quiet kitchen. It's stupid, I know, to use this tone with a masked man wielding a gun, but my sole priority here is my children. Their safety. Their mental well-being—assuming we make it out of here alive. Hearing the steady calm in my voice will keep them centered. "Please just...just talk to me. Leave the kids out of it."

The man plunks an elbow on the counter and leans in. "I'd love to do that, but you know as well as I do that children need boundaries. They need to learn that for every action, there is a consequence. Do you understand what I'm saying here?"

"I understand," I say, but it's not my answer he's looking for. It's Beatrix's.

The man stands there, waiting, while in my mind I tick off the sharpest, most deadly weapons in the house. The knives, the cast-iron pans in the drawer, the tools hanging from Cam's workbench downstairs. Even if I could somehow manage to get to one, can it go up against a gun? I'd have to catch this guy off guard, sink the blade in the fleshy part of his throat or an eyeball, bury it deep before he even noticed it was coming—a challenge with a man so big, so broad, his eyes ever watching from behind the mask. The timing would have to be perfect, my attack smooth and without hesitation. Not exactly a master plan.

And then something else occurs to me, something that sends up a sour, bitter wave.

If I get myself killed, who will watch out for my children?

"Beatrix," the man says, leveling his gaze on my daughter. "I asked you a question. Do you understand what I'm telling you?"

Answer him, baby. Nod. Let him know you understand.

Beatrix's chin quivers, but she doesn't otherwise move. She stares straight ahead, breathing hard.

Frustration mixes with fear mixes with pride. Beatrix is stubborn, just like her father. She has been since the second she came screaming into the world, fists slinging. Just last month, she went through a phase where she existed on saltines and air, where no matter how much I begged or prodded or threatened or coaxed or cried, she refused to take so much as a single bite of anything else. A chef's daughter, and the pickiest eater ever. She wore me down, every single night.

The calories in a pack of saltines may be empty, but at least they're calories.

And now...

Now I recognize that look on her face—the squinty eyes, the puckered mouth—and it terrifies me because I know what it means.

"So you're one of those, huh?"

Beatrix frowns. Her expression says, *One of what?* but she's too proud to say the words out loud. Her left-hand fingers are going nuts, tapping out a silent melody against her thigh—something she does when she's bored or nervous or uncomfortable.

The man knocks his skull with a knuckle, then leans with both arms onto the counter. "A hard nut to crack." His arms are crossed at the wrist, the gun held casually in a fist. It jiggles as he talks, and the positioning is purposeful. "Obstinate. Headstrong. Admirable traits when they come in small doses, but beware, young lady. They can also be your downfall."

I stare at the gun, tracing a line between the muzzle and a freckle just above Beatrix's left brow. One tweak to the trigger and there's a hole in my daughter's head. The thought snags on repeat through my brain and echoes.

If this man shoots my daughter, I will murder him.

"So now I am gonna need an answer. A clear *yes* or *no*. I need to know you heard what I was saying just now about rules and boundaries. I need to know that I can count on you to follow them. Can I do that, Beatrix? Can I trust you not to do anything crazy?"

"The phone's mine," I say, tensing up on my chair. "Whatever you need to say, leave her out—"

"Shh." The man punctuates the hiss with a flick of the gun in my direction. The laughing, chummy jokester from a few minutes ago is long gone, discarded like a crumpled napkin.

The bastard aims the gun at my daughter's head, and I brace, half expecting the pop of a gunshot, the gritty smell of gunpowder.

But there's nothing, only horrible quiet.

I breathe through a flash of scalding panic.

"Answer the question, Beatrix. Can I trust you or not?"

I nudge Beatrix's chest with my elbow. Give her knee a painful squeeze. The tapping stops, and her fingers freeze, then stiffen on her thigh.

Beatrix, for the love of God. Say yes to the man with the gun. Answer him.

Beatrix's chest heaves. Her hands ball into tight fists, her silent struggle obvious. This is Beatrix arming for combat. Planting her flag, sticking to her guns. The seconds stretch, swelling with a torturous silence. Even Bax leans across me to prod her with a finger in the arm.

"Beatrix, please," I whisper. *"Please."*

"Yeah." She frowns at the cheese sticks sweating on the paper towels, the bunches of untouched grapes, and sighs. "You can trust me." The *I guess* is silent but unmistakable.

The man straightens. Nods. Eats another grape, and that's that.

I wilt with relief, even though I know my daughter, and I know she doesn't mean a single word.

SEBASTIAN

3:39 p.m.

That Beatrix kid is a trip. Sneaking the phone out of her mama's bag, slipping it into those ruffly denim shorts. Like I wouldn't notice the iPhone-sized lump in her pocket, or the way her freckles lit up like stars when she passed the thing to Jade. I'm not blind. I saw her hand move to her mama's lap, how when it landed, Jade jerked to attention in her chair. I saw every bit of it.

Then her face when I asked if I could trust her. Even with the gun I've been waving around like a stick of dynamite, this old Beretta Cougar I dug out of storage especially for today, the kid just sat there. Clamping down on her molars, cussing me out with her eyes, looking for all the world like she'd swallowed her tongue just to spite me. My Gigi used to look at me like that, too, when she was about Beatrix's age. I looked at her and I saw my daughter's face and, damn, it was hard to keep mine straight.

But what Beatrix hasn't quite figured out yet is that stubborn streak of hers? It's not a strength but a weakness. It makes her predictable. Easy to manipulate, like kid-shaped putty in my hands. These next few hours are going to be a lot of fun pulling that kid's strings.

"Let's go." I direct the words to Jade, but it's Beatrix I'm looking at, and not just from the corner of my eye. She's the one I'll be keeping my eye on.

Jade's arm tightens around the little guy on her lap. Baxter— what kind of sissy name is that for a boy? Poor kid probably gets the shit beat out of him on the playground. Beatrix, too, though she seems like the nerdy type, an awkward loner who reads a book while all the other kids play. Her gaze sticks to me like a shadow.

Jade frowns. "Go where? Where are we going?"

She looks nothing like she did the first time I met her, at the opening for Cam's restaurant on the West Side. That night she looked like she'd stepped out of a magazine, all glossy hair and glittery makeup and this complicated silver dress that had to cost more than what a normal person pays for a month's rent. She shook my hand, and even with all the people and the commotion, I heard those diamond bracelets rattling. I remember thinking she'd better be careful on the way to her car. A good $50K on that one arm alone. Prime mugging material.

Now, though, in those workout clothes, I barely recognize her. Her hair is loose and wild around her head, her face bare but for two pink spots high on her cheeks. The jewelry is gone, too—only a watch, a diamond wedding band and a honker of a stud perched on each ear. Worlds apart from that flouncy Barbie I saw hanging from Cam's arm. Prettier, too. For a fleeting second, I wonder if I misjudged her.

I gesture to the snacks spread across the bar. "Aren't y'all going to eat?"

"My husband will be home soon," she says, ignoring the

food, my question. "He's home for dinner every night. Take whatever you want and leave, and I'll forget you were ever here."

I lean an elbow on the bar, gesturing with the gun. "And here we were doing so well just now. Your husband doesn't come home for dinner, *ever*. Don't lie to me. Your children understand this. Why can't you?"

She presses her lips into a straight line, and I squint, studying her face. Does she recognize me?

I'm pretty sure the answer is no, though it's not for lack of trying. Her eyes have followed me since the second she saw me in the garage. I've seen the way she's examined my build, clocking the shape of my eyes and my lips and skin and whatever else she can see of my face. I saw her ticking off my features one by one, searching her memory banks for a match. Jade's one of those people whose every thought plays out on her face, which means that so far, she hasn't made the connection.

I straighten, and my gaze sweeps the windows on the back side of the house, checking the view onto the driveway and fenced-in backyard—both deserted. Nothing out there but some squirrels and that big-ass pool, the water like shimmering black glass. It's the front of the house I have to worry about—a solid wall of windows and glass doors.

"Now come on. We need to get our asses upstairs."

Jade frowns, her pretty forehead crumpling. "Why...why do you want to go upstairs?"

"What do you think your neighbors will say when they see a guy in a ski mask marching through your living room? We're okay here, but the rest of this place is like a fish tank."

That's what a couple million bucks in this town will get you—a palace high on a hill where every space winds into the next through mammoth, open doorways. Only three rooms on this level provide any sort of privacy: the master on the back end, the TV room behind Jade and the kids, and the kitchen I've parked us in. Other than that, it's a straight shot for anyone outside looking in, up the yard and through the windows into the library, the dining room, the foyer and living room beyond. Fifty solid feet of unobstructed visibility from the street.

And I've cased this house often enough to know who's out there. Bikers. Runners. Neighbors walking their prissy dogs.

I point to the ceiling. "What's up there, bedrooms?"

I know what's up there. I'm not an idiot. I wouldn't be here without having done my homework. Three giant bedrooms, three full baths lined with marble and tile, ten times more closet space than I ever had even in my nicest house, and along the entire back side of the house, a mack daddy home theater stocked with toys. Blackout curtains, reclinable theater seating, soundproofing in the floor and walls and ceiling. *That's* where we're going.

At the last word—*bedrooms*—Jade's eyes go big and wide, darting from her kids to the stairs on the other side of the wall. She can't stop touching the kids—shielding them with an arm, hugging them to her chest. "Why...why do you want to take us upstairs?"

I roll my eyes, curl my lips in exaggerated disgust just so we're clear. Jade may be easy on the eyes, but she's not my type, and only a real sicko would touch a child that way. "Get your mind out of the gutter, lady, and answer the question."

"The kids' rooms are upstairs. A guest room. The media and playroom." Her voice is thin and shaky, her muscles twitching under her skin like a horse, flicking away flies. She doesn't understand what's happening here—not yet. But she will.

"Any alarm pads up there?"

She shakes her head. "I just told you there are only two, both downstairs."

Staring down a gun and she can still summon up some sass. Any other time I might appreciate Jade's spunk, but not today. Today I can't get distracted by anything trivial.

"And cameras?"

She points to her cell phone, black against the bright white marble. "You already saw the camera feeds on my phone. All six of them."

"Answer the question." I slow down my words, wrap my lips and tongue around them and let them fly like poison darts. "Are there. Any more. Cameras?"

Will she lie? Tell the truth? Her answer is essential to my plan, as are the cameras.

"No." She shakes her head, swallows. "No, there aren't any more cameras."

I sigh. Give her a full five seconds to amend, confess, recant, but she stays quiet. She stares me straight in the face, and she doesn't say a word. Daring me with those blue eyes, as if I don't have full access to her phone, like it wouldn't occur to me to pick it up right now and check.

I pick up her phone, hold it in the palm of a hand. She doesn't so much as squirm on her chair. Impressive.

Game on.

I shift my focus to the lump on her lap. "Yo, Baxter, buddy, I need your help with something."

His body gives a mighty jerk, almost launching himself off Jade's lap, but her arm tightens around him like a safety bar, the kind on roller coaster cars so you don't fly out of the corkscrew curve. She's the type of mother who wouldn't think twice about offering herself up for her children. The kind who would take a bullet for her kids, who would shove them onto the shoulder only to end up crushed by the oncoming truck herself. A lioness, her protectiveness as instinctive as breathing. It's an admirable trait. Not every parent is built that way.

She stares at me, eyes wide over the top of her son's head, and she doesn't let him go.

"Come on, Baxter." I toss the cell to the marble and gesture with my gun—a warning, a promise. He's sucking hard on a thumb, his smooth cheeks puffing and pulling. I smile to calm his nerves. "Get on over here, son. I need you to do something for me."

Jade's gaze sticks to the gun like superglue. "At least let me come with him."

"Sorry, but that's a hard no."

"But Baxter's only six."

"Exactly. Plenty old enough to help me out."

She shakes her head hard enough that her hair whacks her in the face. "But he's terrified. *I'm* terrified." Her voice cracks, and she's trying really hard not to cry.

"What do you think's going to happen? What are you so scared of?"

She gives me an incredulous look, searching for words she can say out loud. Without turning her head, she darts a sidelong glance at her daughter, her expression sparkling with meaning. Little pitchers have big ears—and Beatrix's are practically flapping off her head. This is a kid who knows when to listen.

"I just…" Jade's voice is a soft squeak. She takes a big breath, swallows. "I don't want anything to happen to him."

"Nothing's going to happen to him."

She wavers, frozen like a kid on the high diving board. "How do I know that?"

"Because I just told you so. Everything's going to be A-okay. I won't harm a hair on Baxter's head, you have my word. But only if you put him down and tell him to get over here."

Her body remains perfectly frozen, but something breaks behind her eyes. Her arm loosens some, but she doesn't let her son go. It's almost comical how she thinks she still has a choice.

I load every bit of menace into the parts of me she can see. Hard mouth, squinty eyes, a look that says, *I don't want to hurt you, but I will.* This damn mask isn't making it any easier to get my point across.

"Do it, Jade. *Now.*" I point the gun at her head, then lower my arm just a tad so it's a straight line from the muzzle to her son's head. "Put Baxter down."

Up to now she's been holding it together fairly well, swallowing her tears for her kids' sakes, but two fat ones spill from her eyes now, dragging a shiny line down each cheek. She swipes her face before the kids can see, then pulls herself together as best she can. She whispers in her son's ear and holds him close, kissing him twice on the temple.

And then slowly, carefully, she pushes his bar stool away from the marble and slides him onto the floor.

Two seconds later, he peers around the end of the bar.

I slip the gun into my waistband at the small of my back and crouch down, putting us eye to masked eye. "Hey, buddy."

Any other kid would be bawling right now, but not Baxter. He just stands there, fingers of one hand wrapped around his sister's chair, going to town on the thumb of his other hand. Two round blue eyes watch me from behind a fist, but they don't look scared. They look curious.

I tap him square in the belly. "I meant what I told your mother just now, you know. I'm not going to hurt you. In fact, I want the two of us to be friends, and you know what friends do? They help each other out. I'm going to help you, and then you're going to help me. How do you think that sounds?"

Nothing. Not even a blink.

But he's not freaking out, either, so I take it as a sign.

"Okay, so here's the deal. If you go to the front door and tell me who's down on the street, then I promise not to tell anyone you have a marshmallow sticking out of your ear."

He frowns, and his thumb jerks out of his mouth with a loud *pop*. "I don't got a marshmallow in my ear."

"Yes, you do. Here. Hold still and I'll get it for you." I reach over his head and shake the thing out of my sleeve, catching it in a palm, pinching it between two gloved fingers, showing it to him with a flourish. I'm not the best magician, but I'm good enough to fool a six-year-old.

"That came outta my *ear*?" He sticks a finger in there and jiggles it around.

"It sure did. Next time your mama accuses you of not listening, tell her you couldn't 'cause you had a marshmallow stuck in your ear."

He gives me a knowing nod. "She *does* say that a lot."

"See? Good thing I got it out of there, then, huh?" I grin and poke him in the bony chest. "Now it's your turn to do me a favor. Do you think you can do that?"

He gives me an eager nod. I smile up at Jade.

See? So damn easy.

I hike a thumb over my shoulder, in the direction of the front door. "Go take a look out the front door, will you? I need you to tell me how many people are out there."

I could pull up the footage on the Ring app, but it's like looking through a fish eye, the scale distorted and blurry around the edges. I need the full, 180-degree view, which means I need actual eyes on the street.

The kid takes off so fast, he's like a cartoon version of himself, running in place for a second or two before his rubber soles find traction on the floor. He disappears into the living room and I push to a stand.

"I'm not blind," Beatrix says, glaring across the marble. "I saw you stick that stupid marshmallow up your sleeve."

Of course Captain Obvious saw. From where she was sitting, she would have seen everything—me, pulling the marshmallow from the side pocket of my backpack and sliding it up my sleeve, the way I shook it out behind her brother's ear.

But her anger is a little misdirected. If I cared enough to explain it to her, I'd tell her the person she's really mad at is her little brother, for buddying up to the enemy.

Baxter returns in a flurry of footsteps, his cheeks bright with pride, with self-importance. "There's two ladies down there talking, and a biker, and a big brown truck that almost ran into a mailbox."

"Good job. Those talking ladies. Are they moving or standing still?"

Baxter gives an exaggerated bob of his shoulders. "I don't know. Want me to go look?"

I nod, hold up a finger. "But this time, I want you to stay there. Tell me everybody who's out front, and then when they're all gone and nobody else is coming, I want to know that, too. When you tell us the coast is clear, we'll meet you at the stairs. Got it?"

"Got it." He whirls around and takes off.

I look up and Jade is staring at me. Back straight, cheeks red, perspiration shining up her perfect skin. Silent but for the steady dragon breaths firing up and out her nose. I'm going to need to watch her, too. First chance she gets, this woman is going to come at me.

"The ladies are still talking," Baxter hollers from the front door. "They're laughing and talking and this is gonna take forever."

"Tell me when they start to move, okay? And if anybody else comes by, I want to know." I heave my backpack onto a shoulder, stepping to Jade's side of the counter. "Get ready. When Baxter gives us the all clear, I need you two to *move*."

From the other room, an update: "One of the ladies is turning around. Oh wait, now she's going the other way."

I gesture for Jade and Beatrix to get off their chairs, then nudge them with the gun until they're flush against the edge of the dividing wall. One more step and they'll be standing in the living room, for the ladies and the biker and the big brown truck to see.

"The ladies are crossing the street now," Baxter announces, "but they're walking real slow."

"Are they gone?"

"Almost. Allllmost. Yep, now they're gone. Everybody's gone."

I jam my gun into Jade's spine and hustle them to the stairs.

CAM

3:41 p.m.

Last I knew, George lived in a brick-front town house, one of the overpriced ones that ballooned like mushrooms around a Whole Foods in a busy northern suburb. I don't remember the exact address—after Flavio sent George packing, I blocked his number and deleted every trace of him from my phone—but I'll recognize the place when I see it.

Waze detours me around the perimeter's bumper-to-bumper traffic and dumps me onto Roswell Road, where I run up against a sea of brake lights in Sandy Springs proper. Nothing but gridlock, wall-to-wall cars in both directions.

My blood pressure, already flirting with the danger zone, spikes into dizzying territory. Especially once the light up ahead flips to green, but not a single tire moves because there's nowhere for any of us to go. How the hell do people live in this town?

I stew in the gridlock, while George's last words play on

repeat in my mind, hurled over his shoulder on his way out the door.

You'll pay for this, asshole. When you least expect it, I'm going to make you pay.

This was back in the spring, when the weather finally warmed up enough for us to haul the extra tables out of storage and line them up on the terrace—and thank God because the investor notes for two of my shops were coming due, and these are the type of people who don't like to wait. I needed to fill every table and turn it multiple times because I was still plugging the hole from the last note and the ones before that, pulling profits from one shop to pay the debts on another like a demented game of Whac-a-Mole. Seventy-two cents of every dollar that I earn goes to my investors, which means (a) I'm an idiot; (b) at any given time, I don't have more than a couple thousand bucks in the bank; and (c) I'm a damn idiot.

So there it is, ladies and gentlemen, the truth. Cam Lasky is broke. Despite five booming restaurants, despite the big Buckhead mansion and the custom cars and the hot wife dripping in diamonds, Atlanta's Steak King is in hock up to his rent-a-crown. Lasky Steak is a house of cards. My success is a sham. I am literally and figuratively drowning in debt.

And no. I don't miss the irony. Celebrity chef known for feeding Atlanta's wealthiest bellies can barely feed his own family.

So back in March, when the evenings finally turned balmy, I couldn't afford for George to throw a fit so epic it became known in Lasky kitchens as "pulling a George." I couldn't afford for him to break all those plates and glasses or destroy three crates of hundred-dollar wine, pitching bottle after bottle onto the concrete floor. And I definitely couldn't afford for him to leave in the middle of the dinner rush and take three of the line cooks with him. After I deducted all the damages, his last paycheck was -$1.23.

So yeah. George has a couple of reasons for wanting to take a torch to my best performing restaurant. He would have known how to jig the alarm, too, working it so it didn't trigger at the first sign of smoke. He would have known exactly where to toss the match.

And like Flavio reminded me, he still has a key.

Traffic loosens, and a few minutes later, I screech to a stop at the curb and eye the corner unit on a block-long stretch of townhomes. Three stories of boring brown brick and creamy siding above a monster garage door. Tall and angular, with concrete steps leading to a covered entrance so shallow, you could press yourself to the door and still get a backside soaked with rain. I take in the windows, dark glass obscured with plain white blinds, the leggy plants in the window boxes and on either side of the front door. This is it, all right. The place looks exactly the same.

On the doorstep, I ignore the Ring and rap the door with my knuckle—the kind of knock a friendly neighbor would use to borrow a cup of sugar, maybe, or a delivery person with a package. This is a moment that demands an element of surprise.

I wait, the seconds thumping in my chest like a drumline.

Then again, the Ring would have alerted him to my arrival, which means he probably knows I'm here. I step back and scan the upstairs windows, half expecting to see him grinning at me through the blinds, but there's nothing.

I head back down the steps to the sidewalk, jogging past the truck and around the side of the house, where a six-foot wooden fence surrounds a backyard the size of a postage stamp. I follow it around to the back, stopping at the first gate I come to. Behind it, George's town house looms in a leaden sky.

I push on the gate, but it holds. I'm guessing some kind of latch on the inside where the wood is thin and kind of soggy. I lean on it with a shoulder, and the latch releases with a pop. Bingo.

I swing the door wide and step inside.

Except for a green trash can, the yard is completely bare, a scraggly patch of dirt and grass with not a stick of furniture. No table, no potted plant, not even a ratty lawn chair. The emptiness of it gives me pause, just a fleeting second where my conviction fades.

I haven't seen or spoken to this guy in more than four months. It's possible that George doesn't live here, that he didn't just storm out of Lasky but also this house, this city. What if I'm about to go storming through the backyard of some poor, unsuspecting sucker or worse—a homeowner running for their gun? This is Georgia, where most people have one.

The wooden door bangs shut behind me, followed by a dog starting up next door, muffled barks from a big dog. German shepherd big. I wait, trying to decide.

And then I spot a pair of kitchen Crocs, black and male-sized, just inside the sliding glass door.

I take off across the yard, and this time I'm not the least bit subtle about it. I bang on the doors, peer through unshaded windows onto furnishings I recognize, oversize furniture done up in leather, most of it brown. Not so much masculine as un-inspired, plucked from the pages of a sales catalog.

The living room is a disaster—rumpled pillows and more discarded shoes, a coffee table piled with magazines and books, their spines cracked and the pages dog-eared. Definitely George, who reads more than a librarian. Sci-fi mostly, with an occasional mystery mixed in for fun.

The next window looks onto a spotless kitchen, further

proof that George lives here. Chefs are obsessive about their workspace, and this one is uncluttered and gleaming, with a floor clean enough to lick. A digital clock blinks on the coffee maker, but otherwise no movement, no one home...though the beast next door is still going strong.

Above me, a whoosh of temperature-controlled air followed by a familiar voice: "Yo, asshole."

George's cheeks are a little fuller than the last time I saw him, his head a lot shinier on top. Looks like he finally gave up on that receding hairline and shaved the whole thing off.

He leans both forearms on the second-story windowsill, tipping his chin to the grass I just walked through. "You do know this backyard is private property, yeah?"

"Yeah, but so's my steak house."

"So?"

"So there's a detective looking at the security footage right now, and I gave him your picture."

A double-barreled lie. There's no detective, no picture, but it gets my point across. An accusation, bright and sparkling.

He tilts his head and frowns. "Why would my face be on your security feed? I haven't set foot in the place for what—five? Six months?"

Four and a half almost to the day. George knows this as well as I do.

"Stop fucking around. If you did what Flavio and I think you did, then you're going to jail. Arson's a crime, and you better believe I'll be sitting in the front row at your trial. I'll be the one cheering when they cart you away."

I try not to think about what suspected arson will mean, but it's impossible. It means the insurance money will get tied up in subpoenas and courtroom drama. It means attorney fees I can't afford to pay. It means long waits that end in jail time. My heart fires up, and my insides churn. I can't afford any of this.

George's frown digs in. "Mind telling me what the hell you're talking about?"

"Oh come on. The fire. At the Bolling Way shop. The same shop you swore to burn to the ground."

"There was a fire? For real?" His brow clears, and his lips spread into a smile. "How bad?"

"Why else would I come all the way up here?" I lift both hands, let them slap to my sides. "Bad."

"How bad?"

I stare up at my former sous-chef, a crick tightening on the right side of my neck, the heat bleeding from my body in a single, bracing instant. When I drove here, I was operating on instinct and rage, but George was never that good of an actor.

The wind sends an icy blast up my back. "It's torched, man. A total loss."

He smacks the sill and whoops, a full-bellied laughter that drowns out the birds overhead, the cars on the street, the dog still going berserk next door.

"Dude. *Dude.* Are you serious right now? Are you kidding me?" He pauses to catch his breath, a long stretch of silence to enjoy the hell out of my expression. He laughs some more, all jolly hilarity. "Oh my God. This is too damn good."

"Shut up."

"For real, man. And though I appreciate you coming all the way here to tell me the joyous news in person, what kind of idiot do you think I am? An arsonist would have to be really incompetent to give his former boss a six-month warning. I mean, come on. You and I both know I'm not that stupid."

"It was four and a half. March 24."

"Aww, you remembered our anniversary."

I roll my eyes. "You know what? Forget it. I'm out of here." I turn and march for the gate.

"Wait. Where you going? Who are you going to accuse next—Drew?"

The name slams me in the back, and I stop, my soles sinking into the grass. Drew is a fellow chef, a former employee who I lured to the Lasky brand with the promise of him running his own restaurant. One of the three chefs I fired in an ugly dispute last year because his food wasn't good enough to fill the tables.

"Drew signed a contract, dickhead. Same as you."

A contract that multiple attorneys on both sides agreed was legit. No hidden clauses, nothing sneaky or underhanded buried in legalese. The terms were spelled out in bulletproof, easy-to-understand black and white. I even cut Drew some slack, gave him some extra time to fine tune the menu to appeal to the Perimeter Mall crowd, but I couldn't keep bailing him out when sales were already slipping. A couple more months and we'd be laying off waitstaff, slashing food quality, defaulting on bills. I didn't like it, I didn't want to do it, but it was Drew or the restaurant, that's essentially what it came down to.

So yeah. Drew might have lost his job, but I'm the one who almost lost his shirt. The one who had to pump in a buttload of my own cash and energy to fix Drew's mistakes, who had to work harder and longer to patch up the holes his bad management blew in the place.

But George is not wrong. It's not like Drew wouldn't be more than happy to strike a match to the Bolling Way shop, too. And so would—

"What about Fred and Kelly? Have you been to see them yet? Because they hate your guts as much as Drew and I do."

Fred and Kelly. Once upon a time, chefs at the West Side and Inman Park shops, until sales at those restaurants started sliding, too. Just because you're a chef doesn't mean you should be running your own shop. Not everyone is cut out to be an entrepreneur.

"And what was the name of that line cook up at the Forum? The one you fired when his wife was about to get deported because he was spending too much time on the phone with his lawyer. Simon or Christian or something. Oh, and remember that mixologist you brought down from New York City to revamp the cocktail menu, only to send him packing as soon as he was done? Last I heard, he was slinging gin and tonics at the Dunwoody Country Club up the road. Any one of them would love to see Bolling Way blow up in smoke. Any one of them would have a reason to want revenge."

"You're a real asshole, do you know that?"

"You gotta admit I have a point. You really are your own worst enemy, aren't you? And assuming all those people didn't actually light the match..." He points a stubby finger at my face. "You know what they'd say about the fire, right?"

I shake my head and take off for the gate, not because I don't know but because I *do*. I know exactly what they'll say about the fire, just like a tiny part of me wonders if they might be right.

George's answer chases me out of the yard: "They'd say it's karma."

THE INTERVIEW

Juanita: One of the articles that went viral after the home invasion was an anonymous piece on *Medium*, accusing Jade of being a gold digger.

Cam: Right, and the fact that no one was willing to attach their name to such trash should have told the public all they needed to know.

Juanita: So it's not true?

Cam: When Jade and I met, I was driving a ten-year-old Honda Civic with questionable brake pads and a hole in the floorboard, and my mortgage on the leaky, rickety building that housed my first restaurant was deep underwater. Every penny I made went into that money pit, which is why I was crashing on a buddy's couch in Grant Park at the time. I couldn't afford rent and the health inspector would have had a fit if he found me sleeping under one of my dining tables. All that goes to say, if anybody was the gold digger in this scenario, it was me.

Juanita: How did the two of you meet?

Cam: Jade was one of the designers pitching for the renovation of that place. She walked into my kitchen that day, and I couldn't string two words together. She literally took my breath away. I would have hired her even if she was a talentless hack.

Juanita: [smiling] I guess it's a good thing she was talented, then.

Cam: So darn talented. She nailed the design, and then she helped me execute it on a shoestring budget. Later, she pushed me to expand that first shop into a brand, one that's timeless and recognizable, where people walk through the door and know immediately they're in a Lasky restaurant. That's all because of her.

Juanita: Sounds like building your business was a team effort.

Cam: Since day one. I mean, any decent chef can toss some meat on a grill, but Jade is the reason I went from one shop to five in the span of as many years, why I became known as Atlanta's Steak King. I owe every bit of my success to her. And on the flip side, everything I did was for her, to make her proud.

Juanita: And yet, according to your former general manager, Flavio Garcia, you have no plans to continue after the fire at

Bolling Way. You will not be reopening there or anywhere else in the city.

Cam: Lasky steak houses are a thing of the past. I guess you could say I'm relinquishing my crown.

Juanita: Atlanta's foodies will be sad to hear it.

Cam: They'll survive. There are plenty of other places in town that'll charge them a hundred bucks for some meat and potatoes.

Juanita: I don't understand. How does shutting down honor all the work Jade did to build you up?

Cam: How does anything I've done to build my brand honor her? When I got into this business, it wasn't because I loved cooking. It was because I loved watching people respond to the food I cooked for them. Seeing their eyes roll up into their head at the first bite of the perfect truffled potato. How I could create this...cocoon of good wine and good food, where they'd sit for hours and not notice the dining room had cleared out. *That* was why I became a chef, to make people feel that way.

Juanita: Why?

Cam: Why what?

Juanita: Why did you love eliciting those kinds of reactions to your food?

Cam: [laughs] You really get to the heart of it, don't you? But okay... [long pause] I liked it because it was the only time I saw my father be kind to my mother, when she cooked him a good meal.

Juanita: That sounds…

Cam: Tragic? It was. It *is*. And somewhere along the way, my reasoning got lost, or maybe it ended the way it was supposed to, the same way my parents' marriage ended—in disaster. Because holding up the Lasky brand, running that machine day after day, sucked every bit of joy out of something that, once upon a time, I thought was my destiny.

Juanita: Your former employees would agree. Accusations of mistreatment, claims of wage garnishment, improper management practices, firing staff for no reason other than you, and I quote, "didn't like the look of their stupid face." All in all, it sounds like working at Lasky Steak was pretty joyless.

Cam: For them, and for me. Honestly, shutting down was something I should have done ages ago.

Juanita: So why didn't you?

Cam: Because like me or not, all those people depended on me for a job. They depended on me for a paycheck and health care. My mother depended on me. Jade and the kids depended on me. I'm the one who put a roof over everybody's heads and food on everybody's table.

Juanita: And not just any roof. Your roof covers six thousand square feet in one of the most desirable neighborhoods in Buckhead.

Cam: Do you want it? Because I hear the bank's still looking for a buyer.

Juanita: I can't afford it, which is exactly my point. The asking price is well into the seven figures.

Cam: I'm sure they'll work with you on the price. There hasn't exactly been a run on the place after what happened upstairs. Nobody wants to live there. I certainly don't.

Juanita: But what happens to your employees? With five locations, the number must have been well into the hundreds. That's a lot of waitstaff and dishwashers and bartenders out of work.

Cam: They're the best in the business, they'll find another job. Most of them probably already have.

Juanita: That sounds a bit harsh.

Cam: Does it? I'm only saying it because it's true. My staff were trained to serve the most demanding clientele, and any chef in town would be lucky to have them. And look, did I make mistakes? Absolutely. Are there things I wish I could go back and do differently? Hell, yes. But do you have any idea how hard it is to run a restaurant, much less a chain of them? I did what I had to to survive.

Juanita: Did you garnish their wages?

Cam: [smiling] Let me guess, we're talking about George. For the record, I didn't garnish, I subtracted the costs of the damages he inflicted during one of his infamous tantrums. Ask any of my former employees. George is known for his temper, and the last night he was with us he destroyed my kitchen. There were plenty of witnesses.

Juanita: Okay, but what led up to him breaking those things?

And what do you say to the other complaints, the ones of improper firings and questionable business practices?

Cam: I'd say I made a ton of mistakes. I'd say I got carried away by the glitz and the fame, by the television appearances and fancy parties and people eating at a Lasky steak house just so they could get a picture with me. What's that old saying? The higher your star, the farther it is to fall. That's not an excuse, but I hope it's an explanation, at least.

Juanita: How many lawsuits are you dealing with right now?

Cam: Enough.

Juanita: How many, Mr. Lasky?

Cam: Three. The fourth we settled last week.

Juanita: So when you received the call from Jade that someone was in your home, holding your family for ransom, did you suspect any of your former employees and business partners?

Cam: I suspected *all* of them.

JADE

3:52 p.m.

The asshole separated us.

After he rushed the three of us upstairs, after he tied me to the blue chair in the guest room, he pressed a six-inch strip of silver duct tape over my mouth, took the kids by the hands and led them out the door.

Now they are in the playroom across the hall, doing God knows what, while I am here, helpless, attached to a chair. Losing my damn mind.

What is he doing to them?

What is happening?

I hold my breath and strain to hear, but I can't pick up on anything other than a muffled murmur of their voices spilling into the hallway and my own heart banging against my ribs. From where I sit, I can see a slice of hall, one of the two double doors swung wide, but that room is like a vault. Walls soundproofed within an inch of their life, with double layers of insulated drywall lined with vinyl sheets and pockets of air so that Cam can crank the volume on his movies up to deafening, and the rest of the house doesn't have to listen along.

But with the doors open, I would hear if there was screaming. If God forbid there were gunshots. I think these things, and my entire world teeters on a knife-edge. I am shaking—*no*, convulsing with fear and frustration and fury. If he hurts them, if he so much as touches a hair on my babies' heads, I will kill him with my bare hands.

I thrash against my bindings, but they hold firm. Braided vinyl rope, bright yellow and scratchy, wrapped multiple times around each ankle and wrist then strapped to the brass arms and legs of this blue velvet chair. The rope is too tight to wriggle loose, the slipknot tied with a sailor's skill. No way I can pull free without a knife.

And I can't scream, not with the duct tape over my mouth. Not that anybody would hear me, but still. If I could, I'd sure as hell try.

I tell myself he's not going to hurt the kids. That he's not going to sit them in a chair, press his gun to their little heads and pull the trigger. That the pistol he's been waving around is for me. *I'm* the one he wants to intimidate. If he was here to murder us, he would have done it the moment he stepped out of the shadows. Why go to all this trouble just to torment us? I tell myself he's here for something. Money, probably.

Please, God, let it be money.

I stare at the sliver of empty hallway, and the upstairs layout flashes through my mind. Walls, doors, all the corners and blind spots. There are two ways into that playroom, through those double doors out in the hallway, or an interior door we never use, one that leads to a hidden hallway and the guest room bath behind me. We keep it shut to accommodate the furniture, a marble console table with, next to it, a potted fiddle leaf fig.

Which means if I could somehow manage to break free, I could get to the kids from this room. Sneak through the hidden hallway, shove the door open and the furniture aside. Surprise, asshole. Mommy's here.

Bad odds, though, considering he's the one with the weapon and I'm stuck to a chair.

Still, I look around the room for something I could use, taking in the furniture and decor—the rosewood and brass bed, the matching nightstands, the Herman Miller dresser, all of them impractical. The closet is empty, nothing but plastic hangers and a flimsy wicker hamper, and there's nothing useful under the bathroom sink. I consider the bedside lamps, two complicated things of metal and glass anchored to the wall. A third lamp, a floor model, weighs practically nothing.

The vase, a couple of books, a vintage lucite bowl, a flawless Ritts from the sixties. A little bulky, maybe, but solid enough to bash in somebody's head. I just need to get to it first.

I struggle against the rope, but the damn thing only pulls tighter.

Beatrix's face. Oh my God, her face when that man tied me up. While Baxter chattered away about some stuffed gorilla he wanted to fetch from his room and the Xbox game Santa gave him for Christmas, Beatrix stared at the back of the man's head and said nothing. Empty eyes. Slack jaw. The kind of expression she gets from watching too much TV, or on a car ride that's taking too long. No fear. No fury. Just... nothing. Her face was like a dead zone. When this is over, she's going to need a lot of therapy.

Assuming we survive.

I shove the thought aside before it can turn into a sob, force myself to think about Baxter. At least he's doing okay. I hear his singsong voice floating on the air, no longer scared. He's too young to understand how dangerous things are, how the man is manipulating both kids in order to manipulate *me*. That bullshit marshmallow trick with Baxter, the begrudging admission he pried from Beatrix—those stunts were a message to me.

See? he might as well have said. *I control your kids, which means I control you.*

That's the kind of psycho I'm up against.

With all my might, I heave my body backward in the chair, then lurch my weight forward, but nothing happens. The legs don't lift from the floor. The chair doesn't so much as wobble. I remember the first time I sat in the thing, one sunny afternoon in the Jonathan Adler showroom. I loved the weight of it, the sturdiness, the way the horizontal brass bars at the base of the legs kept the chair stable, and always flush to the ground. Now the damn thing doesn't even budge.

And honestly, even if I managed to tip it, then what? The legs aren't legs but connected brass bars, a closed square holding up either side of the chair. Even if I were able to wriggle the rope down the legs, I can't just slip it off the feet and be free. I could maybe tip this thing, but then what—crab-run down the stairs with a forty-pound chair on my back? I won't make it very far, and I'd never leave my kids.

Shit.

Shit.

He knows this, of course. He knows as long as he stays with my kids, then I'm going nowhere—not without coming for them first. He knows if I did somehow escape, I'd come straight to them, which means he'll be ready for me. I picture him sitting in a chair facing the door, tapping the gun on his knee. Waiting.

But why? For what? What does this man want from me?

Laughter comes from the other room, and my stomach roils in an oily wave. This is torture. He's *torturing* me. SpongeBob's voice bursts from the speakers. Is he tying them up? Turning up the volume so I won't hear their screams?

I stare at the doorway across the hall and my hands shake with terror. With *rage*.

What is happening?

I have no idea, because I am tied to a goddamn chair.

I am struggling against the ropes when I hear footsteps— big ones, coming my way. Rubber soles slapping the hardwood, the feet carrying them too big, far too heavy to belong to one of the kids.

I stare at the door, the breath going solid in my lungs. From across the hall, the TV blares sounds from *The Loud House*, thumping the air in thundering bursts. I've always hated that show.

He comes around the corner, a slouchy black shadow palming a gun. He sees me and stops in the doorway, feigning surprise. "There you are. The kids and I have been looking all over for you."

I scream into the tape, "Let me go!" It comes out as a long, frantic squeal that ignites the back of my throat.

He steps into the room, his sneakers swishing on the vintage Moroccan shag, and settles the gun atop the dresser on the far wall. "So…how you been? What have you been up to? Been keeping yourself busy?"

I scream into the duct tape again, the silver strip flexing a bubble that pulls like razors on the skin around my lips. I strain against the rope, the yellow strands cutting into my sweaty skin, marring ditches into the velvet armrests.

With his free hand, he cups the lump that is his ear. "Sorry, but I didn't quite catch that." His grin inflates, and he laughs again, an exaggerated sound. "It's called enunciation. You should try it sometime."

He stands there for a few empty seconds, letting his stupid joke flutter and die. Christ, how I loathe this man.

His gaze darts around the room, taking everything in, pausing on the lamps, the vase, the lucite bowl. I wonder if he's doing what I did, cataloging them as possible weapons. When he looks back at me, he's no longer smiling. "You have a real nice house here. Really nice. Did you do all this yourself, or did you use a decorator?"

Even if I could respond to that, I wouldn't. There's no way I'm going to explain myself to this man. How I've forgotten my mother's smile but I remember every detail of the flouncy curtains she spent months cutting and stitching, or the way she would fill the house with flowers and branches she cut from the yard. I'm enough of an armchair psychologist to understand the reasons I've spent my life since surrounding myself with pretty things, or why I gave up a career that fed the hole in my soul to spend more time with the kids. This man doesn't deserve to know that about me.

Plus, if I'm right, if it's money this guy is after, there's no good answer to his question. Yes, I used a designer—me. And while I didn't pay a design fee, I also didn't pinch pennies. Every inch of this place bears my fingerprint. This house, these carpets and tables and meticulously sourced decor, it's some of my finest work.

So instead I sit quietly, taking in his eyes, hazel and almond shaped, the way they droop down at the outside corners. They're frighteningly familiar but in the same way a Labrador retriever is, or a pink-edged tulip. Seen one? Seen them all.

He moves closer, a rabid animal on the prowl.

For all my aggression earlier, now I shrink into the chair, pushing my body backward into the stuffing, but there's nowhere for me to go. The chair I'm strapped to is already pressed to the wall.

"Hold still." He bends down, and I squeeze my eyes shut and wait for it—his hot breath against my skin, his gloved hands clamping down around my throat.

This is it. This is where I die.

Something brushes my cheek, and I flinch. The sensation stops, then starts again, a steady pawing on the skin just below my cheekbone.

I crack an eye and there he is, a black shadow looming over me. One hand braced on the back of the chair, the other too close for me to see what it's doing, what *he's* doing. But I feel and hear it, the flicking of his masked finger picking at a corner of the duct tape.

His breath is moist on my face. He smells like soap and fabric softener and something bitter, like the remnants of an afternoon cup of coffee.

He manages to work a corner of the tape loose, peeling a piece of it away from my skin. His hand freezes, his gaze meeting mine head-on. "This is going to hurt. Are you ready?"

I don't even have a chance to nod before he rips the tape off in one red-hot snap, shucking the top layer of my skin with it. I'm too shocked to scream. My face, my lips, my cheeks and chin. All of it is on fire, a dousing of acid smack in the face.

He straightens, standing above me with the tape dangling from a hand. I glance down, half expecting it to be dripping snot and spit and blood. "Let's try this again. What was it you were saying?"

"Where are the kids?" My words come out on a gasp, but they're all I can think about. Where are the kids? Where are they, where are they, where are they?

"The kids are fine. Watching some cartoon in the other room. I put Beatrix in charge of the remote."

I don't tell him this is not a good idea. That neither sibling should be in charge of the channel choice. Cam's system is complicated, the remote cost a fortune, and Beatrix and Baxter can never agree on what to watch. They're not used to unlimited screen time. The only way this ends is in screaming and tears.

"Please, I want to see them. I need to tell them to be good. I need to tell them—"

That I love them.

The words stick to my throat, eating up all the air and smearing my vision with tears. As hard as I tried to keep them in check downstairs, there's no stopping them now. They roll down my cheeks, burning the raw skin around my mouth, the salt lighting it on fire. I strain against the ties on my wrists, my ankles, and I sob.

I need to tell my children I love them before it's too late.

The man backs up a few steps, sinking onto the edge of the bed. "The kids are fine. You can talk to them later. First, you and I are going to make a phone call."

I'm listening, but my gaze is glued to the door. I suck a breath to yell out to them, then reconsider. They seem calm, for now at least. If they're tied to a chair like I am, if they're distracted by the television, calling out to them would only cause panic.

"Jade." He snaps, three quick flicks of his fingers to get my attention. "Are you listening? I need you to pay attention. We're going to call your husband, and I want you to tell him he is needed here at home—"

"Fine. But first take me to the kids. I want to see Beatrix and Baxter first."

He sighs, an aggravated sound that rumbles in his lungs. "I already told you. The kids are fine. And you are not exactly in a position to negotiate."

"Please."

"We're not talking about the kids right now. They're not important."

His words ignite a bonfire in my chest, and I lean forward on the chair. "What did you do to them?"

"Jade." He bares his teeth, talking through them, low and controlled. "This isn't about the kids. This is about you and me, don't you get it? I need you to focus on what is happening, right now, right here in this room. On you, making the call to Cam."

So he knows *both* our names. It's an important tidbit I tuck away with all the other pieces I've gathered about him.

"I can't."

He frowns, two black-brown brows appearing from under the mask. "What do you mean you can't?"

I wave my hands, strapped by the wrists to the chair. "I need my hands to hold the phone. You'll have to untie me first."

Even with both hands free, the lucite bowl would be too much of a stretch, a good five feet of air between it and my fingertips. I could never clear the space fast enough, not with the rest of me attached to this chair. He'd see me lunging from a mile away. He'd smack my arm down, go for his gun, shoot me for even trying.

The man rolls his eyes. "Please, I am not an idiot." He hikes up on a hip, drags my cell phone from his pants pocket. "I'll pull up his number, and then we'll put him on speaker."

"Let me see the kids first."

"Jade. May I remind you that you are unarmed and tied to a chair?"

"Please. I'll call Cam. I'll say whatever you want me to say to him, but I need to know my children are okay. Let me see them, *please."*

He stares at the floor, sucking his bottom lip, thinking.

Dragging it out. Making me sweat. Enjoying it. The seconds stretch and dilate.

His gaze whips to mine. "If I do that, if I take you in there and let you have this little reunion you want so badly, how do I know you won't try something? How do I know you won't find yourself a weapon, or go for mine?" He glances over his shoulder at the gun, an ominous hunk of black metal on the dresser, as if I need the reminder. The threat is plenty clear, and the pressure in the room changes in an instant. He turns back, giving a slow, sad shake of his head. "I don't think so. I don't think I can trust you."

"I won't try anything. You can trust me. I swear."

"Call me a cynic, but I don't think I can."

"But I told you about the cameras. I didn't lie about those."

He doesn't respond. He just sits there on the edge of my guest room bed and stares me down, his eyes hard, his expression— what I can see of it—ice-cold. I tell myself to shut up, to stand down. There's no winning this argument. And yet I can't stop myself from begging one last time.

"*Please,*" I whisper, cheeks heating, eyes stinging. "Please let me see them."

I know that I'm being reckless, putting my life, my children's lives on the line here, but I can't think of anything but them in the other room, knowing I'm in here strapped to a chair. They must be so terrified. I need to see with my own eyes that they are safe. To comfort them, as much as the sight of them will comfort me.

The man heaves a sigh.

"Fine, you can see them, but not until after." He stabs the air, one gloved finger pointed to the ceiling. "*After* you make the call, *after* I know I can trust you to do what I say. If you do everything I tell you to, I will take you into the playroom for a little visit with the kiddos."

He's lying.

The black thought slips into my mind like a monster, ringing loud and clear in my sister Ruby's ever-cynical voice. *There's no way he's taking you to your kids, Jade. If you believe him, you're a bigger fool than I thought.* It hits me as a prophecy because she's right. No matter what I do or say, he'll never follow through. I know it with gut-punching certainty.

Bend to this man's will, gain his trust, catch him off guard. That's the plan. It's not a great plan, but it's the only plan I've got. I stare up at him, looking him straight in the eye. All I have to do is cooperate for now and wait for the exact right moment.

I swallow and speak the words he wants to hear. "What do you want me to say?"

JADE

4:07 p.m.

Cam picks up on the second ring, his voice bleating from the speaker of my iPhone.

"Yo, babe, I was just thinking. With Bolling Way in ashes, why don't we get away? Just you and me and a sunny Caribbean island. What's the one with the pink sand again? I've always wanted to see that."

"Cam."

"There's nothing I can do here anyway. Flavio can handle things with the insurance, and honestly, I could use a break. Everything was already so nutty, and now this fire. If I don't take a minute to step away from this craziness, I'm going to crash and burn."

His voice is tinny, ringing with Bluetooth and high-speed wind. I picture him flying down Peachtree in his truck, clueless I'm calling for what is essentially a ransom call. If only he would stop talking long enough for me to tell him.

"Cam."

He yammers on—about the fire, a former sous-chef leaning out of an upstairs window, karma.

"Omigod, would you *shut up*?" This time I scream into the phone. I scream so hard the back of my throat catches fire.

He stops midsentence.

"Stop talking and listen to me, okay? This is an emergency."

There's a long, empty beat of airy silence. "Is this about that skeevy guy again, because—"

"No, but I need you to listen carefully." I stare at my husband's name on my iPhone screen, and I want to scream. I want to cry. I don't want to be making this call. "There's a man here, at the house. He says that—"

"A man. What man? Who?"

If only I knew. I've spent the past hour asking myself the same question, flipping through mental headshots of Cam's salaried staff, the chefs and general managers I've met throughout the years, but there were a lot and the restaurant business is notoriously fluid. Talent bounces around, floating from restaurant to restaurant based on the latest newspaper reviews and Glassdoor rankings.

"Cam, listen to me." My voice is shaky and raw, the words scratching in my throat like twine. "This man has a gun, and he says he will kill me if—"

"A *gun*, are you *serious*? Babe. If this is a joke, it's not funny."

"It's not a joke. This man says he will shoot me and the kids unless you do exactly as he says. I'm only allowed to tell you this once. Are you ready?" I glance up at the man, and he nods his approval.

"Hell no, I'm not ready. Where are the Bees?"

Beatrix and Baxter. Instant tears at the affectionate term, said in such a desperate tone, used in such a blood-chilling context.

I gulp hard breaths, staring at the man's knock-off Adidas sneakers. Cam is a solver. He spends all day every day tearing down roadblocks and putting out fires. But he's not staring down the barrel of a gun, or attached to a forty-pound chair. He still thinks he can turn this thing around.

"The kids are in the playroom. Watching TV."

"Where are you?"

"I'm in the guest room." I squeeze my eyes tight, breathe through a slice of white-hot panic. "He tied me to the blue chair."

"You're tied to a chair. Are you for real right now? Because you're scaring me."

I'm scaring me, too. Hearing the words roll off my tongue has me electric with fear, but I can tell Cam isn't there yet. It's not that he doesn't believe me, it's just that he's still processing.

"He has a gun, Cam. He says he wants money."

"Jesus." Tires screech, and a car honks in the background. "Hold tight. I'm on the way."

"Cam, *no*. If you come without the money, he'll kill us. If you call the police, he'll kill us. Do you understand? You can't call the police. He says if you do, if he sees somebody sneaking through the yard or hears so much as a siren in the distance—" I don't think I can say the terrible words out loud, but I know I have to "—he says he'll kill the kids first and make me watch. He says he'll give me plenty of time to see it, and then he'll kill me, too."

"Let me talk to the kids. I want to talk to them."

Before we made this call, before the man pulled up Cam's contact card on my phone and hit the number for his cell, the parameters were clearly defined. This is one of the scenarios we talked about. If Cam asks to talk to the children, I am to tell him no.

I look at the man now, and he shakes his head.

"You can't. They're in the playroom."

I stare at the phone as I say it, trying to ignore the gun in his other hand, the barrel pointed at my forehead. I'm praying the last word will spark something in Cam's mind. A memory. A recollection of the three nanny cams, concealed in strategic spots around the playroom. The same ones he teased me for installing, the ones he claims were an unnecessary expense seeing as I was never going to hire a nanny.

"Are they... Are the Bees okay?"

"For now." Another answer the man and I rehearsed, one that's meant to put the fear of God in Cam.

The kids' earlier bickering from the back seat of my car rings once again through my head, wrapping like barbed wire around my heart. I will never fuss at them again. I will never lose patience when they want another hug, another story, another few minutes of my attention when I've finally found a moment alone.

I squeeze my eyes shut but it doesn't staunch the tears. "But, Cam, you have to do exactly as I say."

"Tell me. I'm ready."

"I need you to go to the bank and withdraw—it's a specific number. Maybe you should write it down."

"I'm ready," Cam says without missing a beat, and I don't push the issue. This is a man who can't remember to pack socks or take out the trash, but he never forgets a recipe, a measurement, a budget line. Cam knows exactly how many packs of butter he has in the cooler at any given moment. He knows the market price of a twenty-eight-day aged filet mignon down to the cent. He doesn't need to write the number down.

"I need you to get $734,296 in cash and bring it to the house. Do not call the police. Do not tell anyone what you need the money for. Just get it and bring it home. When you get here with the money, he'll let us go."

"Who is he?"

"I don't know. He hasn't told me his name."

"Is it…is it *him*?" Cam doesn't have to say who he's referring to. The pock-skinned, man-bunned man.

"No. At least I don't think so."

"Who, then? What does he look like?"

The man touches the side of the gun to his temple, a not-so-subtle indication to mention the mask. Before the call, he told me I was allowed to, but only if Cam asked.

"I don't know. He's wearing a mask."

The man nods, gives me a close-lipped smile. *Good dog.*

"It sounds like I'm on speaker. Is he listening? He's standing right there, isn't he?"

Finally, Cam is asking the right questions, gathering up the facts with his businessman's mind. But before this call connected, the man was very specific about what I was allowed to say. The instructions, that I'm separated from the kids, that we're fine for now but that Cam needs to hurry—those were all parts of the script. Everything else is on a case-by-case basis.

I look at him for guidance, and he gives a slow shake of his head. Panic heats the space behind my breastbone because I don't know what that means. Am I supposed to lie and say he's not listening? To not answer the question?

Cam reads the truth behind my silence. "Mister, I don't know who you are, but I want you to be assured that I will get you the money. I'll get whatever you want. But I'm begging you, please don't hurt my family."

I wait for the man's response, but he stares at the phone in his hand as the silence stretches. He's thinking, I guess, considering how to answer—*if* to answer. He looks at me, and his lips move, pink and exaggerated like a silent film star.

Police.

I frown, not understanding until his gaze flits to the phone.

"Did you hear the part about the police, Cam? You can't call them. He said no law enforcement of any kind. He'll kill us if you call them."

"I heard you. I won't call them. You have my word."

The man rolls his eyes. Across the hall, the television fades into a commercial break and the house falls quiet, only a soft hiss coming from the phone. I stare at it, stomach acid burning up my throat as my mind bubbles with terrible thoughts. *He doesn't believe Cam. He doesn't think he'll bring the money.*

Icy fingers clamp down on my heart and squeeze. "How long will it take you to get here? Do you remember the amount?"

"Seven-three-four-two-nine-six. I remember. It's a strange amount."

I said the same thing, too, and pretty much word for word. The man refused to tell me anything other than I better hope Cam will be able to scrounge up the cash.

But in the minutes ever since, in between his careful explanation of what I am to say and him punching the call into my phone, I've quietly come up with an answer: the number is not random. It's the bottom line on a bank statement he fished out of our mailbox, maybe, or the purchase price for a building Cam is bidding on for one of his restaurants. Otherwise why not demand an even $800,000? Why not shoot for a million or more?

Another realization is that as strange as the number is, it also could present a problem—it's too big to just walk into a bank and withdraw. Aren't there waiting periods for that kind of cash? Precious minutes to wait out the red tape.

And his investment strategy these past few years has been aggressive. Expanding his business, turning every bit of profit into capital for the next location. What if he doesn't have enough money liquid? Cam might have to gather up cash from different accounts, liquidate some of his assets. He might not have enough time.

Or maybe that's the whole purpose.

Terror churns in my stomach because maybe this is no typical ransom plot. Maybe this man's promises of a happy reunion is a lie. Maybe no matter what kind of miracle Cam works, the day culminates with a bullet in each of our heads.

If that's true, if this whole exercise was intended to fail, then that means nothing I do, nothing Cam does, will change how this day ends. As much as I want him to hurry, every minute he's not here means another minute the kids and I are still breathing.

Another minute I have to figure out how to get us out of this alive.

"Where are you?" I say. "How long before you can get here?"

"I don't... I don't know. It's going to take me some time to pull that kind of cash together. I'm going to have to empty the safes, move some things around between accounts, and the banks close in what—an hour? It would be a lot quicker to just transfer the money, all I need is a—"

"No." Another one of the scenarios the man and I discussed, and he was crystal clear. "No bank transfers. It has to be cash, and you have to bring it by seven. He says one second later than that and we're dead."

"Seven o'clock *tonight*?" Cam's voice cracks through the speaker, incredulous. "I don't... That doesn't give me anywhere near enough time."

"Yes. He was very specific about the time." I don't mention that the man smiled when he said it: *Tell your darling husband seven o'clock or else.* Almost like a dare.

In the background, squealing wheels pierce through the roar of an engine. "Look, sir, whoever you are, listen to me. I will get you this money, but you have to understand there are forces out of my control. It's rush hour. Traffic is a nightmare, and the banks are going to take forever. I can probably stitch together a couple hundred thousand today, and then tomorrow morning first thing I'll get you the rest. I swear to you I'll pull through, but I just don't—"

"*Cam.*" The gun's barrel is flush to my forehead, jabbing it into the bone, pressing hard enough to leave a bruise. Icy metal against scalding skin.

I think about my children in the next room, my husband on the phone, how if this man pulls the trigger now, they will hear everything. The gunshot, my insides splattering onto the wall. This will be their last memory of me, the exact moment they heard me die.

He pushes harder.

"He wants the money today, Cam. *All* of it. By seven."

A long pause filled with exhaled air, hard and sharp like Cam had been gut punched.

"Okay. *Okay.* I'll figure something out. I don't know what, but I'll do it. Hold on, babe, I'll be there as soon as I can."

"Please hurry." A shuddery spasm traps in my throat, a sob struggling to escape.

"Jade, just…hold tight, okay? Take care of the Bees, tell them I love them. I will be there as soon as humanly possible. I love y—"

Click. With a rubber-tipped finger, the man pushes End.

CAM

4:19 p.m.

The air in the truck's cab reeks of sweat and terror. The light up ahead flips to yellow, and the sea of traffic in front of me glows eerie red, brake lights as far as I can see. I screech to a stop behind a white SUV, slam the steering wheel with the heel of my hand, my whole world turning crimson.

A masked man. A gun. My wife tied to a fucking chair.

The call was coming from *inside the house.*

And the kids are, what—splayed on the carpet on the playroom floor? Strapped to one of the recliners, a sock stuffed into their mouths? The horrible, awful vision slips like black smoke across my mind, and I pound the wheel and howl into my car because I don't know. I don't know if they're bound and gagged, if they're conscious, if they're even really alive. *For now,* Jade said when I asked if they were okay, and as much as I believe my wife, I know one thing with one hundred thousand percent certainty: never believe the asshole with the gun.

Calm down, Cam. You can't save any of them if you drop dead of a heart attack. Calm down and breathe.

But it's hard getting any air with this Mack truck sitting on my chest. My heart is a clenched fist, punching a fast, erratic beat against my ribs. I'm on the verge of blacking out—an all too familiar sensation these days, like floating out of my body and watching myself die from three feet above.

Only you don't die from panic attacks or atrial fibrillation or whatever the hell else the ER doc told me these episodes could be. You only feel like it.

The light turns green, but traffic doesn't move, and I lay on the horn. The woman in the SUV takes her sweet time, pausing to wag a bird over her shoulder before she shifts her foot to the gas. The car eases forward, and I ride the brake and her bumper. I glance over both shoulders, edging closer to the lanes on either side, but I'm closed in by wall-to-wall traffic, and it's not going to loosen anytime soon. Atlanta's notorious rush hour is just getting started.

Calm down.

Think things through.

Don't come to me with a list of problems, I'm always preaching to my staff. *Bring me the solutions.* Identify the issues, evaluate your options, tackle the items one by one. This is what I am constantly telling them.

Now it's my turn.

Problem number one: I don't have $734,296 in cash. I don't have that anywhere in a nearby universe. Cash flow may be the lifeblood of the restaurant business, but that doesn't mean I have piles of it lying around. Whatever cash I have on paper, none of it is liquid.

And contrary to popular belief, the restaurant business doesn't run on cash, not since an Atlanta bartender was killed in a late-night burglary a few years back. Overnight, every sit-down restaurant in town instituted a no-cash policy—Apple Pay or cards only. Even with the tip jars at the bars, even if I raided the valet stands, there's no way I can come up with that kind of money, not before the 7 p.m. deadline.

Which brings me to problem number two: just under three hours for this mission impossible, and that includes driving time in bumper-to-bumper traffic. I'm still a good four minutes away from the office, and the banks close in—I glance at the clock on the dash—forty-eight minutes.

The vise around my chest twists tighter, sending a surge of adrenaline to my heart. It bangs against my ribs in an almost painful pulse, brisk and erratic. The last time I felt this way, an ER doc whipped out the heart paddles.

The lane to my left opens up, and I swerve into it and gun the gas, blowing past the SUV.

Problem number three: no police.

Honestly, this is the only one of his demands I can get behind. The idea of a bunch of armed cops swarming up the lawn, busting through doors and crawling through windows... I've seen enough movies to know how that scenario ends, and the thought of something happening to Jade and the kids makes my double-beating heart explode into quadruple time. Whatever made this guy decide today was the day to force his way into my house and hold my family at gunpoint, it's not because he has any other options. His back is against a wall, and he's obviously desperate. I don't want to think about what will happen to Jade and the Bees if I fail.

So, on to solutions, then.

1. Gather up the money. Get as much as you can from the bank before it closes, and then whatever it takes. Loan shark, armed robbery, murder for hire. Whatever I have to do to scrounge up the cash, and do it fast.

2. Deliver it at the house before seven tonight.

3. Alone.

Oh, and 4. Don't drop dead of a heart attack before you get Jade and the kids out alive.

I take a right at the light, tires squealing as I veer onto a two-lane road that runs along the rail yard, empty train tracks stretching out to my left. A shortcut from the southern tip of Buckhead to my office on Atlanta's west side. If it weren't for the blue-haired lady in front of me, a two-minute trip. I gun it around her ancient sedan, and the road opens up.

I pull up the number for my banker's cell and hit Call.

"Cam, hey," Ed says, picking up on the second ring. "I was just about to call you. I heard something about a fire?"

An instant reminder of the day's first disaster. Now it barely makes a blip.

"Wow. Word travels fast, huh?"

Ed makes a sound that's not quite a laugh. "Big city, small town. And you know how people here love to talk. I heard it from my wife, who heard it from the manager of the Restoration Hardware across the road. Was it bad?"

"Catastrophe territory, which is why I'm calling. I need to know how much is left on that line of credit and how quickly I can get to it."

I know how much is left on the line of credit: a couple thousand and some change. Peanuts compared to what I need, but I also know how Ed ticks. He hates being confronted with a big ask. He likes to be buttered up, warmed up, massaged, and he gets a kick out of solving money problems. It's basic psychology, really. People are more open to a proposition if they're part of the solution.

There's a rapid clicking through the phone, Ed's fingers flying across the keyboard. "As I recall, it was somewhere around a couple thousand. A little more, maybe, but not much. If you give me a second, I can pull up the numbers."

"What's the chance of you guys increasing it?"

The clicking stops. "By how much?"

"By another half million, maybe more." I wince. So much for buttering him up.

Ed blows out a long, slow breath. Silence on the line.

A couple of years ago, Ed would have signed off on the loan without question. Lasky runs tens of millions of dollars annually through his bank, and for what's coming up on a decade. A consistent flow every year like clockwork—only now most of it goes to my investors. As my banker, Ed knows they're the ones with the money, not me.

"Come on, Ed. You know I'm good for it."

"I know you're a fantastic chef and a hardworking businessman, yes, and that you've been an ideal client for the past seven-plus years. But I also know you've taken on investors and are probably already overextended as it is. And you read the papers. The market is volatile, and every banker I know is treading water, praying the economy doesn't tank like the *Titanic*. I've been ordered to sit tight until further notice."

"Sit tight on what—me?"

"Not you. Lasky Steak."

"That's the same damn thing!"

Ed doesn't respond, mostly because he can't dispute it. I am Lasky Steak and Lasky Steak is me.

I swallow, trying not to throw up. "So no more loans."

"None. Like, zero. Not unless something's changed since the last time we talked and you can put up some serious collateral. And so we're clear, it's not only you. Nobody is handing out free money right now, Cam. We're all in a waiting pattern."

I swerve into the office lot, a long strip of asphalt that runs alongside the squat redbrick building where Lasky Steak, Ltd. is pressed between a furniture distributor and a chocolate shop.

I sling the truck into a spot by the door, grab my cell from the cupholder and flip the audio onto my phone's speaker.

"Okay, then. What about my IRA?" I slide out of the truck and race up the alleyway with my phone and keys. I don't expect to find anybody inside. This place is mostly for me, more living room and test kitchen than office space, an escape I picked up for a steal soon after Beatrix was born, because I couldn't get a lick of work done at home. I fumble with the keys in the lock, but it's cranky and refuses to cooperate.

"What about it?" Ed says.

"What's it worth and how fast can you cash it out?" The dead bolt gives, and I trample inside, tapping in the code for the alarm. I don't bother with the lights, or even closing the door behind me. I'm not going to be here for long.

"Besides the fact that you'd have to pay a penalty fee *plus* taxes on the entire amount, did you hear what I just said about the stock market? Don't touch your IRA, Cam. You'd take a huge hit."

"I need to know what it's worth."

"God, I don't know. Half a million if you're lucky."

The number sticks to my stomach like an ulcer. I haven't logged in to the account since the last time the stock market took a nosedive. Too painful, especially since my strategy was to wait it out. I'm young, not quite forty. I figured I wouldn't have to touch it for a while.

But a half million? Shit. It should be at least double that.

"Do it," I say, my shoes squeaking on the polished concrete floor. "But there's one caveat. I need the money today."

I'm moving fast through the dim space, past the factory-style windows high on the exposed brick walls, hung with the twinkle lights I inherited from the caterer I bought the place from. Jade didn't do much other than throw some vintage rugs over the polished concrete floor, add some couches and chairs—"conversation corners," she calls them. And in the middle of the room, a glass chandelier over a giant oak table she designed herself, littered with cookbooks and papers. I can't walk by the thing without thinking back to the night we broke it in; Baxter was born ten months later.

On the other end of the phone, Ed chokes on a laugh, a loud phlegmy bark. "You can't... That's... Look, I want to work with you, I really do, but that's impossible. Your IRA isn't liquid. We're going to have to sell off the stocks first, and there are transfer times—"

"I need the money, Ed. Like yesterday." I settle my cell on a shelf in the storage room, giving him time for the realization to sink.

A long, painful silence.

I plug the code into the safe, and the lock slides open with a metallic *thwunk*.

"Is this about the fire?" Ed says finally. "Because if it is, I can maybe help get the ball rolling with the insurance company. You're with Hartford, right?"

"This isn't about the fire." I turn around, scanning the shelves for a box, a bag. Something small and inconspicuous. I spot a shoebox on the top shelf filled with old receipts and dump them onto the floor.

"Then what?"

What would happen if I told him the truth? Would he tell his boss, call the cops? I'm pretty sure bankers have an ethical obligation to report suspected crimes, so better to keep Ed in the dark.

"I don't have time to explain. You're going to have to trust me on this."

"And *you're* going to have to give me some kind of indication of what's going on before I can agree to do this. I can't help you without an answer."

Normally I could volley like this for days. Winning Ed over with words, cooking up steaks and uncorking a bottle of my best red, plying him gently to my side, but every second I spend arguing is another second I don't have the money. The clock is ticking. My heart feels like it's about to explode. I don't have time for this shit.

I grab my phone from the shelf and hold it an inch from my face. "What's going on is that I need you to give me my money. *Give me my damn money, Ed. It's mine. Give it to me!*"

There's a long patch of empty air, and I force myself to pause. To take a deep breath and blow it out. Get my temper under control just enough to sound remorseful as I start again. "Come on, Ed. You *know* me. You know I wouldn't ask unless this was life or death. The truth is I'm desperate, man."

The silence stretches again while in my head, I'm doing the math. The rest of the line of credit, the few piles of cash in the safe, cash advances on my three credit cards. If I'm lucky, $100K, which means without that IRA, I'm screwed. Jade and the kids are screwed. I don't have anywhere near enough.

I slide the money into the shoebox, along with what I really came for: my gun, a tidy black Smith & Wesson. The three magazines, eight 9mm rounds apiece, I drop into my jacket pocket. That's twenty-four bullets I can sink into the asshole in the mask. I grab the box and head for the door.

Ed blows out a breath heavy enough to rattle the line. "Fine. But you'll have to give me a minute to run things by my boss. Maybe we can work something out where we extend the line of credit if you sign over your IRA. Just to bridge the time it takes to sell the stocks."

"Thanks, Ed. I really, really appreciate it. I owe you one."

"Don't thank me just yet. Alissa still needs to sign off on this plan, and even then, I don't see how any of this takes place today. It's going to be tomorrow morning at the earliest before I have that kind of cash."

I close the door and jog down the alleyway to the truck. "Life or death, Ed. I need the money by closing time."

Ed puffs another defeated sigh. "Then you'd better let me go so I can get busy."

THE INTERVIEW

Juanita: After that phone call from Jade, why wasn't your first call to the police?

Cam: Because those were the marching orders. Bring home $734,296 by seven and don't call the cops. Jade made it perfectly clear what would happen if I didn't obey.

Juanita: Seven hundred, thirty-four thousand…

Cam: And two hundred ninety-six dollars.

Juanita: That's an awfully big number.

Cam: Yeah, no kidding. And an hour before the banks were set to close.

Juanita: Almost like he wanted you to fail.

Cam: Or like he wanted to torture me, because I sure as hell didn't have that kind of money lying around.

Juanita: How can that be? You owned five restaurants consistently named as the best restaurants in not just the city but the country. Before the fire, your Buckhead steak house had a six-week wait for a Saturday night table. You were featured in magazines and newspapers, and were a regular guest on the morning news shows. You even beat out Bobby Flay on *Iron Chef*. You're very successful.

Cam: *Was* very successful. *Was*. But after *Iron Chef*, investors were tossing me money like they'd just hit the jackpot in Vegas, more cash than I ever thought imaginable. Like a fool, I grabbed on with both hands, never stopping to think through the consequences of opening another shop before the one before it was paid off. Because here's the thing about investors, Juanita—they really like you a whole lot better when you pay them back.

Juanita: What happens if you miss a payment?

Cam: Depends on the investor. Most were pretty reasonable. A thirty-day cure provision, meaning I had a month to get my act together and cough up the money. After that, it depends on the terms of the contract, how much I was willing to put up as collateral.

Juanita: What were your terms?

Cam: They were 50 percent interest in the shop, 50 percent of the profits and a personal guarantee.

Juanita: So, a lot.

Cam: Everything but the wife and kids.

Juanita: And the others? The ones who were less reasonable?

Cam: [smiles] They were the first to get paid back.

Juanita: Did you ever consider shuttering one or more of your restaurants?

Cam: Of course I thought about it. For about three seconds.

Juanita: Why so short?

Cam: Because in the restaurant world, closing your doors for any reason is equivalent to failing. Especially if people were ever to find out the truth, that I closed because of money problems. The Lasky brand would have suffered. The rest of my shops would have fallen like dominoes.

Juanita: And then there's also the fact that Jade had no idea you were experiencing money problems.

Cam: [sighs] And then there's that. The point is, I had no choice but to keep trying to dig myself out of the hole.

Juanita: What made you decide to keep your money issues from her?

Cam: God, I don't know. A million and one reasons. Because her father never liked me. Because her sister would have never let us hear the end of it. But I guess it all goes back to the fact that I was too proud, *am* too proud. I mean, all that time I told myself I kept going because of her, but that's a lie. It was because of me. Because I couldn't admit I was a failure, because I couldn't stand the thought of ending up just like...

Juanita: Like your father?

Cam: Yeah, like him. I remember what it was like after he lost all his money, the way Mom and I went from this giant mansion to a seedy hotel, all the whispers that would start up the second she left a room. Do you know that's the reason I chose steaks as part of the Lasky brand? Because to me it was the ultimate status symbol, being able to afford a hundred-dollar meal on a regular old Tuesday.

Juanita: So your ambition stemmed from not wanting to make his mistakes.

Cam: If you'd asked me a year ago, I'd say it was because I didn't want to put Jade and the kids through what I went through as a kid, but that's not the truth. It was about *me*. I didn't want to go through that again. So okay, maybe I was an asshole to my employees, but it was because I was drowning, trying to keep my business afloat while taking on water.

Juanita: Even more reason for calling 9-1-1. The Atlanta Police Department has a Special Weapons and Tactics unit. They have officers specialized in hostage negotiation, ones with specific skills and decades of experience. They know what to do in hostage situations, because they respond to more reports of home invasions in a month than many other cities do in a year.

Cam: [sarcastic laugh] Doesn't say much for our fair city, does it?

Juanita: My point is, the police would have known what to do.

Cam: Or they would have come in, sirens wailing, busted down my front door and started shooting until somebody was dead. Which as you know, they did.

Juanita: You could have told them not to use the sirens.

Cam: I did what I had to do, what I thought was the best thing at the time.

Juanita: But police officers are trained for this exact situation. They know how to respond in order to save lives.

Cam: Look, lady. You and whoever's on their cushy couches at home can sit there and judge me all you want, but let's talk again when it's your wife chained to a chair, begging you to hurry home with money you don't have while your children scream bloody murder in the background. Until then, until you've stood in my shoes with the weight of a thousand elephants on your chest because you can't cobble together the ransom to save the people you love most, I suggest you save your judgment for someone else because you don't know what that's like. You can't know until you've been there.

Juanita: Point taken. But tell me this, knowing what you know now, if you could go back and do things over, what would you do differently?

Cam: [leans forward in the chair] Every single goddamn thing.

JADE

4:19 p.m.

The man watches me from above. "Who's 'him'?"

I frown, more concerned with the strip of duct tape dangling from his fingers like a shiny silver snake. My skin still stings from where he ripped it off the first time, and I'm not looking for a repeat.

"Please don't put that over my mouth again. I promise I won't scream."

Screaming would only scare the kids, which I really don't want to do. They're being so brave, so sweet and quiet in their playroom, and I know from experience this peaceful state won't last long. Especially if they hear their mother across the hall, screaming her face off.

And even if I did scream, the nearest house is a quarter acre away, separated by multiple layers of stone and plaster and double glass. No way anybody outside would hear, not even if they were standing on the front stoop.

He moves closer, and I crane my head back until it's flush against the wall. "You promised to take me to my kids. You said you'd let me see them after the call."

"Yeah, well, I lied. Now answer the question, Jade. Who's 'him'?"

"What?"

"Just now. Cam asked if I was him. You said you didn't think so. Who's 'him'?"

I'm barely listening, still reeling from the fact that I don't get to see my kids. I stare at the door and the slice of empty hall and try not to cry. "Just some guy who's been following me around town."

"You have a stalker? How very Buckhead Betty of you. But how do you know I'm not the same person?" He waves a gloved hand in front of his masked face, a demented Vanna White. "It's not like I'm giving you much to go on here."

Admitting I have a stalker is one thing, but granting him insight in my thought processes, my fears, is another. I give him the most obvious answer.

"Your build is different. He's shorter and smaller, skinnier. And he has a man bun, which I'm pretty sure you don't have under that mask."

He barks a laugh. "A man bun. No, I don't have a man bun." His tone says *ridiculous*.

I add another item to my mental list: mainstream hairstyle, traditional cut. Or possibly bald. Either way, not the type to sport a man bun.

"But it is interesting, don't you think, that another man has been following you, too. What do you think he wants?"

I lift a shoulder but remain silent. I'm not about to get into my theories with this man—not that I have all that many. Until that guy showed up at Beatrix's violin lessons today, I always just assumed running into him was random.

And I don't miss this man's choice of words, that someone *else* has been following me. I think back to all those times I raced through Whole Foods, bracing for the man-bunned man to pop around the corner. Was I so distracted by looking for him that I didn't notice the other, more sinister man trailing me up and down the aisles? Did he follow me to the gym, the coffee shop, the post office, Beatrix's violin lessons, too? As I go about my normal day, am I really that oblivious?

He sinks onto the edge of the bed directly across from me, the mattress springs creaking under his weight. "But it does make you wonder, though…" He shakes the tape from his fingers and it flutters to the floor, landing upside down on the rug.

I stare at him, waiting for him to finish.

"How much do you know about your husband's business?"

I try not to let on how surprised I am at his words, how much this question disturbs me. It's a little surreal how perfectly he dropped it into the conversation, too, in a voice so casual and offhand, shooting it off like a poisonous dart. These words were meant to rouse suspicion. I'm not about to give him the satisfaction.

"Cam and I are partners. He tells me everything."

The truth is, this only *used* to be the case. Cam and I fell in love while building his brand. Some of our best date nights were spent making the rounds, bouncing from restaurant to restaurant so he could check on things in the kitchen while I schmoozed with the customers and made sure the lounge pillows were fluffed and the flower arrangements fresh. Yes, it was work, but there was plenty of time for socializing as well—sending over free apps whenever we spotted friends, popping by their table for a glass of wine, offering folks a free cocktail at the bar. Every night was work and one big party all rolled into one. Once upon a time, it was how Cam and I connected.

But that was before kids, and homework and bedtime rituals and early-morning carpools that had me crawling under the comforter by ten. Cam and I make it a point to eat lunch together most days, but we rarely talk about work. Not for a while now.

"What about Cam's business?" I say.

Across from me, the man's lips spread in a hideous smile, and I know I'm giving this asshole exactly what he wants, but my reasoning is more than just bald-faced curiosity. Every hint he drops, every tiny tidbit he buries in a sentence he thinks I won't notice…they're all clues. At some point this man will make a mistake and say something revealing. The more I know, the more chances I have to survive this thing. At some point, I will catch my enemy off guard.

"I can't decide if you're playing with me," he says, his words slow, thoughtful, "or if you really don't know."

He falls silent, a long, strategic pause as he watches me with dark, observant eyes. He's waiting for me to engage, to beg him for information, but I don't respond. If Cam were here, he'd tell me I'm being too proud.

Baxter's singsong voice carries across the hall, the sound too low for me to pick out his words from the TV soundtrack, and his chatter both soothes and terrifies me. It means Baxter and Beatrix are conscious, that they're safe—as the man said, *for now.* Assuming Cam can scrounge up three-quarters of a million dollars and somehow make it home by seven—two colossal assumptions. I just have to keep the kids alive until then, but how am I supposed to do that when I'm stuck in this chair?

The man twists around on the bed, facing the open doorway. "Yo, Bax."

I try to think of something to stop him, to keep his focus on me, on right here in this room, but my mind is thick as peanut butter.

A stomach-fluttering pause, then a high voice floats across the hall: "Yeah?"

The man glances back, just long enough to flash me a wink. "Everything okay over there?"

This is all for my benefit. This man is manipulating me again, dangling my most precious carrot and daring me not to snap it up. Calling out to the kids now is punishment—for not taking his bait fast enough, for not playing along with his stupid, diabolical game. I'm a rat, trapped in his maze.

The words burst out of me, high and frantic. "If I really don't know what?"

He lifts a finger to his lips and tilts his head, pointing his ear at the door.

"The commercials are taking forever," Bax calls out. "But can you come over here? I got a cramp."

The man puffs a laugh, turning back to me with a look I recognize through the mask. *Crazy kids.* He doesn't know that this is classic Baxter, and that "cramp" is an excuse. A word that can mean virtually anything, from help changing the channel to bringing him a snack, getting him a glass of water, reading him another book, giving him your undivided attention. He says it so often, the word has infiltrated the Lasky family lexicon. When the recycling bin needs to be rolled to the curb, I tell Cam I have a garbage cramp. When Cam wants sex, he tells me he has a penis cramp.

And now Baxter is using the word with this man as if he's here to help us, not hold us hostage. He's too young to understand what's really happening here. He's too trusting to be scared. One stupid magic trick downstairs, and Bax is buddying up to the monster.

"If I really don't know what?" I say again, red-hot adrenaline thumping in my veins. "Please tell me what you know about Cam's business. Because if there's some kind of problem, if he's hurt you in any way, I can help. Cam listens to me. Please let me help."

"You want to help."

It's not a question, but I nod anyway, a series of frantic and fast bobs of my head.

The man pushes off the bed. "I gotta tell you, Jade, I wasn't expecting you to be this accommodating, not with that temper of yours. Remember when you lost your shit after the valet couldn't find the key to your car? You threatened to have him fired."

Oh, I remember. We were trying out a new sitter, a friend of a friend of a friend's nanny, a high-strung girl who had just called in a panic after Baxter projectile vomited his spaghetti dinner over the antique Beni Ourain and was running a 102-degree temperature. Cam was in the kitchen, cooking for a CEO roundtable, leaders of Atlanta's Fortune 500s crammed into the private room, and his truck was in the shop. With my car stuck in the lot, it took me twice as long to get home in an Uber.

But the bigger point is that *he* remembers, which means he was there. He saw me throw that fit.

A Lasky employee, then? A client?

"Tell you what," he says when I don't respond. "Let's stick a pin in this subject for now. Just until I get back, so...don't move, okay?" He laughs—another stupid, pathetic joke. "Hang tight while I go check on the kids."

As soon as he's gone, I lurch forward at the waist and tug at the rope with my teeth. The guy is smart, positioning the knot on the far side of my wrist, too far for me to reach with my mouth, so my first task is to somehow rotate the rope until the knot is on top. I bite and pull, bite and pull, nudging the rope along with little flicks of my wrist. It drags over the skin of my arm in millimeter increments, painful and excruciatingly slow.

Words float in disconnected fragments across the hall.

...Mommy...talk to her...very important.

Bax again, speaking in Baxter code. The more trifling the request, the more urgently it is delivered. He wants to tell me about a pretty blue bird that's perched on the windowsill, probably, or an unreachable itch in the center of his back. How long have we been upstairs—twenty minutes at the most? Even with the cartoons blaring, it's long past the limit for a six-year-old to sit still and be quiet. The question is, how much will the masked man tolerate?

The man's voice comes in a low murmur, too faint for me to hear.

I work at the ties and do the math. My watch says it's a few minutes before 4:30—a little more than a half hour until the banks close and two and a half hours before Cam's deadline. Whoever this man is across the hall, whatever he thinks he knows about my husband, I wonder what he knows about the restaurant business. Three-quarters of a million dollars is a lot to have just lying around, liquid cash Cam could stuff in a bag when his system is geared to cashless transactions, credit cards and Apple Pay and touchless payment apps. Even if Cam raided all the tip jars and valet stands, there's no way he'd get anywhere close. He's going to have to make a trip to the bank.

Questions beat through my mind like razor blades.

Who is this guy? A fired waiter? A bartender or chef? He's stronger than me, faster, too. Even if I managed to wriggle myself loose from this chair, can I sneak across the hall and surprise him with the lucite bowl to the temple? Can I kick the gun from his hand and then use it to shoot him in the face?

And then, darker, more dangerous thoughts: three-quarters of a million dollars is a *lot*. What if Cam can't get to the bank in time? What happens to us then?

For a bleak moment, I think about how the kids and I will end this day. How difficult Cam's task is, how helpless and outmatched I am stuck to this damn chair. One false move, and the man could kill everyone in this house—*bang bang bang*—and still have bullets left over for Cam when he arrives. Maybe that's been his plan all along, to kill us, then take the money and run. Maybe this whole afternoon is just part of his evil game.

By now my right wrist is slick with spit, and the knot has rotated a good inch. Only a half inch more and then—

Beatrix's scream pierces the upstairs hallway.

SEBASTIAN

4:27 p.m.

Confession time. This Beatrix kid is a pain in my ass.

Her little brother, Baxter, I can manage. That kid is just begging for some attention, which I pretend to give him while he rambles on about the pair of squirrels fighting over an acorn in the yard. Unsurprisingly, the big one won.

But Beatrix's scream was meant to piss me off and blow out my eardrums. And what a scream it was, one of those top-of-the-lungs, glass-shattering shrieks made for a horror movie soundtrack, loud and high enough to echo around my skull. The dull throbbing behind my mask is just painful enough to be distracting.

And the remote, which I'd stuck in her hand after duct taping her arms to the armrests, she somehow manages to hurl across the room like a Frisbee. That's what Baxter called me over for, to tell me the channel needed changing and Beatrix had accidentally dropped the remote on the floor.

I take in the distance from her fingertips to the remote, lying upside down by the far wall. Eleven feet, maybe more, and pitched high enough to clear the coffee table. All that, with one flick of her wrist. I hate to admit it, but it's impressive, really. Somebody sign this kid up for baseball.

But still.

That doesn't change the fact that Beatrix is trouble. That stubborn act of defiance downstairs in the kitchen, the remote, her feral scream just now. She might be skinny, but she's a spitfire with a vicious streak to go with that ridiculous hair. On a normal day, I bet she's a handful.

And that finger tapping. A constant and random rapid-fire drumming of her left hand. A nervous tic? Some kind of secret code? I check in with her brother, who's staring open-mouthed at the TV. Completely oblivious.

Across the hall, Jade blubbers for her daughter, begging Beatrix to tell her what's wrong, assuring her that everything's okay. It's a lie, of course. Jade knows that everything is *not* okay. Not even close. Not unless Super Cam can swoop in and save the day.

"Beatrix, *please*," Jade hollers from across the hall. "Answer me! What's happening over there?"

Beatrix lies on her plush leather recliner like a slug, her glare stuck to the ceiling. Chest heaving, limbs splayed, slack at the ankles and the forearms where they're pinned down by multiple layers of duct tape.

But at least she's comfortable. I made sure of it when I put her there. I reclined the damn seat as far as it would go. I attached the tape to her socks and not the bare skin of her ankles so it wouldn't pull the fine blond hairs. I even let the siblings sit next to each other instead of on opposite ends of the couch in case the little one got squirrely.

"You gonna put your mama out of her misery?" I say, and

Beatrix's gaze whips to mine. "Sounds like she's having some sort of panic attack." I shrug like I couldn't care either way.

Beatrix gives me her best eye roll, then looks toward the door. "I'm okay," she shouts, and her tone is begrudging at best. "He didn't hurt me."

I settle my gun on a shelf at the far wall and pick up the remote, giving her my best stern-dad look. And Lord knows I've had plenty of practice. Gigi was a handful, too, but at least with her, I knew where the bad behavior was coming from.

"Wanna tell me what this is about?" I wag the remote by my ear. "How come you threw the remote across the room?"

"She dropped it," Baxter says, taking up for his big sister.

I ignore him. "Is this how you treat electronics in this house, like they're disposable? Like they're a worthless piece of trash? Are you really that much of a spoiled brat?"

Behind me, the television blares a commercial, an annoying jingle for some kind of sugary cereal. I punch the mute button with a thumb. "Beatrix, I asked you a question. I'm going to need an answer."

Baxter looks at Beatrix.

Beatrix glares at me. "To which one? That was three questions."

I almost laugh. *Almost.* This kid's too smart for her own good, an added complication I need to figure out how to tame—and fast. Too much planning has gone into this day to let a sassy, spoiled kid ruin everything.

"Hey, mister?" Baxter says, but I don't look over. I don't acknowledge him at all. Let this be a lesson to him, too, to not interrupt when other people are talking.

"Do you know how much a remote like this one costs?" I say to Beatrix. "Hundreds and hundreds of dollars. And look here, you cracked the screen. These things don't just grow on trees, you know."

She looks away, bored. *Bored.*

I'd forgotten how impossible nine-year-olds can be. My fingers itch to spank her.

I settle the remote in the bowl on the coffee table and sink onto the edge. "Look, if you and I are going to get through this afternoon in one piece, you're going to have to do better. To *be* better. You told me downstairs I could trust you. Now I need you to prove it. And just so we're clear, throwing remotes around and letting your mama get all riled up isn't the way to do it. Don't you hear her over there?"

That breaks through the noise in Beatrix's immature brain. She stops seething long enough to cock her head, to listen to her mother sobbing across the hall. I see the second she feels regret.

"You did that," I say, pointing a long finger at her face. "*You* made your mama cry. That's on you."

Her angry scowl bleeds away.

Baxter wriggles in his chair. "Mister, I really gotta—"

"Zip it." I hold up a hand in his direction. "This conversation is between me and your sister. You're going to have to wait your turn."

"But it's *important.*"

A cramp. He's cold. A dancing chipmunk on the windowsill. A cloud that looks like a question mark. Baxter believes that they're *all* worth everyone's attention.

"Kid, you really need to learn the definition of *important*, you know that? Now pipe down. I'll deal with you in a minute." I turn back to his sister, working to soften my tone. "Hey, I've got an idea. How about you and I start over? Let's just wipe this messy slate clean and begin again, how does that sound? You promise to be good, and I'll promise not to hurt you or your br—"

I stop. Sniff the air, at the exact same time Baxter empties his lungs. *"The poop is coming!"*

CAM

4:38 p.m.

I stare at the broad backside of the fussy fortysomething lady blocking the teller's window and will her to hurry the hell up. Twenty-two minutes and counting until the security guard locks the big glass door behind me and flips the sign to Closed, and this woman is standing here like she has all day.

She leans against the counter, oblivious to the line six people deep behind her, and shouts into the bulletproof glass, "I really need that money today."

Yeah, welcome to the club, lady.

I can't see the teller from where I'm standing, but a tinny voice spurts from the speaker at the edge of the glass. "I understand that, ma'am, but the bank typically needs twenty-four hours' notice for a cashier's check. Did you place the order online?"

The lady shakes her head, but her brown bowl cut doesn't budge. From her shoulder, a wrinkly canvas bag says "Abs are cool but have you tried doughnuts?" in pink and purple rhinestones. "That's what I'm here for, to place the order and get the check. That's why I got in my car and drove all the way over here, because I need it today."

I shift to my other foot and sigh, loud and obvious, and I'm not the only one. Hushed curses and heaved sighs swirl from the folks behind me, all clutching their wallets and checking their watches. Another teller ambles by behind the window with a stack of twenties, looking everywhere but in the direction of the glass. A Next Window Please sign stands propped at the other three teller windows, the blue canvas stools behind them empty.

I look around for a manager, another bank employee, anyone I can ask to light a fire under this transaction, but if they're here, they're hiding. Even the security guard is gone, vanished behind the thick locked doors.

"I can put a rush on your order, ma'am," the teller is saying, "but there is an added fee, and we'll still need time to pull the check together. And considering we close in…twenty minutes, I'm afraid the check won't be ready until tomorrow."

Twenty minutes. The words hit me square in the chest, seizing my heart into a concrete ball, and I battle to catch a breath. My ribs feel like they're packed in cement, the muscles locked up tight. The air can't make it to the bottom of my lungs.

My phone buzzes with an incoming call, and I yank it from my pocket, my chest deflating when I see the screen.

Not Jade.

Not Ed.

I swipe and press it to my ear. "Hey, Mom."

"Well, don't sound so disappointed. I was just calling to see how you're doing."

No way in hell I'm telling her about Jade and the kids. Mom

is a worrier. She'll spiral and call me every two seconds. I love her, but I wish I hadn't picked up.

"I'm okay, but I can't really talk right now."

"Aw, sweetie. Don't take it so hard. I know the article was not the most flattering, but you can recover. Maybe you can get that PR person of yours to work some magic and have some of the worst parts retracted."

"What worst parts?"

Mom keeps talking, her words tumbling over mine. "And maybe while you're at it, you could talk to your attorney. I mean, I'm not saying you should sue, but they might be able to twist an arm or two."

"Mom. What are you talking about? What article?"

"The one in the *AJC*. 'The Joylessness of Cooking,' that's what that reporter titled the piece of trash. And don't you worry, I've already written a letter to the editor complaining about journalistic bias."

I wince. Great. A letter from my mother, published in Atlanta's largest newspaper. Just what I need.

At the front of the line, the woman smacks her bag to the counter. The teller leans around her form and mouths, *Sorry*. I stare at the woman's backside and try not to faint. Nineteen minutes and counting.

"Sweetie, did you hear me?"

"She actually used the word *joyless*?"

Then again, maybe that's what I get for letting the reporter, a peppy twentysomething food critic, shadow me for a day. She tagged along as I trekked from kitchen to kitchen, where I was careful to put on my best, most agreeable face.

But I've caught enough flashes of my own sourpuss in the window, or shimmering in a pot of hot oil. I know how I look, which is why I can barely stand a mirror for more than a second or two. You don't have to be a genius to see how miserable I am, how joyless my job has become.

Mom sighs, long and loud. "Oh, honey. A whole bunch of times."

The woman in front of me stabs a stubby finger into the glass, gearing up for another argument, and my body goes electric. I tell Mom I love her but I have to go.

"Jesus Christ, lady, come *on*," I say, clutching the phone in a fist. "Just pay the fee and move on, will you? You're not the only person here with business to do."

"Yeah," the person behind me says. Another voice farther back, deep and male, grunts in approval.

The woman takes it from the top, punctuating her argument with a finger stabbing at the glass, but I am no longer listening. Her voice bleeds away with a slicing pain in my side. A heart attack? My lungs' last gasp for air? I press the spot hard with the heel of my palm and fan the credit cards in my other hand, comforting myself with the math. Three Mastercards and one Visa for a total of $26,000 in cash advances, plus a platinum Amex with a $10,000 line. That's just over $35,000 in advances I can walk out of here with today, assuming this woman gets the hell out of my way. I eye the way she's sprawled against the countertop, the hot breath of her tirade fogging up the glass, and my heart punches a hard, frantic beat. This woman is going nowhere.

Stay and wait this out, or come up with a plan B? After all, the $35,000 is a drop in the ransom bucket. It's not going to get me anywhere close to the $734,296 I need to save Jade and the kids. It won't make even the tiniest dent.

Especially if Ed doesn't pull through.

I scroll through my phone, checking the call log and emails inbox, swiping through my messages. Still no word. I pull up Ed's contact card and fire off a text: Status?

I stare at the screen and wait for a response. Tiny letters under the blue bubble tag the text as *delivered*. But there are no dancing dots, nothing to indicate he's even seen it.

I check the time—4:44—and try not to scream.

There's movement in my periphery, and my head pops up to spot the second teller slinking back into view. He stops at the first window, nodding at what I'm guessing are marching orders, his squinty gaze pinned at the woman holding up the line. He sighs and checks his watch, and I roll my eyes.

Dude, we *know*.

Just please, for the love of all that is holy. Hurry it up already.

He sinks onto the stool at the second window, and I'm already there, spilling my cards into the stainless steel feeder before he's removed the Next Window Please sign. "I need the max cash advance on these five cards."

He picks up the cards and arranges them in a neat line on his side of the glass.

The rhinestoned lady shoots me a smirk, a serves-you-right curiosity burning in her eyes, and I clench my teeth and try not to slug her. She has no idea what kind of tragedy has brought me to this place, just like I don't know what's motivated her. People will do all sorts of things when they're desperate for cash. Lie. Cheat. Steal hundred-dollar steaks from the freezer in order to feed their families. Max out every line of credit in order to survive.

So fuck me and fuck this lady.

I fish my license and another card from my wallet and drop both into the slot. "I need whatever's on this account, too." The Lasky account I use to pay bills and run payroll, the last twist to the noose around the Lasky windpipe. Another $10K, which means the payments I signed off on last night will be dead in the water. Emptying it out will be the death knell.

With a finger, the teller slides the card next to the others. "So you want me to close this account?"

I shrug. "Empty it, close it out, I don't care. As long as you give me what's in there."

He sticks it in the reader by his monitor and recites an amount that churns in my gut. "That's $13,514.83."

"What about the payment to ADP, is there any way to stop it?" Taking back the money from payroll, that's apparently the kind of asshole I am.

The teller shakes his head, gestures to the cards spread out before him. "Do these cards all have a pin?"

"Yes. Well, all but the Amex."

"Sorry, sir, but I can't do anything without a pin." He drops it back in the slot with a metallic *ding* that echoes in my bones.

I grip the counter with both hands, fighting a wave of dizziness. "How do I get a pin?"

"I believe you have to call their customer service." He stuffs the Visa into the reader. "Enter the first pin onto the pad, please."

I tap in the pin, then flip over the Amex, dial the number on the back, and drop it back in the slot. "Do this one last. I'm getting a pin for it right now."

The process is excruciatingly slow. I cast an apologetic glance over my shoulder at the people in the line as the teller counts, then double and triple counts the Visa cash into a fat stack. With a Sharpie, he scribbles the total onto a paper label he uses to bind the bills, then clips the stack to the card. We move slowly down the line, repeating the process for each card while I listen to canned music in one ear, occasionally broken by a woman's soft voice: *Thank you for calling American Express. All our representatives are serving other customers. Approximate hold time is…six…minutes.*

Six eternal minutes to think about all the ways I've messed

up. All the wrong turns I've made, the questionable people I've chosen to partner with in order to expand the Lasky brand. That first bistro, in that tiny house in Peachtree Hills, feels like forever ago. A kitchen barely big enough for three chefs shoulder to shoulder and just enough tables to eke out a salary, but I loved that old rickety place.

It's a juice shop now, but I wonder: If I went back to that concept, if I traded the Lasky Steak empire for a tumbledown bistro in Peachtree Hills, would I be happier? Would Jade love me as much if I wasn't Atlanta's Steak King?

What the hell happened? When did I lose my way?

By now, the woman to my left is gone, and the teller is punching in numbers and counting out cash with an accountant's efficiency. Before too long, it's one last straggler and me, a man in dark blue scrubs.

Approximate hold time...three...minutes.

Keys rattle in my other ear, the security guard flipping the locks on the doors behind me, a jingling that alerts me to closing time. Five o'clock on the dot. I peel the phone away from my ear and check the notifications.

Still no response from Ed. *Goddammit.*

Images of Jade whiz by in my brain—tied to that blue chair, staring down the barrel of a masked madman's gun. Helpless while the kids scream for her from across the hall. I wonder if she's conscious, if she's beaten and bloody, if he's broken any of her bones. Why didn't I ask? Why didn't I insist on talking to the Bees? I consider calling her back, right after—

An Amex representative, a real person this time, sounds in my ear, and my knees buckle in relief. "Thank God. I need a pin for my card."

The teller gives me a look, one that says he's glad there's a thick slice of bulletproof glass between us, then goes back to counting out the cash while the Amex representative walks me through the steps. By the time the teller has clipped to-gether the last stack of money, I have a working pin.

When the last stack is counted and marked and fastened, the teller points me to a glass-enclosed room at the far end of the building. An office, boring and generic—a desk, two chairs, a computer monitor and a giant poster on the wall. The room is dark, much like the rest of the bank. The security guard turned the lights off ages ago.

I turn back to the teller. "If you don't mind, I'm kind of in a hurry. I'll just take the money and go."

"Sir, I will deliver the money to you in that office." Not so much a question as a demand. He gathers up the piles of cash and drops them into a zippered bank bag. "We'll have more privacy there."

I turn, taking in the space around me, all of it empty. Even the security guard has moved on, disappearing with his rat-tling keys behind a padlocked door. I am the last man stand-ing. We have all the privacy in the world.

The teller leans the Next Window Please sign against the glass and takes off with my bag of cash. I match him step for step, following him down the glass until he disappears behind a wall. A few seconds later he steps out of a door farther down, the bag of cash tucked under an arm. I hustle to the office, where he flips on the light and closes the door.

"Mr. Lasky, are you aware that according to the Bank Secrecy Act, we are required to report cash withdrawals of $10,000 or more to the IRS?"

I plop into one of the chairs, thinking how to best respond. No police. That's what Jade said. She said at the first sign of sirens, the man will start shooting, and he'll start with the Bees. A fresh wave of panic climbs my chest at the thought.

I can't let that happen. He said no police.

The IRS, on the other hand. The IRS is a bureaucratic behemoth, like most governmental agencies only speedy when they're on the receiving end. It'll takes weeks, months even, for them to follow up on this report. It's already past five. The earliest they could get to it is tomorrow morning. All I need is a few hours.

"Okay, fine." I stretch a hand across the desk. "Report away."

On the chair across from me, the teller grips the bag of cash with both hands. He's not blind. I watch him clock my sweaty face, the leg I can't seem to stop jiggling, my frenzied eyes with a bank robber's glint. He knows something is wrong. I might as well be wearing a sign: "Meth addict, need money for drugs."

"I am also required to ask why you want such an unusually large amount of cash."

I frown, my chest going hot. "It's my money. Am I not allowed to withdraw however much of it I want?"

"Of course you are. But I am required to include the reason for the withdrawal in my report, and refusing to provide one will result in a denial. Either way, I still have to report you to the authorities."

I breathe through a sour slice of panic and try to come up with an explanation that will result in me walking out of here with that money—*my* money. Something legal, something that won't send up an immediate red flag with the police.

Stick with the truth, or at least something pretty damn close, and look the person right in the eye. Say the lie without blinking, then smile and change the subject. I've only been doing it for months now.

"There was a fire this morning at one of my restaurants. That means my employees are out of a job. People who depend on me for their livelihood, to feed their families and cover their health care costs and pay for the roof above their heads. This money is for them, just until the insurance comes through and we get the place back up and running." I smile. "Now, if you don't mind, I've got a kid's ball game to get to."

It does the trick. The teller scribbles something onto a form and slides the money across the desk.

Thirty seconds later the security guard reappears to sift through his keys while I shift from foot to foot, and then he opens the door and I'm out of there, racing to my car with a bag stuffed with $49,000 and some change, thanking a God I definitely don't deserve for the fire that killed my business.

THE INTERVIEW

Juanita: You mentioned your father—

Cam: Pretty sure that was you who mentioned him, but okay.

Juanita: Right. *I* mentioned your father, but only because you implied you weren't eager to follow in his footsteps.

Cam: Not many people would be.

Juanita: Because he lost his business, a chain of three thousand-plus hardware stores that went belly-up after the divorce? Or because his investors then sued him for using off-the-books accounting to overstate profits and conceal debts? His conviction left your mother and you penniless.

Cam: Yeah, well, in the end, so was he, so... [shrugs]

Juanita: You say that like you think his bankruptcy and subsequent prison sentence were a justified result of his behavior. Do you see these things as some sort of karma?

Cam: Not really a fan of that word, but yeah, I do. My father drove everyone he'd ever loved away, and then when his life went to shit, he blamed those same people for deserting him. Money was the only thing he cared about, so I'm not going to lie. When he lost all of his, it wasn't necessarily a bad day.

Juanita: He died in prison.

Cam: Yes. Penniless and friendless, alone and bitter. The old man dug his own grave. And before you ask, no. We never reconciled.

Juanita: And your mother?

Cam: You'd have to ask her. That's her story to tell, not mine.

Juanita: But considering what you've been through, surely you must have gained some understanding into your father's behavior. Surely you must feel some regret for the way things between you ended.

Cam: No on both accounts. Not even a little bit. My father walked out on his family and never looked back. He replaced us with a girl half his age, who up and left after his company tanked. He never once apologized for what he did to us, not even when he got sick. I lost my father many years before he died.

Juanita: And what would you say to the people who say "like father, like son"? Who put you in the same boat as him, as someone primarily motivated by money?

Cam: I'd say they have it completely, one hundred percent back-ass-ward. Unlike my father, I wasn't motivated by money, but by the way money eased the weight of my responsibility to the people I love. Jade and the kids, my mother. Every single thing I did was for them, to feed and clothe and take care of *them*. I would have *never* left them in the dust to fend for themselves. The last thing I ever would have done is walk away.

Juanita: And yet you took your wife's jewelry without her knowledge or permission, essentially theft. You pawned some of her most precious pieces and replaced them with fakes so she wouldn't know.

Cam: And then I used that money to pay my children's tuition. For Beatrix's violin lessons and the homeowner association fees on my mother's condo. Don't get me wrong. I'm not proud of what I did, but at least I stuck around. I did it to save my family the heartache of losing everything including their friends—because make no mistake. A bankruptcy is a surefire way of learning who's in your life because they want what you have. I was trying to save them from that.

Juanita: By being the polar opposite of your father.

Cam: Exactly.

Juanita: And yet, just like your father, you've also been accused of underhanded business practices. Things like employing undocumented workers and paying them under the table, for example.

Cam: Have you ever been in a restaurant kitchen? Something like 95 percent of the folks working the cleanup lines are Latino. They are the hardest workers doing the dirtiest jobs.

Lasky's policy was to hire only the ones who had individual taxpayer identification numbers, which means they could pay the IRS without alerting ICE. Whether or not they actually filed is none of my business.

Juanita: But were they legal?

Cam: Also none of my business. And look, judge me all you want, but I did what it took to keep my family and business afloat.

Juanita: So again, like father, like son.

Cam: Well, Juanita, I guess it's true what they say. In the end we all become our parents.

JADE

4:47 p.m.

It happens so fast, if I blinked I would have missed it.

Beatrix in exaggerated tiptoe, slipping out the open doorway of the playroom into the hall. Back hunched, arms stretched out for balance, legs spread wide so the frilly cuffs of her shorts don't brush together when she walks. It's a Looney Tunes version of a tiptoe, skillful in its absolute silence, a careful and precise movement she's clearly practiced. It makes me wonder how many times she's done this while Cam and I were reading or watching TV downstairs, oblivious to our daughter sneaking about above our heads. Dozens, probably.

She swings her head to the right, peering down the long hallway that leads to the kids' bedrooms. It's the direction Baxter and the masked man just disappeared down, only a few seconds earlier. Baxter was moving fast, his face strained with hurry, one hand gripping his bottom in a way that typically means he's going to need a change of pants. He was in too much of a panic to notice me sitting across the hall, strapped to a chair, and the man didn't look over, either, though I didn't miss his grimace.

I can hear them now, the low murmur of voices muffled by a door and two walls. Baxter's bathroom, which is good news since it's the farthest away. The last door at the end of the hallway, tucked around not one but two corners. Assuming the man is waiting just outside the bathroom door, there's still a wall between him and Beatrix.

Beatrix turns for the stairs, and almost by accident, her gaze lands on mine.

She flinches so hard, her sneakers squeak on the hardwood floor. I wince at the sound, and my heart seizes, then trips into high gear. I hold my breath and listen for signs of someone coming.

Beatrix must be thinking the same thing, because she looks in the direction of the voices, and I watch her face for a reaction. My daughter is like me, an open book. Everything she ever thinks is telegraphed straight to her face, as easy to read as blinking neon letters. If the masked man is bearing down the hallway, coming for her, I'll see it on Beatrix's expression.

But her face doesn't change. Her back slumps in a silent sigh of relief, and she looks back.

Heart pounding, I study my daughter from top to toe. I take in her dry eyes, count her fingers, search her skin for blood or bruises. The bow on the hem of her pink polka-dot shirt has come untied, and her shorts are rumpled at the crotch from sitting, but there's no rips or bloodstains. Her hair is pillow-mussed, that cowlick I'm always trying to wrangle into submission pushing the hair high on the left side of her crown, but otherwise she looks fine. Frightened, but fine.

And then I notice the marks on her socks, and I wonder if she was tied to a chair, too. No, *taped* to the chair, one of the reclining theater seats in the playroom. That was the sound I heard before, the harsh creak of the duct tape ripping off leather so Baxter could race to the bathroom.

But it doesn't explain how Beatrix managed to wriggle free.

Especially if her bindings were anything like mine, double and triple wrapped around my skin, as unforgiving as steel cuffs. Other than a slimy arm and a dull throbbing behind my front teeth, I've gotten nowhere with the knot at my wrist. Clearly, I am not one of those mothers who could lift a car to save her children, or bust out of chains like the female version of the Hulk. I strain against my bindings, but my arms and legs don't budge.

I'm stuck.

Helpless.

But not Beatrix. She stands there and stares at me, her eyes big and wide and round.

Go, I mouth, but I don't dare call out to her, not even a whisper. And honestly, go where? Not back to the playroom, certainly. The man will be back in what—thirty seconds? A minute? Not enough time for Beatrix to get very far. And as soon as she opens any of the doors downstairs, she'll trip the alarm.

At the sound of the first siren I start shooting, and the first two bullets are for the kids.

If Beatrix is lucky, she might escape, but Baxter and I surely won't. There are no good answers here.

Go.

Beatrix nods, but her feet don't come unglued from the floor.

I hold my breath and listen to the noise coming from farther down the hall. Baxter is still chattering away, the occasional word piercing the low hum of water running through the pipes. Washing his hands at the sink, I'm guessing, which means he's close to finishing up. The man is still silent, nearby but unaccounted for, which terrifies me. He could be waiting by the door. He could be halfway to the hall by now. What if he comes back to check on Beatrix?

I shake my head at her, but I don't know what I mean by it. *Don't get caught? Don't leave me here?* Both, probably. My hands ball into tight, frustrated fists.

On the other end of the hall, a toilet flushes. A door creaks, followed by footsteps.

Go! I mouth the word again, stretching my lips around it so she understands, leaning forward and adding another: *Run!*

And this time—finally, thankfully—she does.

I first tried my hand at acting in middle school, mostly to escape from the dark cloud of misery hanging over our house—a silent father who spent his evenings dozing in front of a TV, a surly older sister eating her feelings and everything else in sight, rooms that without my mother's touches had grown faded and dusty. I coped by cloaking myself in someone else's skin—a lighthearted mermaid falling in love for the first time, or the dancing, singing, footloose daughter of a strict preacher father. Anyone but a sad and lonely eighth-grader longing for her mother.

It's those old, sucky acting skills I call upon now when I hear noises at the end of the hall. I sit up straight as my body goes rock-hard, my fingers digging into the velvet armrests of the chair. I wipe my expression clean and force my muscles to relax, my face to look normal—or as normal as a mother's face can be, tied to a forty-pound chair.

An animated Baxter comes first, his stuffed gorilla Gibson pinned under an arm, skipping like he's headed for a birthday party at Chuck E. Cheese. He blathers on about the shows he wants to watch, the popcorn his mommy would let him have.

I stare at him, gritting my teeth and trying to appear fearless, courageous. My son doesn't so much as glance over.

The man follows behind. He comes into view, and my heart clenches.

Showtime.

I can't quite see him from this angle, but I know the second he spots Beatrix's empty chair. I hear his grunt of surprise, the stumble in his footsteps when he comes up on an empty room. He curses, a long string of expletives followed by Baxter's high-pitched giggle.

"*Beatrix!* You get your butt back in here, missy. *Right now.*"

There's a long stretch of silence while he waits for an answer. I hear the low volume on the TV, fast and heavy footsteps, breaths huffing with emotion, but nothing from Beatrix. Of course there's not. By now she's had a good thirty, maybe forty-five seconds to get wherever she's going, and I already know her tiptoe skills are stealth. I picture her downstairs, sneaking from room to room, trying out all her normal hiding spots until she finds the best one.

The man stomps into the hall. "You better believe I'm going to find your scrawny little butt, so you might as well come out now. Come out and take your punishment like a girl." He looks at me, eyes flashing. "Where is she? Where'd she go?"

I frown, blink my eyes in stage-managed confusion. "I thought she was with you."

Jesus, that was bad. Overacted, leaned way too hard into the enunciation and my voice cracked on the last word.

"Bullshit. If she'd come this way, she would have run right past you. No way you didn't see her, not unless she—" He lurches backward, one long leap from the hallway into the playroom. I clock his movements by sound, footsteps moving deeper into the playroom, solid furniture scraping across the floor, a door creaking open. The hidden hallway to the guest room bath. He knows about it, too.

"Beatrix, now's the time to get out here, hon." The man's voice is muffled now, and it's coming at me in stereo—from the playroom across the hall, louder from behind me, somewhere deep in the bathroom. Heavy footsteps come from that direction, too, elephant stomps moving closer. "Beatrix!"

Baxter steps into the hall in a fresh shirt and Batman pajama pants, and I choke on a sob. I hate that he's seeing me like this. I hate that I can't protect him.

He sees me and waves. "Hi, Mommy."

It rolls over me like a hurricane—how helpless I am to help him, strapped to this chair. If I told Bax to run, he'd never make it far. If I told him to hide, his giggling would give him away. I can't do anything to protect him because I am *tied to a chair.*

I suck down my tears. Push a smile up my cheeks so as not to frighten him. "Hey, big guy. How're you doing?"

"Good." He bounces his shoulders. "I had an accident, though."

"That's okay, baby. It hap—"

"*Jade.*"

He's here now, coming in long, angry strides out of the bathroom. He pulls the gun from his cargo paints and aims at my head, not stopping until the metal makes contact with my forehead. I squeal and rear back until my head is flush against the wall.

"Did she come through here? Because if she did and you lie about it, you and I are going to have a big problem."

"I already told you, I don't know. I don't know where Beatrix is."

I say it with conviction because it is not a lie. Also, if he shoots me now, Bax will see. He will watch his mother be murdered. Pretty much number one on the list of how to mess up a six-year-old for life.

"Beatrix didn't come through here, I swear."

I say the words while in my head, I'm listening for the beeping of the alarm pad. If she'd left, out the window or one of the doors, the alarm would be wailing. There's nothing but silence from downstairs. Wherever she is, Beatrix is still inside.

The man stares at me through slitted eyes, his mouth going thin with realization. He's done the same math. He knows Beatrix is still in the house, too.

"Where, Jade?"

"I don't know. You were supposed to be watching her."

"I was dealing with your son's shit."

At the last word, Baxter giggles, a high and teetering delight. For him there's nothing merrier than when his father has to drop a dollar in the curse jar, because it's money that belongs to the kids, split evenly down the middle. Every couple of months, we empty the jar at the bookstore—and they come home with armloads of books. A cook line is an animated place, where tempers flare hotter than the grill flames. Cam's language has always been colorful.

I can't help but feel some sort of grim satisfaction. Dealing with someone else's shit is never fun, even worse when it comes from a child who is not your own. I know it's a tiny win, but I'm taking it.

He jabs the gun hard into my forehead, metal on bone. "Where is she? Hiding in a closet? Under a bed? Did she go downstairs? She must have, because if she'd come the other way, I would have seen her."

I don't dare move. I barely breathe. And I sure as hell don't answer. No way I'm giving him any indication of where Beatrix might be. With any luck, she'll stay there until Cam comes home and this is all over.

Suddenly, the pressure is gone. He takes a couple of steps backward, parking his feet at the edge of the carpet. "You know what I think? I think you know exactly where she is. And I think you're going to tell me."

He drops the gun into his pocket, exchanging it for a pocketknife he fishes out of another. No, not a pocketknife, a switchblade, the kind killers use. He presses the button with a thumb, and the blade, long and serrated and curved like a deadly claw, shoots out with a sharp click.

A gun *and* a knife.

I stare at the razor-edged tip. "I… I already told you, I don't know where she went."

He stalks closer, and I push myself backward, even though there's nowhere for me to go. I'm already deep in the seat's stuffing. The chair squeaks but doesn't budge.

"You don't know this, but a little while ago, your kids and I had a little talk, didn't we, Bax?"

From the doorway, Baxter gives a solemn nod.

"I told them what would happen if one of them opened a door or a window and tripped the alarm." He glances behind him, to Baxter sucking his thumb. "Want to tell her what I said, buddy?"

Bax's answer comes from behind a fist. "Nothing good."

"Exactly. Nothing good will happen. Only bad. So I'm asking you again, Jade, where is Beatrix? And please note that this is a question, but it's also a warning. I want you to think long and hard before you answer, because if I find out later you're lying, I'll take out Beatrix first, and then Baxter. And I will make you watch."

Baxter plucks his thumb from his mouth with a soft pop. "Take us out where?"

I stare into the man's eyes, too afraid to blink mine. "I swear to you. I do not know."

"Take us where?" Baxter says again, frowning at the man's back. He's alert now, slowly becoming aware. Something is very wrong here.

My brain races with panicked thoughts, trying to come up with one that will buy us some time. "What about the money?"

The man cocks his head. The knife is fisted in a gloved hand—a threat and a promise at the same time. No prints, no DNA left behind. A backpack full of tape and rope and weapons. A sore knot ices over in my chest. This man has come prepared. He knows what he's doing. Maybe he's done this before.

"What about it?" he says.

"Cam isn't stupid. He's done hundreds of deals, and he'll know to demand proof of life before he gives you anything. You won't get a cent if all of us are dead."

Baxter's eyes goggle at the last word, and he shoves his thumb back in his mouth and sucks hard enough to make his cheeks pucker. Our eyes meet, and I recognize that expression, the way one eyebrow squiggles up and the other down in a way that makes Cam laugh and call him Lord Farquaad.

It means Baxter is a ticking time bomb, one single bad moment away from a meltdown.

The man puffs a breathy laugh, sour meat and bitter coffee. "Cam's not going to have much of a choice in the matter. Now come on."

I know I should be projecting calm. I should be stuffing down my own fears in order to protect my son's emotional well-being. A child should never feel unsafe in his own home. I should be reassuring him everything is okay.

But this is life and death. Literally. And everything is *not* okay.

The man rushes me with the knife, and I throw myself

backward, but there's nowhere for me to go. My skull connects with the wall, setting off a burst of fireworks behind my eyes. The room spins with a wave of pain, of terror. I'm vaguely aware that I'm screaming.

Baxter lets out an earsplitting, high-pitched howl, and I know I should console him. My screams are only escalating things, spiraling Bax higher and higher into a panic, like tossing kerosene on a fire.

But I can't make myself stop. All I see is the knife, streaking closer to my skin. I can't look away and I can't stop screaming.

The man touches the tip of the blade to the flesh of my arm, and—

"Baxter, *go. Run.*"

—saws through the rope in two seconds flat. I suck in a shocked breath, watching him hook the blade under the knot I'd just spent forever twisting to the top of my wrist and give a good tug. The blade slices through the rope and suddenly, my arm is free.

I fall silent, but not Baxter. His back is still flush to the wall, his eyes squeezed into tight slits, his mouth wide in one long, continuous wail.

The man glares over his shoulder. "Baxter, that's enough. *Quiet.*" He turns back, his gaze brushing over mine. "Either you shut him up, or I will."

"Shh, Baxie. Quiet, okay? I'm not hurt. See? Look at me, sweetie. I'm fine."

The blade is cool and hard where it touches my skin, but the pain isn't sharp, just a solid pressure where he wriggles the knife between my other wrist and the looped strands of braided vinyl. My ankles are next. The pieces fall away one by one, fluttering to the floor in sloppy yellow coils. My limbs come free, my skin stays intact.

Baxter is still bawling, his back pressed to the wall, but I don't motion him closer. I don't dare, not until the man folds the knife in two and drops it back into his pocket. He steps back, and I hold out a shaky arm.

Baxter skitters in a wide arc around him, then launches himself into my lap. His crying stops almost immediately, but he curls into a tight ball and buries his face in my chest, squeezing his eyes shut. I wrap my arms around him and clutch him close, pressing kisses in his hair.

The man watches from by the bed, his calves pressed against the mattress. He shakes his head. "We don't have time for this. We need to find your devil daughter."

I plaster on my fiercest, most determined look, and this is where I make the silent vow: before this day is over, I will kill this man. I will steal his gun, cut his throat, smash his head, pummel him into a bloody, broken heap. Surprise him, hurt him, use his rope to hog-tie him, seal his mouth and nose off with his own duct tape. I will do whatever I have to do, but this man *will* take his last breath today.

And I will enjoy every second.

"Fine." He rolls his eyes, training the gun at my forehead. "The little guy can help us search, but next time he screams like that again, I'm locking him in a closet."

JADE

5:07 p.m.

With Baxter on my hip, we search every inch of the ground floor.

We start in the rooms where a man in a mask can move around freely without fear of being seen from the street: the master bedroom; the attached bathroom, after I've lowered the shades on the window looking out onto a neighbor's guest-house; the closet beyond with a long sheet of glass high up on a wall, a rectangular slice of trees and birds and sky. We check closets and peer under furniture, open chests and dump out drawers, shove clothing aside to poke a gun into the darkest corners. The whole time, I hold my breath and pray I won't find my daughter.

But everywhere we look, there's no Beatrix.

Which is more than a little surprising, since she's never been the most original kid when it comes to hide-and-seek. The giggling lump behind a curtain or a half-closed door, or the body attached to the feet sticking out from under the bed. Wherever she is, she's well hidden. I just pray to God she stays that way.

"Baby, I can't hold you much longer," I whisper to Baxter as we're moving through the front rooms—the study and the dining room, the galley butler's pantry lined on one side with windows. "I'm going to have to put you down, just for a minute."

"Nooo." Baxter clings tighter, wrapping his legs around me and clamping on with extraordinary strength. The kid's always been an acrobat. He's had a six-pack since he was two.

We're both all too aware of the man. He sticks close, never letting us wander more than ten feet away, jabbing the air between us with the butt of his gun, urging me from room to room.

I jostle Baxter higher on my hip and keep moving.

We come around to the back of the house, where I jiggle the last door handle and tug on the last window, even though the red light on the alarm pad said the system was still armed. That means Beatrix is still in the house somewhere.

"These are locked, too," I say. "Everything's locked."

He stands at the edge of the room, on the far side of the wall separating the living space from the kitchen. Anyone on the front doorstep right now might see the toes of his shoes, the muzzle of his gun, but the rest of him is well out of sight. Everything about the way he's standing is intentional. It's chilling how familiar he is with our home.

"Any other way out?"

I shake my head. "Not without tripping the alarm, no."

"Does she know the code?"

This gives me pause, even though my headshake is immediate. I don't think Beatrix knows the code, but she pays attention. She hears things even when I think she's not listening.

It's possible she knows the code, and it's possible that in all the commotion upstairs we didn't hear her disarm, then rearm the system and leave, but the doors are all locked. She couldn't have done that, not without a key. I think about the spare in the kitchen drawer, or the one on a key chain in the bottom of my purse, but I don't say a word.

"What about the basement?"

There's no way Beatrix would have chosen the basement for a hiding spot, not without me or her father at her side. For the kids, the basement is a dark and hostile place, filled with spiderwebs and skeleton walls and dusty shapes looming in the darkness. They're terrified of the place—which is a good part of why Cam and I have never considered finishing it.

He juts his chin at the bookshelves behind me and beyond, the hallway that leads to the basement door. "Let's go take a look."

Baxter wriggles deeper into my chest, clutching me tighter. "Mommy, I don't wanna go downstairs." My sweatshirt pulls on a shoulder from where it's bunched in one of his tight fists.

"It's okay, sweetie. We won't be down there long."

The man orders me to do a quick check of the street, then hustles us across the living room and down the hall, where I flip the dead bolt and pull open the door. A chilly draft rushes up from the darkness, and I shiver—not from the cold but with the beginning wisp of a plan.

The basement is where Cam keeps his tools.

I feel around the wall for the light switch, and a bare, dusty bulb flicks on, shining light on the steep wooden stairs, rickety and builder-assembled to pass code, but just barely. I follow them down, down, down into the darkness.

The stairs dump us onto a concrete slab, and I blink into the pitch-black basement. The air is a good ten degrees cooler down here, and it smells of underground, of dirt and dust and creatures living and dying.

I flip another switch, and it lights up the first room, an unfinished square tomb piled high with plastic boxes and furniture. A high chair, a crib, our old queen mattress and box springs, the plate rack that came with the antique buffet in the dining room but I found too fussy. Everything is neatly stacked, one on top of the other like giant blocks, then arranged against vertical studs waiting for drywall. Beyond it, the space that runs the length of the house is cloaked in blackness.

The man calls out into the shadows, "Beatrix, if you're down here, sweetie, now would be the time to make yourself known. Come out now and I promise not to hurt you."

No answer. Only the sound of Baxter's shallow breaths against my shoulder. I cover my son's head with a hand, his fine hair tangling in my fingers.

"Are there any doors or windows?"

I turn, gesturing to where dim light trickles like water from somewhere deep in the darkness, a window well concealed behind thick hedges. Even on sunny days, very little light makes it through.

"Stay here while I check," he says. "Move and both of you get a bullet."

While he's gone, I shift Baxter to my opposite hip to give my bicep a break. He's a deadweight, forty-two pounds of bone and muscle dragging on my shoulder, my back, my neck where his arms hang from it. My entire upper body is on fire, muscles shaking, joints throbbing. But I know what would happen if I put him down: he'd scream and wail and pitch a fit, and I need to save that for when I need a distraction.

"Locked up tight." He jabs me in the back with his pistol, a harsh gesture that means *move it*.

I lurch forward with a hot burst of adrenaline. If I didn't have Baxter hanging from me like a monkey, that would have been my chance. I could have lunged for him. I could have grabbed his wrist with one hand, the gun with the other, and wrestled it from his grip like some badass TV spy. I probably would've gotten shot, but maybe, just maybe, I could have knocked off his aim to somewhere it wouldn't kill me. An arm, maybe, or a foot. Bloody and painful, but not fatal. And then I'd grab the gun and shoot him in the face.

But I can't fight back—I wouldn't even dare try—not with Baxter clutched to my hip.

That's when it occurs to me: the most terrifying part of being a parent isn't this monster holding the gun. It's the idea that something I do or don't do could get my children killed. That I could be to blame for their deaths. That they would die, and I would be both a witness and the cause. How would I ever live with myself?

Then again, I probably wouldn't have to.

Beatrix first, and then Baxter. And I will make you watch.

The third bullet in the gun pressing between my ribs would be for me.

I think of what that would be like for Cam, walking in on three dead bodies, and my eyes go hot with tears. I should have told him I loved him. I should have led with those words before anything else. I should have started the call with the most important.

The man shuffles us farther into the darkness, nudging me down a strip of concrete studded on either side—a future hallway lined with future rooms. He finds the light switch and flips it on, two more dusty bulbs that cast a buttery yellow glow.

"Yo, Beatrix. We know you're down here, girlie. Might as well come out from whatever old box you're hiding behind.

I promise you nothing bad will happen. I won't hurt you, but only if you show your face *right now*."

Still nothing. Just a long stretch of strangled silence while I listen for movement above our heads, footsteps or the squeak of a floorboard. Wherever Beatrix is in this house, she's good and hunkered down.

"Now you." The scratchy male voice comes with another stab of the muzzle.

"Now me, what?"

"What the hell do you think? Call for your daughter. Tell her to come out of hiding. She'll listen to you."

Doubtful. There's no way my voice is going to coax Beatrix out of hiding, not with a masked man standing right here, holding me and her brother at gunpoint. Beatrix may only be nine, but she's not stupid, and nobody has ever accused her of being overly obedient. Just ask any of her teachers.

And then there's also the fact that I don't want my daughter to be found. I want her to stay hidden until seven, until Cam arrives with his big bag of cash and this man does whatever it is he came here to do.

My mind is finally coming around to what I've known in my gut for almost an hour now—this is no textbook ransom plot. Yes, this man held a gun to my head while I assured Cam our lives would be spared, as long as he brought home the money on time.

But he's already proven he is a liar.

"Do it," the man says, digging the gun into my ribs. "Tell your daughter to get out here."

I turn, calling into the darkness. "Beatrix, sweetie. If you're down here, I need you to come out now. It's time for you to come out."

My voice trembles, a combination of fear and red-hot fury. Now I know how the circus lions feel, why they sometimes lose it and chomp off their tamer's whip-snapping arm. If I didn't have two children to protect, I'd go for this man's blood, too.

The only sound is Baxter breathing into my shoulder.

The man gives another thrust to the gun, jabbing it deeper into my bone. "Tell her it's safe."

"I don't think she's down here."

The pressure between my ribs releases, the pain dulling to a low throb. My muscles release until I realize the gun isn't gone; it's just moved. The muzzle is pressed into Baxter's thigh.

"Say it." The mask casts purple shadows on his face, making him look like a monster. His teeth, the golden flecks in his eyes—they flash yellow in the darkness, standing out like ugly headlights.

"Beatrix, sweetie, it's safe for you to come out. I'll show you how to play the Partita no. 2. You said you wanted to try a piece in C minor."

The partita reference, I'm hoping, is a tip-off. Partitas are known for their difficulty, and this one from Johann Bach is long, and it's fiendish, and it's in D minor, not C. It's the piece every violinist aspires to, one of the most difficult ever written, a good fifteen minutes of pure, uninterrupted hell. Me referring to it now is a secret message buried in what sounds like an ordinary sentence.

Come out means stay hidden. *It's safe* is a warning of danger.

Without warning, Baxter pitches with all his weight to the left. "Mommy, *there*." He stabs a finger into the darkness, at the spot where a bulky HVAC unit cloaks the concrete in ragged shadow.

The man whips his gun to the unit, and I stumble in that direction, too, mostly to hold on to Baxter. It's like last summer biking on Hilton Head, when he leaned so far out of his seat I almost steered us into the bushes. Now he comes close to tumbling out of my arms, his weight dragging me with him.

"Good job, Baxter," the man says, grinning. He keeps his eyes and the gun trained on the spot. "We got you, Beatrix. You can come out now. Tag, you're it."

"Not Beatrix. My bouncy ball with the stars on it and the dinosaurs. I thought I lost it."

I let out a hoarse laugh, then swallow it when the gun swings back our way.

But now that Baxter's seen the ball, there's no ignoring it. I crouch down and pick it up, my gaze sweeping the concrete for a box cutter, a nail, something sharp and deadly. A weapon would be a game changer. But my hand comes away with nothing but rubber and dust.

I push to a stand, brush the ball off on my shirt and place it in Baxter's sticky palm.

"Keep moving," the man says, glaring because I'm taking too long. "You better hope she shows up soon."

What I really hope is that Beatrix is upstairs right now, throwing open the front door and sprinting down the driveway, arms flailing at whoever happens to be jogging past, hollering for them to call the police. With us deep in the bowels of the basement, now would be her chance. We wouldn't hear the alarm pad's warning beep from where we're standing, not until the sixty seconds were up and the sirens started wailing. By then she'd be far from the house. I might die here in this dusty basement, but at least Beatrix wouldn't. With any luck, she'll live to be a hundred.

The man shoves me in the shoulder, pressing me forward. "Let's go."

The thought of Beatrix growing up like I did, without a mother, punches the air from my chest, a dagger twisting in my heart. No waving to me from the first chair of the Chicago Symphony Orchestra. No scolding me to stop bawling in the front pew when she gets married. No handing me my first grandchild. These are the things both of us will miss if I die here today.

But Beatrix can still finish school. She can still fall in love, get her heart broken, celebrate birthdays and weddings and Christmases. It won't be long before she forgets my face, my voice and smile and smell, the way I tug on her ringlets or tickle that spot behind her ear, but she's still so young. Her grief will turn wooly and imprecise, a general malaise for the loss of a mother she barely knew and can no longer remember.

I know because it happened to me.

That's why I gave up the career I loved, why I'm room mom and snack mom and library reading-time mom, why I cart them all over town, to soccer and music lessons and trips to the library and zoo, why I swallow my impatience at having to ask them three times to clean their room and sweetly ask them a fourth. I tried my best to fill the gap my mother left with all the love I have for my children. If nothing else, Beatrix will remember that her mother bent over backward to care for her, that I filled the house with happiness and love.

I just won't be here to see it.

"Move it."

With the man on my heels, we search the rest of the basement. I sweep the space from back to front, calling for Beatrix until my throat is sore. Every move is a calculated risk, every box I peek behind a potential land mine. Because as soon as I find Beatrix, she will be punished. And if we don't, Baxter and I will be. Maybe not with a bullet to our heads—not yet, not until Cam gets here—but in the meantime, his switchblade can do a lot of damage.

By the time we come into the last room, the one with Cam's workbench, I'm ready. I cling to the shadows by the shelves and keep up the pretense, calling for Beatrix as I move deeper down the line. I'm just waiting for the right moment.

I find it at the wine shelves, where I shriek and jump back, jiggling Baxter from my hip. The relief is instant—my throbbing back loosens, and my deadened fingers go tingly. Baxter's feet hit the floor and instantly bounce back up. He leaps onto my leg and latches on, climbing me like a playground slide. I shake him off and stomp on the floor with a shoe.

Baxter skitters backward. "What? What is it?"

I stomp again, moving closer to the shelving. "A cockroach just crawled over my foot. A big one."

The cockroach ruse is lame, I know, and it's a good thing it's dark down here because my cheeks have got to be an ugly purple. I am stomping empty air, everything about me visibly rattled, but at least it fits the ridiculous scene. And at least my lie does exactly what I needed it to: it got Bax off my arm and gave me room to move, while also sticking the man's gaze to the floor.

I eye the distance between me and Cam's workbench. Six, maybe seven feet.

"It went under there." I gesture to the row of hard-shell suitcases, lined up under a bottom shelf by color and size.

The man makes a disgusted sound. "Leave it."

I whip the suitcases one by one away from the wall, wheeling them into a messy spin behind me. They crash into the room like bumper cars, backing up Baxter and the man even farther. Bugs have never been Baxter's favorite, but bees and cockroaches are the stuff of nightmares. He shoves his thumb into his mouth and starts sucking.

The man leans a shoulder against a wall stud. "What the hell are you doing?"

"I'm looking for the cockroach."

"Why?"

"Why else? So I can kill it."

It's bullshit, of course. But moving down the line of suit-cases has me edging closer and closer to Cam's workbench, taking stock of the tools hanging from a pressed-wood peg-board, assessing which would make the most deadly weapon. A box cutter, a lug wrench, a drill bit, a big, fat, sharp nail. Any-thing I can wound him with, maybe sink into an eye socket.

"You're not supposed to stomp on those things, you know." He's put even more space between us now, a good ten feet at least. "Their eggs squirt all over the soles of your shoes and then you drag them all through the house. A couple of days from now, you'll have a hundred baby cockroaches."

I look over my shoulder, but in my head I'm running through the logistics. One more step toward the stairs and he'll lose sight of my right arm. One more suitcase and I'll be standing in reach of the workbench.

"I'm pretty sure that's an old wives' tale," I say, creeping closer to the bench. "And it's too late anyway. My Terminix guy told me by the time I see one roach, there are a million more crawling around behind the walls." It's why I pay him to spray the shit out of this place every other month, so we *don't* have bugs. I shove a box away from the wall and stomp on the empty floor. "Bax, go get the broom, will you? I think I saw it at the bottom of the stairs."

Baxter shakes his head. His feet stay rooted to the floor, his gaze to the spot where I just stomped on empty air.

The man doesn't move, either. "What? Why?"

I whirl around, positioning myself one more step to the right. Two feet, no more, the line of tools within arm's reach. I pick my target in my periphery, a blue-handled screwdriver at the end of the board, thin and six inches long. One un-watched second, that's all I need.

"So I can sweep it out before it disappears behind the wall."

"Just leave it and let's go. Did you hear that, Beatrix?" He leans his upper body back into the hall, craning his neck to holler into the empty rooms. "We're going back upstairs, so that leaves just you down here with about a million cockroaches."

He turns back, rounding us up with his gun and marching us back toward the stairs. Baxter whines for me to carry him again, and I hoist him onto a hip and drag us both up the stairs.

But as we're coming up to the main level, I tug my right sleeve over my hand and prick the pad of my thumb with the screwdriver, and a thrill travels up my spine. It's a Phillips-head, the point sharp enough to break the skin.

Bring it on, asshole.

I'm ready.

CAM

5:24 p.m.

I sit in my truck in the bank parking lot, traffic drumming on the other side of the bushes at my bumper, and scroll through the messages on my phone. Missed calls from my mother, a buttload of bills and marketing emails, a flurry of texts from Flavio and a local Housewife hounding me to cater a dinner for the cast and a hundred of their closest friends. I ignore them all, searching for the one I need, but it's not there.

Ed's silence cannot be a good sign. It means he couldn't talk his boss into fronting the funds for my IRA or, at best, that he doesn't yet have an answer. Either way, I'm screwed.

Jade's words ring on a constant loop through my head, the way her voice sounded on the phone, how fear turned it high and thin. The sound of it shoots a new jolt of adrenaline through my veins, turning me radioactive. I can't shake the image of her beaten and bloody and tied to that chair, helpless to stop the bastard from going after the Bees—an image that breaks me.

I run a shaking hand down my face and force myself to focus.

Stick with the plan.

Get the money.

Go get Jade and the Bees.

This mantra is the only thing keeping me sane.

I pull up Ed's contact card and tap the number for his cell, my leg jiggling against the steering wheel. To my left, a neat line of crepe myrtles flutter under a stiff wind, and I start the car and crank up the heat even though I'm sweating. Panic sweat, the kind that makes you feel cold and slightly nauseous, like you're coming down with the flu. I gun the gas and the vents spew lukewarm air.

One ring. Two rings. Three. I suck a breath and hold it there, ready to let loose a primal scream if Ed doesn't pick up.

On the fourth ring, a slurp of garbled static beats through the truck's speakers, followed by a fumbling of metal against fabric and finally, thankfully, Ed's voice.

"Hey, Cam. I was just about to give you a call."

Relief shoots through my veins like a drug, and I settle the phone in the cupholder, then throw the gearshift in Reverse. "Ed, please. For the love of God, *please* tell me you've got good news."

I look over my shoulder and punch the gas, swinging the truck backward into the mostly empty lot. I've already thought about the best way to Ed's office, on the fourteenth floor of a high-rise on the Buckhead loop, already plugged the coordinates into Waze. I screech to a stop and shove the gearshift into Drive, but Ed's next words freeze my fist around the stick.

"I've got some news, yes, but I'm not certain it's the good news you're hoping for."

A sick tremor works its way across my torso. "Please, Ed. I'm begging you. I am desperate."

"Yeah. I'm getting that, Cam, and I want you to know that I really went to the mat for you. My boss may be all smiles at those soccer games and cocktail parties we're always inviting you and Jade to, but here at the bank Alissa is a hard-ass, and she plays by the rules. I have very little wiggle room in these matters."

The parking lot in front of me smears, a hazy gray wash of asphalt and skeleton branches and gauzy air. "I don't have time for guessing games, Ed. Just tell me what she said so I can figure out how I'm going to plug the hole."

"Basically, it's a yes *but*. Yes, Alissa agreed to extend a loan to cover the time it takes for us to cash out your IRA, *but* there are two strings attached. First, she capped the loan at $350,000. Now I realize your IRA is worth much more than that, and that's great news on the back end, but as far as extending the money up front, Alissa was pretty adamant. Three-fifty is as much as we'll be able to get out of her."

I don't have to do the math: $350K, plus the cash in the bag on the seat next to me, is a little over half of what I need for the ransom. That leaves one hell of a hole, but it's an amount that feels a little more feasible. My mind kicks into overdrive, racing through a mental Rolodex of people I know with that kind of cash. Business-owner pals whose fields are cash driven, friends who flaunt wives hung with diamond jewelry and Birkin bags, who blather on about yachts and vacation homes and who have homes with panic rooms and safes stuffed with cash.

Only problem is, why would they give any of that money to me?

And then I replay Ed's words and realize there's more. He just said there were *two* strings, *two* conditions to the money.

"What's the other one?"

At Ed's sigh, my body turns to stone, bracing for what comes next.

"The earliest I could get you the cash is tomorrow morning."

His message is a gut punch. "Tomorrow morning is unacceptable, Ed. I need this money tonight. I need it *now*." I slam my fist against the steering wheel.

"I understand that, but even if we could get through the paperwork today, an amount that large takes time to pull together. I'm up here at the executive offices, which means I don't have that kind of cash just lying around. I'd have to call down to a local branch, but it's already past five. I doubt I could even find anybody to pick up the phone."

He pauses, sitting through a silence I know I'm supposed to fill, but with what? I've got nothing.

"I'm sorry, Cam. I know you were counting on this, but truly, my hands are tied. As much as I want to help you out here, and I really *do* want to help, it's the best I can do. Come by first thing tomorrow morning, and we'll get you sorted out."

I slump in my seat, resting my forehead against the wheel and breathing through a brutal wave of panic. I see a younger Jade, her curls hanging wild like they used to before she started straightening them, grinning above me in bed. A purple-faced Beatrix, waving wrinkly fists and raising hell in her hospital bassinet. Sweet, innocent Bax, sacked out under the Christmas tree atop his Woody blanket. *Devils by day, angels at night*, Jade is always joking, but the truth is, Bax is an angel when he's awake, too.

And now—

"Please, Ed. *Please*, I am *begging* you." A sob is stuck in my throat like a brick, so thick it hurts to swallow. "I'll take any amount you can offer me, at any interest rate. I don't give a shit what you charge me for it, I just need that money today. This is life or death for me. I know that sounds cryptic, and I can't tell you anything more, other than that it's true. If I don't get this money today, people are going to die."

Another long pause. More silence waiting to be filled.

"Look, I..." Ed clears his throat. "I feel obligated to ask what this is all about, because honestly? From where I'm sitting? This sounds like something the police should be involved in. Is everything okay, Cam? Is Jade?"

I wipe my eyes, fist the steering wheel, and drive the truck out of the lot to God knows where. Where do I go now? Whom do I ask for money now? I follow the asphalt around the building and to the road, and everything around me goes black around the edges. For a shivery second I think I might pass out, but I shake it off, clenching down on my teeth until my vision turns solid again.

"I know our relationship is mostly professional, but I like you," Ed says. "I consider you a friend, which is why I'm going to ask you again. Do you need help? Do I need to, I don't know, send in the cavalry? Because I'll do it if you need me to. I'll make that call. All you have to do is say the word."

No police.

And for God's sake, no sirens.

"Thanks for trying, Ed. I've got to run." I hang up and pull into traffic.

I drive down an unfamiliar street and try my damnedest not to throw up. $49,000 and some change. That's all I've got to show for ninety full minutes of hustle, and now it's too late. The banks are closed. Ed packed up his papers and clocked out, and I have less than an hour and a half to scrounge up seven hundred grand from God knows where. What a nightmare.

Ed's final words to me echo in my head. *I'll do it if you need me to. I'll make that call. All you have to do is say the word.*

For the first time today, I wonder if involving the police isn't my best option. There are loads of home invasions in this city, drama you hear about every day on the news. Surely the cops have a SWAT team, a playbook, skilled negotiators who know what not to say. Surely they know to turn off the sirens. Surely they know how to avoid a standoff.

Only, how many of them end in tragedy?

My mind swirls with real-life scenarios I saw on the news. The pregnant lady shot in the stomach by a stray bullet, the girl who watched her twin sister get gunned down, the mother who escaped out the basement window only to have her entire family murdered when the cops busted down the door. I had to flip the channel because their stories were so tragic—and these are just the ones I can remember.

I think about what that would be like, having to live with the knowledge that my mistake cost me my family. Even if the cops came in quietly, even if they snuck through the trees in the neighbors' yards and managed a surprise attack, they'd have to get inside the house somehow. They could probably get the alarm company to disarm the house, but he'd hear them coming from a mile away. Plenty of time to kill everyone including himself before the cops stormed up the stairs. What if they blow it? That kind of mistake is forever. You can't put the pin back in that grenade.

No. I can't risk it. It's a potential death sentence. Involving the cops has got to be the absolute last resort.

So then…what? Call the house and explain? Beg him to hold off until the banks open in the morning? That would give me the rest of the night to pull together another four hundred thousand and think through my defenses. An automatic weapon. A Kevlar vest so I can take the bullets meant for Jade and the Bees. If I can hold him off until tomorrow, I'll have time to come up with a plan.

Still, I imagine Jade, sleeping on that blue chair with a gun pointed at her head, sharing fifteen extra hours of oxygen with a psycho kidnapper. One wrong move, one moment of impatience and his trigger finger could get twitchy. The kids would be witnesses, so they'd die, too. *Boom boom boom*. My whole family, lying in a sticky pool of their own blood. Wiped out in an instant because I couldn't come up with the ransom.

Which means there's only one answer, only one possible recourse: get the money and bring it to the house by seven. It's the only way to keep Jade and the kids alive. Failure is not an option.

And then I remember the fire.

The one that licked my Bolling Way kitchen to death and took out my best source of income. The one that sparked in an outlet next to the cooking oil, exploding into a fireball when it hit the ceiling's flammable noise panels.

Now it's like pulling a crumpled lottery ticket from your pocket and seeing the winning numbers, like ripping open the candy bar to uncover the golden ticket. All this time, I've been sitting on a pot of money I didn't even think about. A flicker of hope sparks in my chest, and my lungs swell with gulped air. I yank on the wheel and swerve onto the dirt shoulder, tires kicking up rocks and garbage as the truck skids to a sloppy stop.

Flavio picks up on the first ring. "Finally. I've been leaving you messages all afternoon. Where are you?"

I look around, blinking through my windshield at the run-down terrain. Boarded-up buildings and chop shops behind chain-link fences, an occasional fast-food joint—the cheap and dirty kind. Scaryville, as Jade would call this place. Bank-head, I'm guessing.

"Running a couple of errands. What's the word from the insurance adjustor?"

There are still all sorts of obstacles, I know, but if I could somehow manage to get my hands on a check, I could take it to one of those check-cashing places—Western Union or one of the sketchy ones that stay open late for suckers like me, desperate people willing to pay an obscene rate for quick cash. But even then, even if I had to forfeit what? Ten percent? Twenty? The payout will still be more than what I need. I'd walk away with plenty of cash for Jade and the kids.

"That's what I've been calling you about," Flavio says. "He wants to know about the building on Pharr."

I frown. "What about it?"

"Actually, he's standing right here. Why don't I let you talk to him." Not so much a question as it is a statement, and one that ticks a warning beat in my chest.

There's a shuffling on the line, the cell phone exchanging hands, followed by a new voice, deep and heavy on the syrup.

"Hey, Cam, Matt Brady here. I'm sorry you and I haven't had a chance to chitchat before today, though I surely regret what's got us on the phone now. I want you to know, however, that you and I will get to the bottom of this fire. I assure you, I'm here for the duration."

My restaurants are filled with men who talk like this, in flowery sentences delivered in dignified twangs that echo of cotton fields and weekend hunting lodges. They pull up to the valet stand like they just arrived from the country club, in custom shoes and neck scarves doused in designer cologne, and they buy buckets of Screaming Eagles for them and all their friends. They run big companies and sign big checks.

What they do *not* do is take a job as an insurance adjustor.

"Thank you for that, Matt. I appreciate your dedication to the cause, but as I'm sure you can understand, I have lots of people counting on me for their livelihoods. How soon do you think we can get them some compensation?"

I may not have grown up in the South, but I can play good ol' boy like the best of them.

"Well, I suppose that depends in large part on the conversation you and I have here today. What can you tell me about the Pharr Road establishment?"

"I can tell you the building on Pharr does not belong to me. I haven't taken ownership yet, and just between you and me, whether or not I move forward on the purchase is kind of up in the air."

He makes a humming noise. "Still. I find it a little interesting you put down that kind of earnest money on a building just around the corner from your existing restaurant on Bolling Way. Less than a quarter of a mile to be precise, and featuring a rear lot that'll fit fifty-plus cars. I checked the zoning, and what do you know? The City of Atlanta has earmarked it for restaurant use."

The rubber band around my chest wraps tighter. I don't like where this line of questioning is headed.

My laugh tries for casual but misses by a mile. "All that's true, but have you seen the place? It's a real dump. One I no longer have the time or the funds to renovate. Looks like Lasky will be staying put."

"How much do you think it'll cost to fix it up? You're a businessman, Cam. I'm assuming you've done the math."

Hell yeah I've done the math. Four thousand square feet of prime real estate smack in the second wave of the Buckhead development, easily accessible from both Buckhead and Midtown, and an owner who's beyond desperate to sell. A no-brainer, assuming I could cough up the money—which I can't. Not without another investor with deep, deep pockets.

"I don't see what this has to do with—"

"How much, Cam?"

I fight the urge to scream. The clock on my dash ticks to 5:30, and we still haven't gotten to the payout or talked about the possibility of him writing a check for the money I need to save my family. I white-knuckle the steering wheel, my body a sizzling bundle of reflexes and raw nerves.

"A million, give or take, for the reno plus furnishings. And then there's the cost of the building—which again, isn't mine."

"But it's under contract. You put down a significant chunk of earnest money."

"Money I'm fully prepared to walk away from. Recent developments have changed my investment strategy somewhat."

"Are you referring to the fire?"

"I'm referring to the hole in my bank account!"

I wince at his stretch of silence.

"Look, I'm sorry. My nerves are shredded. The truth is, Bolling Way is the only shop keeping me afloat, which means I need that insurance money as soon as humanly possible. I needed it yesterday."

"I'm afraid that's not how this works. What do you think, that I just drive around town with a trunk full of money? I don't even own a checkbook. There's a process for these things, which starts first and foremost with you filing a claim. Then, once that's approved, we have up to thirty days to process the payment. Now, I'm not saying it will take that long, but you see where I'm going with this? It's going to take some time."

"Okay. Well, what about an advance?"

"You could request an advance, but that's only meant to tide you over for the first few days. Advances are typically a very small portion of the total estimated amount, and even then, it'll be tomorrow before I can work through the paperwork."

The reality hits me like a fist in the face—no insurance money today, no way of plugging that $700,000 hole—along with a more urgent problem: a man coming at me on the other side of the windshield. A crackhead, that much is obvious from the slant of his mouth, his vacant expression, the way his limbs flop around in a sloppy gait.

My hand reaches into the space below my seat, my fingers closing around the handle of the Smith & Wesson. I flip the safety and drag the weapon onto my lap, holding it steady.

"Flavio can handle the claim," I say while looking the crackhead straight in the eye, holding his gaze, daring him with mine. He peers through the side window, sizing me up, too. I see his eyes settle on the logo on my shirt, then wander on to the truck's rims, the oversize tires and custom grill.

Not today, dude. You do not want to fuck with me today.

"Whatever information you need, Flavio can provide." I watch the crackhead in the side mirror, his gait slowing at the back bumper. My body is on high alert, but my heartbeat finally eases up, settling into a deliberate, steady rhythm. "Now, if you don't mind, I'm kind of in the middle of some—"

"Just one more thing." Matt's genteel twang is gone now, replaced with something flat and razor-sharp.

"Yeah, what?" I clock the guy's slouchy stride, the way he ducks his head under that hoodie, how his hands swing long and free.

"Earlier this afternoon, I had a very enlightening discussion with a Mr. Spivey at the Abernathy leasing offices. He says you're scheduled to start paying rent at the end of the year."

Abernathy, the landlord. My gut twists with unease because yet again, I know where this conversation is headed.

"*Was* scheduled. *Was.* Obviously, this fire changes things. Mr. Spivey already told Flavio they'd work with us on the lease."

"That's not what Mr. Spivey related to me. He said the two of you have been involved in a bit of a tiff. He accused you of trying to wriggle your way out of what's supposed to be a five-year lease."

"That's all true," I say, because there's really no use in denying it. Tim Spivey has probably fifty emails from me and my attorney throwing every excuse at the wall to see if one would stick. The Bolling Way shop was making a killing, not just for me but for the entire development. More diners meant more shoppers, hordes of happy, tipsy folks with plenty of money to spend. I was willing to stay, but only if they dropped the monthly payments on the last two years of the lease. Preferably, to zero.

"Next time you talk to Mr. Spivey you can tell him a move to Pharr Road is off the table. Lasky Steak is going nowhere."

"I'll do that, Cam, but just so we're clear. You do understand how it looks, right? A catastrophic fire smack in the middle of a lease dispute. The timing is beyond convenient." His accent is back, the words delivered slowly, precisely, like a doctor reporting bad news.

"I don't like what you're insinuating."

"Oh, I'm sorry, I must not be making myself clear. I'm not insinuating anything. What I'm doing is making an accusation, and I'm not the only one. The investigator agrees the fire looks suspicious. He even threw around the word *arson*, and multiple times. If that's the case, if the fire was intentionally set by you or someone directed by you, then that would qualify as insurance fraud. A felony."

The words are like an ambush, prickling my skin with alarm. "Check the security footage."

"I have. Seems the camera was turned on, but the wire from the unit to the monitor had come loose. The last recording from your security company was taken just before midnight last night, a good ten hours before the fire. The footage from today showed a blank screen."

In other words, no way to prove who set the fire—and more importantly for this particular conversation—no insurance money from Matt today. Maybe ever.

He's still talking, something about next steps and legal matters, but I'm not listening because a shadow has fallen across my side window. The crackhead, going for my door handle.

I press the gun to the window, the muzzle flush to the glass.

There's a sluggish delay, a full couple of seconds before his eyes have focused on the weapon aimed at his chest, and then they widen in shock. He stumbles backward, almost stepping into traffic, missing a passing bus by a foot before he takes off in a dead run.

Matt's voice fills the cab: "Did you hear me, Cam? I said I'm sending your case to the Special Investigations Unit for potential insurance fraud. That's the first step into an investigation as to the origin and cause of this fire."

I toss the gun onto the passenger's seat and shift into gear. "That's great, Matt. It's just really fucking fantastic."

I hang up and hit the gas, pulling out with a growl of motor and clattering of kicked-up gravel, my mind stuck on two facts. I have no idea where to go next, and I'm just so royally screwed.

THE INTERVIEW

Juanita: In the months since the home invasion, there have been rumors of you stiffing contractors and suppliers—

Cam: [scoffs]

Juanita: —that you created a namesake charity and used those funds to pay off your children's private school and business liabilities—

Cam: [rolls eyes]

Juanita: —and that what you claimed was the best dry-aged specialty beef was really just meat you purchased in bulk at Costco.

Cam: Would you like the number for my distributor? I'm sure

he'd be more than willing to give you a couple of choice sound bites. I still owe him more than fifty grand.

Juanita: The point is, these stories are such a far cry from your reputation as Atlanta's Steak King that it's jarring. Would you like to hear a few of the words used to describe you on social media and in the news?

Cam: Not really.

Juanita: Slimy. Shameless. Selfish. Self-centered and self-dealing. A crook like your father. A con artist and a villain. People sure love to hate on Cam Lasky, don't they?

Cam: What can I say? I'm a despicable guy.

Juanita: Don't you want to at least try to defend yourself?

Cam: No.

Juanita: Why not? I thought you were here to tell the truth. To look into the camera and set the record straight.

Cam: Do you honestly think after everything that happened that I give the first shit about my reputation? Come on, Juanita. I mean, *look* at me. See how I've paid. So no, I'm not going to try to defend myself because what I did is indefensible. That's the truth I want people to hear, that I am a sorry, stupid man. That I carry a truckload of guilt and regret and shame. I'm sure your viewers will be beyond thrilled to hear how miserable I am.

Juanita: And Jade?

Cam: What about her?

Juanita: If she were here right now, what would she say? Would she say she still loved you despite what you did, that she forgave you?

Cam: [lengthy pause] Knowing Jade? Sure. But your question should be whether or not I'd believe her.

JADE

JADE

5:32 p.m.

We are back up on the main level, Baxter, the masked man and me, parked in the hallway between the master bedroom and the stairs. He orders me to stand against the wall, and my shoulders brush against the series of family portraits in matching black frames, stern-faced grandfathers and great-great-aunts I've never met and history has long forgotten, hanging from brass hooks on the wall. I wonder what they would think of the screwdriver up my sleeve, if they would see it as brave-hearted or reckless.

"What do you think?" he says, flipping off the basement light just inside the door. "Should we leave it open or lock her down there?"

I don't respond, mostly because he doesn't seem to expect an answer.

He leans his head into the stairwell and shouts, "Congrats, Beatrix. You're locked in the dungeon with a million cockroaches," then slams the door and twists the dead bolts with a snide grin. "If she's down there, we'll know it pretty darn soon."

Baxter lays a clammy hand on my cheek and turns my face to his. "Mommy, Beatrix is not in the basement." His voice is a shout-whisper, the kind he uses to tell his deepest, darkest secrets—like what I'm getting for Mother's Day weeks before he and Beatrix present me with a package. Baxter thinks if he whispers something, he's not spoiling the surprise.

But I wish he'd keep quiet, especially if he happens to know where his sister is hiding.

And even if he doesn't, every word Baxter utters, every move he makes, puts him square in the spotlight, when it's so much safer for him to fade into the background. I need him to keep quiet because I want this man to deal with *me*, not my children.

He stares at Baxter like he's stuffed with gold. "Do you know where your big sister is?"

The screwdriver is like plutonium, tingling against my skin. If I slid it out of my sleeve right now, I could hold him off of Baxter for a second or two, but I only get one chance. The worst thing would be to waste it.

He steps closer, and Baxter and I lean back, knocking one of the frames from the wall. Great-Great-Grandpa Wally, who played shortstop in the army baseball league. His picture crashes to the floor with a sickening crunch, scattering glass shards across the hallway.

"No." I shake my head. "Of course Baxter doesn't know."

Baxter *might* know. The kids play hide-and-seek often enough, and he knows all the best spots, places our captor didn't think to look. Squeezed into the dead space between the laundry hamper and the long dresses in my closet, for example, or curled up inside the covered ottoman in the study. Bax can probably even rattle off a couple I don't know about.

The man's gaze whips to mine. "No offense, but when it comes to your kids, you're not the most reliable witness. I prefer to hear it from the horse's mouth." He scratches a gloved finger over Baxter's knee. "Hello, horsey."

It isn't really a question, and Baxter doesn't answer. I clutch his body tighter to mine.

"Come on, little guy, I thought you and I were friends." A slight edge has snuck into the man's voice, a not-so-subtle warning. "Friends don't keep secrets. Now tell me where your big sister's hiding."

But this time Bax isn't falling for it. By now he's seen too much—the awful words this man has been slinging around, the gun in his fist and the switchblade in his pocket. Baxter knows the masked man is not his friend. He shrugs against my shoulder and mumbles, "I don't know."

"You don't know."

Baxter shakes his head.

"But you just said she wasn't downstairs."

He nods.

The man's eyes go a little wide, a universal gesture for WTF. "Then how do you know?"

"'Cause the scary man who bangs on the pipes lives down there. How come you wear a mask? Do you have superpowers?"

Just then, a familiar sound sticks the breath to my lungs. A key, rattling in the front door.

All heads whip in the direction of the noise, even though we can't see the door from where we're standing. Not with the four-foot stretch of wall, a solid boundary between the base of the stairs and the front door, blocking the view. I stare at the alabaster plaster, breathless.

The man's whisper laps at the side of my neck. "Who's that?"

I shake my head, the burning in my arm muscles bleeding away into a panicky tingle. Is it Cam, returning home already with the money? I hold my breath and wait, clutching Baxter to my chest, straining to hear. Five full seconds of frozen terror.

There's a sharp sound of metal on wood, followed by a whoosh of outside air.

And then two things happen all at once. A long steady beeping erupts from the alarm pad bolted onto the bedroom wall, and a familiar voice sings out a hello.

Tanya Lloyd, the neighbor from across the street.

"Jade, are you here?"

With impressive speed, the man tugs me down the hall and into the bedroom. "Tell her not to move," he hisses, flipping open the cover on the alarm panel and ticking in the code. *"Do it."* Just in case, he raises the gun six inches from my face—as if I need convincing.

"Hang on, Tanya," I shout, pointing my face into the hallway. "Stay where you are. I'll be right there."

My words don't stop her footsteps from moving deeper into the house. Tanya is our nosiest neighbor, the kind who parks herself in her bay window when the kids are at school so she can keep an eye on the street. She knows every neighbor within a five-mile radius. She knows their kids' names and their dogs' names and what day their lawn and pool service comes. She knows who's pregnant and who's getting married or on the verge of divorce, and which houses are about to go on the market weeks before the broker hammers a For Sale sign in the grass. If one of our neighbors forgets to pick up their dog's shit from our front yard, Tanya calls to tell me who it was, and exactly which bush it's under. She is a one-woman security patrol, and she drives Cam and me up a tree.

And now she's here, in our house. Standing in the foyer. If she comes in any farther, and she will, which way will she go? Left, into the kitchen and the television room beyond? Or right for the stairs—in full view of us, standing just inside the bedroom doorway.

And speaking of bedrooms, it feels strange to be standing shoulder to shoulder with a masked man in mine. The space is too personal and far too intimate. Everywhere I look are pieces of me and Cam. The framed photos of the kids, naked but for their diapers, on the wall. The romance novels piled up on a nightstand strewn with discarded earrings and Chapstick and lotion bottles. The neat pile of freshly laundered sports bras on the bed, which I wish to God were tucked in a drawer. I don't want to be here with him. It's too disturbing, like some kind of BDSM nightmare.

On the other side of the wall, Tanya's footsteps go dull and blunted, which means she's moved from the foyer marble onto the living room hardwood.

Please go left please go left.

Turning right would get us killed. Me, Baxter, Tanya. Three unarmed innocents. Turning right would involve her in this nightmare, too.

And then something else occurs to me. What if she's here because she saw Beatrix make her escape? What if she saw her…I don't know, shimmy down a drainpipe, race down the hill, sneak through the bushes to the neighbors'? If anybody saw Beatrix make a run for it, it would have been Tanya. What if *that's* what she's coming here to tell me?

Tanya's footsteps are clomping around, moving nearer. "Where are y'all? Are you upstairs?"

"Get rid of her," the man whispers, and now he sounds like Cam. Cam has never been a Tanya fan. Not since the welcome-to-the-neighborhood party she threw us, where after one too many cocktails, I offered her a key. Cam wanted me to march over there and demand it back, because he knew she'd equate the key with an open-door policy. She uses it at least once a week to pop over for drinks, to deliver our mail or just to say hi. She's sweet, but she needs constant coddling, like an insecure, jealous spouse. She wants nothing more than to be needed.

And now that's one battle won because boy do I ever need her.

I scurry down the hall with Baxter on my hip, my shoes slipping in the broken glass, stopping at the bottom of the stairs. I spot Tanya in the living room, pinching a fuchsia-tipped bloom of an orchid plant between two fingers, I'm guessing to see if it's real.

"Sorry, sorry. We were in the bedroom. Hey, Tan."

She whirls around, her oversize shirt swinging around her hips, and I know what she sees: wild hair, lipstick chewed off, haunted eyes. I saw myself in the bedroom mirror just now. I know I look a mess.

But Tanya is her usual put-together self. Dark jeans, white shirt topped with a chunky necklace. This one's made of long fingers of polished black horn studded with diamonds. Tanya once told me she knew every time her ex-husband had an affair, because he'd come home with another stunner for her jewelry collection—and she has amassed quite the collection.

"There you are. I was just bringing by some mail I picked up for you last week. Y'all should really put a lock on that mailbox, it's a surefire way to— Aww, Baxie, what's the matter, sugar? You look like you've been crying." She steps close enough to brush his cheek with the pad of her thumb.

One more inch, one tiny twist of her head, and she'll spot the masked man slinking silently down the hall to my right, the gun he's aiming at my temple.

"He's just tired. It's been kind of a crazy day."

Her glossed lips purse with sympathy. "Poor baby. I hope you're not coming down with that nasty bug that's been working its way through the club." She presses the back of her hand to Baxter's forehead, then one of his cheeks. "You're a little warm, but nothing too bad. Are you feeling okay?"

She's standing less than a foot away, close enough I can smell her spicy-sweet perfume and the caramel she stirred into her afternoon coffee.

"Baxter's fine." I run a shaky hand over Baxter's head, flattening the tangle of fine hair at the crown. My next words are as much for him as they are for me: "He's fine. Everybody's fine."

She smiles, but I can't manage to match it.

"Well, you can never be too careful, you know, and you don't want to push too hard if you're not feeling well. Bill McAllister tried that, and he passed out on the ninth tee. One minute he's standing there, bragging to his caddie about the birdie he just scored, the next he's lights out on the green. They carted him off in an ambulance, you know."

Tanya blabbers on, oblivious as ever to my discomfort, but I'm no longer listening because out of the corner of my eye, movement. A black smudge, shifting from me to Baxter. The man didn't say it, but he also didn't have to. One wrong move and he'll shoot us both dead.

I transfer Baxter to my other hip, putting my torso between him and the muzzle of the gun. If anybody here is taking a bullet, it will be me. I'm going first.

Take that, asshole.

I stare at Tanya's mouth and will the chattering to stop—*Leave, there's a gunman standing* right here, *run back across the road and save yourself*—but my mind is as thick as molasses. I need her to stop talking long enough for me to give her some kind of sign. A subtle clue that she will recognize as a call for help, but the gunman won't.

"Jade, I swear. You are such a dreamer. Did you hear a single word I said?" She watches me, eyebrows raised. I shake my head, and she laughs like I'm the silliest thing ever. "I have a question for you. And before you say no, just promise you'll hear me out, okay?"

I don't respond. My mind is racing, trying to come up with words that pry loose some understanding, some urgency in Tanya. She takes my silence as an affirmative.

"Okay, so I'm putting together a fundraiser for my niece, you know, to help out with some of the medical costs. Poor thing's not getting any better. If you're the praying type, say a little prayer she gets in that trial, will you? Her insurance is being so difficult."

I mold my face into something that I hope resembles sympathy. Tanya's niece needs new lungs. Doctors say she won't survive the next year without them.

"Anyway, you know how you told me once Baxter went back to school this fall you were thinking about getting back into decorating?"

She pauses just long enough for me to nod. I don't remember telling her as much but it's something I could have said after a glass or two of wine.

"Well, that got me to thinking, what if you offered up some free room makeovers for the silent auction? We could take some before and after pictures at my house, or if you have a girlfriend who could use some pointers, her place. Doesn't matter where, as long as the pictures are good because you *know* the people who come to these things. They spend stupid amounts of money on their homes, and I thought maybe this way, we could raise money *and* drum you up some business. A win-win, don't you think?"

This. This right here is why despite all her faults, I harbor a soft spot for Tanya Lloyd. On the one hand, she lets herself into my house to ask me a question she could have easily posed by phone. It annoys the hell out of Cam, and any other day, it would annoy the hell out of me, too.

But anybody else would have marched over to ask me to donate something from Cam. A cooler filled with Lasky steaks, a dinner for twelve in the Lasky private room, a Lasky gift card.

But Tanya didn't ask for any of that. She didn't even hint at it. I mentioned once in passing that I missed playing with fabrics and textures and patterns, that finding the exact perfect color combination was once upon a time as satisfying to me as an orgasm. My sister would have called me shallow, my friends would have forgotten that conversation ever happened, but not Tanya. Tanya filed that little tidbit away and pulled it out not to use to her advantage—okay, maybe a *little* to her advantage—but also to mine.

Cam is wrong about Tanya. She can keep the key.

She grabs on to the arm I have wrapped around Baxter. "Well? What do you think?"

I think I don't want her to leave. I think I need to figure out a way to signal for help. And if she picks up on the clues I'm about to slide into this conversation, I think I will love her forever.

"Sounds great, sign me up. Oh, and hey, did you ever ask your brother about next weekend?"

Tanya doesn't have a brother, just three sisters who live on the outskirts of town, walking distance from where they stuck their mother in a memory care facility. That's what she calls it, often and on repeat every time the two talk, that for the life of her she can't understand why anybody would "stick" her in such an awful place. Tanya carries a lot of guilt for being miles away, but the point is, she has no brother.

She frowns. "My brother..."

"Yeah, he was going to come over and help Cam move the concrete table to the other side of the backyard, remember?"

"I see." She's puzzled, I can tell, but not quick enough to make the connection that something might be wrong. Not yet. She needs more.

I widen my eyes, flit them in the direction of the man with the gun. "Do you?"

"No, Jade. I don't."

I shake my head, a quick and subtle back-and-forth, were it not for the man watching from five feet away.

Don't say it. For the love of God, keep your big mouth closed.

But Tanya Lloyd, neighborhood busybody and unsuspecting philanthropist, says the quiet part out loud: "Hon, what is going on? Because I know you know I don't have a brother. Is everything okay?"

JADE

5:39 p.m.

I stare at Tanya, and I don't know how to stop this train. My little blunder with her fictional brother just now could have gotten her killed. It could still, if she doesn't let it go.

I think about what I will do if the man comes after Tanya, how I can protect any of us with Baxter hanging from my hip. I feel the body-warmed metal of the screwdriver against the skin of my arm, painfully conscious that I've now got *three* people to worry about, *three* innocent bystanders to protect instead of just my two children. I need to come up with a way to reframe this battle and move it to a safer place—somewhere without the risk of collateral damage.

"Sorry, Tanya. I must be confused. I've just got so much on my mind, I guess I forgot."

Tanya doesn't seem the least bit offended. "No worries, sugar—for a minute there I was worried you were dipping into the afternoon sherry. Speaking of, did you hear? Suzanne

Foster down the block just checked herself into rehab. Though I suppose nobody who's ever been to one of her book clubs would be the least bit surprised. That woman's liver must be big as Brazil."

Baxter wriggles to be let down, and I slide him down my leg. We didn't exactly have time to go over the rules here, but I'm guessing the man aiming a gun at my temple wants us to stay in his sights. As soon as his feet hit the floor, Baxter takes off toward the back of the house, to the TV room and the chest full of toys. I watch him go, bracing for some kind of payback. At least he's out of shooting range.

"Did something break?"

I follow Tanya's gaze to the floor behind me, where shards of glass sparkle like fallen snow on the hardwood.

"Oh, that," I say, letting my gaze drift over the man. He's pressed to the wall, his back to the living room, but all I see is his gun, mere feet away from my head. It's like staring down a rabid animal. He lifts a gloved finger up to his lips. *Shh.*

I turn back to Tanya. "It was a picture. I accidentally bumped it off the wall."

"Oh, well, better clean it up quick, then. If your kids are anything like mine, they don't know where their shoes are half the time. If one of them runs through that mess, you'll be digging glass out of their feet till Christmas."

My lungs swell with breath, and the words come out before I can stop them. "Can I get you something to drink?"

Light. Casual. An Oscar-worthy performance, and it's the polite thing to do, though I don't have time to think through a game plan, and I definitely don't want to consider the consequences. In my periphery, the man moves closer, the muzzle almost to the edge of the wall. The gesture is a warning, a promise of coming punishment.

Tanya shakes her head. "Thanks, but I can't stay. I just ran over to—"

"Are you sure?" I flash her my most gracious smile, and then I do it. I step forward, shifting my body to the other side of the wall, putting me officially out of shooting range. "I've got a bottle of that Sancerre you like so much in the fridge."

Last time she was here, she drank almost the whole thing by herself.

Her gaze wanders in the direction of the front door, where she has a view of her house across the street. "I'd love to, hon, but another time, okay? When I left there were seven kids jacked up on Sour Patch and Coca-Cola, and I gotta go wrangle those rascals off my chandeliers before they burn the place to the ground."

Don't leave. Take us with you. The words scream through my head, and then I think of my Beatrix, curled up somewhere in this house, and my skin goes slippery with fear. I can't leave, not without *both* my kids.

But Baxter can. He can leave. If I can somehow get Tanya to take Baxter with her, to take him by the hand and lead him to safety across the street, he'll have told her about the masked man who tied his mother to a chair before they step through her front door. I'm surprised he hasn't already.

Probably because he was too focused on getting his hands on his big sister's karaoke machine—in this house, it's the root of the most vicious of sibling battles. Beatrix doesn't allow her brother to touch so much as a dial, and now Bax is going to town with the disco lights. If that doesn't smoke Beatrix out of her hole, nothing will.

Tanya is still talking. "...over the weekend sometime and we'll do a walk-through of my house. I have a couple of rooms that could use some rearranging. I can get my cousin to come over and take some pictures. He's not a professional photographer, but he's pretty decent."

Shit. She's wrapping up. Adrenaline zings through my veins, and I blurt the first thing I can think of.

"Oh my God," I gasp, and it sounds real—those old acting skills again, and this time they're more convincing.

Her eyebrows shoot to the ceiling. "Oh my God, what?"

"I just realized I forgot to take Beatrix to her dentist's appointment, and now we're about to be late."

"Now? I don't know of any dentist in town who works past five."

"This one's open until six thirty."

Beyond her in the den, Baxter's figured out how to turn on the mic. Heavy breathing punctuated with an occasional and serious *"testing testing one two three,"* syrupy with synthetic echo.

Tanya waves her hand in a "who cares" gesture. "Don't worry about it, then. They're probably hours behind by now, which means you've got a good thirty, forty minutes of leeway."

"Still. Would you mind taking Baxter for a bit? You know how Beatrix can be such a handful, and she's terrified of the dentist. I promise I'll swing by to get him as soon as we're back. Shouldn't take longer than an hour or so."

Tanya checks her watch and pulls a face. "Oh, sweetie, I would, but I've already got two extra kids in the house and you know what those Montgomery twins are like. They—"

"Please." My voice cracks on the word, and I force myself to slow down, to calm down. "Please, Tanya. You'd really be helping me out."

"Oh… I don't know. It's really not the greatest time, and I haven't even started on dinner."

"I'll return the favor anytime. Any weekend night you want. You can go out with the girls."

Still, she looks undecided, so I latch on to her arm, all five fingers locking on to her wrist. My upper body pitches forward, leaning into Tanya's personal space for a change, getting right up in her face.

Help.

I mouth the word, and just in case, I dart my eyes in the direction of the man and his gun concealed behind the wall, clamping down hard on her wrist. Her face twists in pain, in confusion.

"Sweetie, are you okay?"

When I don't respond, Tanya frowns, her gaze sinking to my lips. I carve them around the word again: *Help.*

Three breathless seconds pass while she holds my gaze, three seconds while my heart booms so hard in my temples I wonder if I'm having a stroke. Tanya pats my hand, peels my fingers one by one away from her arm and stares with wide eyes into mine. "Hey, Bax?" She yells it without turning her head.

My knees go slushy, my eyes wet with relief. She's going to take Baxter out of harm's way, which means if I survive this shit show, I will have a lifetime supply of flowers and Sancerre delivered to her doorstep. I will kiss her on those coral lips and bow down to worship her pedicured feet. I will take out a full-page ad in the *AJC* telling everyone in Atlanta and beyond how she saved Baxter's life by whisking him out of the danger zone and carting him across the street to safety.

He pokes his head around the corner, the microphone in a fist. "Yeah?"

Tanya turns to him with a held-out hand. "I was thinking about pizza for dinner. How does that sound?"

Bax looks at me for confirmation, and I nod. Pizza is his favorite, and normally it wouldn't take him long to decide. Now, though, he stands there, uncertain.

"What about my shoes?" He looks down at his bare feet, sticking out from the Batman pajamas.

"You don't need 'em," Tanya says, coaxing him with a smile. "I already told the kids we're eating in."

Baxter frowns, his gaze bouncing between us, and I pray he doesn't say anything about the man hidden behind the wall. I pray he goes back to ignoring the man with the gun, to playacting like this is an ordinary afternoon, and we're not being held captive in our own house. On the way down the driveway, he can tell Tanya all about the masked man, just not now. Not yet.

Baxter shrugs, tosses the mic to the couch. "I guess."

Now that she's caved, Tanya seems anxious to get across the road. She plucks Baxter's hand from the air and drags him toward the door. "Okay, well, call us on your way home, and clean up that glass before somebody gets hurt."

I try to think of what to say—*Take care of my baby, wait, don't go*—but come up empty. Instead, I stare at their retreating backs, the way her shirt is gathered around her hips, how it's snagged up on one side by something in her back pocket.

At the door, Baxter turns to wave, and I blow him a kiss.

"And thanks again for helping out with the auction, Jade. You and I are going to raise so much money for my sweet niece. I'll see you when you get back." She turns to holler over her shoulder, "Good luck at the dentist's, Beatrix."

And then, just like that, the door swishes shut, closing with a sharp click.

I take a shaky step into the living room, just far enough to watch Tanya lead my son down the hill, and tears sting my eyes, but I manage to hold my shit together because Baxter is safe and Beatrix is hidden and I can't cry, not now. Not until Cam shows up with a big bag of money he trades for me and the kids, not until the cops kick down the door and slap some handcuffs on the maniac at the other end of the hall, not until after they rip off that mask and I know who's under there and why he chose this house out of all the bigger, nicer ones on the street. Not until Cam and I have both kids safe in our arms, a Lasky family sandwich. Then, and only then, will I allow myself to cry.

From behind me comes a tightly controlled voice. "You're going to pay for that."

JADE

5:46 p.m.

"What do you think, that I'm stupid?"

The voice comes from directly behind me, as low and threatening as when he stepped out of the shadows in the garage. I flinch, half expecting his gloved hands to wrap around my throat and squeeze, or the cold sting of the gun pressing into the back of my head—but there's nothing but hot breath in one of my ears.

"I don't think you're stupid."

I say the words, the desperate questions cycling through my mind. Did Tanya pick up on my clues? Will Baxter tell her about the masked man? Will she run home and call the police? Maybe...just maybe she thought to alert the neighbor on East Brookhaven. I can't remember his name, but Tanya will, and she'll know he's a former navy SEAL turned real-estate investor who would know how to defuse the situation until the police can get here. My gaze sweeps the windows to the patio and backyard beyond, searching for a muscular body creeping through the trees, but there's nothing out there but squirrels.

"Nice try, getting rid of Baxter, but I could have sworn I told you to get rid of *her*. Did I not just tell you to get rid of *her*?" He puffs a disappointed sigh, his breath stirring up my hair, tickling my neck with the strands.

In my head I'm doing the math. Sixty seconds for Tanya and Baxter to walk down the hill and across the road. That's a whole minute for him to tell her, for her to piece the clues together. The brother that doesn't exist. My obvious desperation for her to stay. My silent pleas, two of them, for help. Surely, *surely* she knows by now. Surely she's speed-walking across the road, hurrying home to her phone.

I just pray the police know to come without sirens.

"It was the easiest thing in the world," he says. "*Sorry, Tanya, I'm really busy. I'm going to have to ask you to leave.* That's all you had to say."

Now, finally, I dare to turn around. "I never ask her to leave, and you heard what a talker she is. That's probably the shortest she's ever been in my house. She would have gotten suspicious."

He licks his lips. "Maybe, but what about the Sancerre?" He leans into his Southern accent as he says it: *San*-cerrrr. "What about giving her your son? If he tells her about me, if she picks up the phone and calls the police, you know what's going to happen, right?" He points the gun at my head, closes one eye in aim and mouths a single word: *Pow.* "And Beatrix is here somewhere. She'll get one, too."

I take in the distance, two feet at most, the gun clutched in a fist, and something occurs to me. A memory from four, maybe five years ago, when my girlfriends and I took a self-defense class. An hour-long, hands-on workshop on the best way to survive an attacker. The beefy instructor told us to defy our instincts and move in rather than dodge. To strike instead of flee. The best defense isn't a defense at all, he said, but a full-throttle attack. You might get hurt, but it's your best chance to walk away alive.

And now, with Baxter safe with my neighbor and my hands free, it's the best time.

I rehearse the moves in my mind. A quarter turn so he won't see me slide the screwdriver out of my sleeve, or the flash of steel when I grip it in a fist. I'll have to make sure it stays hidden while I stay within striking distance, and then I wait. The second he looks away or twists his body just so, I will come at him from behind.

"So here's what we're going to do. You are going to walk over to the front door, slowly and calmly, and flip the locks. I will be listening for the dead bolt to slide into place, so I will know if you try anything. And if you do, I want you to know it's not you I'm going to punish. It's the little girl hiding somewhere in this house. Do you understand?"

I nod.

"But first we need to set the alarm. And here's the deal. Before the nosy neighbor lady, I might have trusted you enough to leave you here for a few seconds while I did it, but that's over and done. You just showed me I can't trust you, which means you're just going to have to come with."

He grabs a handful of my shirt and tugs hard, and I lurch forward into the hallway, almost slipping on the glass. By the time I'm upright, he's behind me, the gun aimed at my torso, and we march single file to the alarm pad in the bedroom, where I tick in the code.

"Just 2-9-2-1," he says from over my shoulder. "No funny business."

When I'm done, he tips his head in the direction of the wall and beyond to the front door. "Now go."

On my way, I pause to peek into the rooms on either side of the foyer, searching for signs of Beatrix.

Nothing in the dining room, but there's also no place to hide other than inside the antique buffet, which is jammed full of dishes we hardly ever use—the gold-rimmed wedding china that can't go in the dishwasher and the hideous Christmas service Cam's mother gave us as a wedding present. No way she could squeeze in there, not without making a racket.

I look to my left, in the study.

Many more places for her to choose from here—behind the doors of the built-in cabinets under the bookshelves, for example, or tucked inside one of the covered ottomans. I do a quick scan of the room, but the only sign either of the kids have been here is the mess spread across Cam's desk, colored markers and tape and a messy stack of blank papers one of them pulled from the printer.

There's movement at the bottom of the hill. A teenager being tugged down the road by a black Great Dane, who stops to sniff around the mailbox.

I glance behind me. The man is tucked out of sight, hidden behind the wall to the stairs. From his angle, he won't be able to see how slow I'm moving, the way I'm shaking the screwdriver out of my sleeve while waving my free arm at the girl and her dog. I'm clearly in distress. Maybe this girl will see a panicked, frenzied woman freaking out inside her own front door and think to call for help.

Look up look up look up.

She doesn't look up. The dog lifts its massive leg and squirts its scent all over my gardenia bush, but the girl is too absorbed by whatever is on her phone. She keeps her head down, scrolling with a thumb.

"Jade." The voice is low and impatient, and it carries an unmistakable warning. "What's taking so long?"

Down at the road, the beast gives a mighty tug, and the teenager lurches forward, her phone popping out of her hand. She catches it in midflight and doesn't miss a beat. Walking and scrolling, walking and scrolling. *For Christ's sake, girl, look up.* Not once does she lift her head.

Shit. Shit shit shit.

My ears ring with building pressure and the realization comes to me like a whisper. It's up to me now. I clasp the screwdriver in a tight fist, testing the point on my palm. Good and sharp, but I'll have to come at him hard. His neck, his temple, that soft spot between his shoulder blades. I'll have to put all my weight and strength behind it. One chance, that's all I get.

"You're gambling with your life here, Jade. With your children's lives. If you want tonight to have a happy ending, I suggest you stop playing around and lock the damn door."

With one last hopeful gaze up the empty street, I steel myself to what happens next. No more waiting on the cops or some heroic neighbor. No more waiting for Cam to save us. Now is my chance. I'm not about to miss.

I fill my lungs with air and courage, then flip the dead bolt.

JADE

5:50 p.m.

I turn away from the door and I don't break stride. I take the long way across the foyer tiles, making an arc around the entryway table so I can pick up some speed, gain some momentum. This man is bigger and stronger than me, but if I come on hard and fast, maybe I can take him by surprise.

I'm going to have to surprise him.

At the edge of the foyer, I pivot, turning my torso so the thin slice of steel I wriggled out of my right sleeve is concealed. I feel the weight of the screwdriver in my fist, the hard solidness of the butt my thumb is wrapped around.

One shot. That's all I get. One risky, raging shot. Better make it count.

"Who's Ruby?" He leans against the short slice of wall at the bottom of the stairs, waiting for me. The gun dangles in a hand, his other wrapped around my iPhone. He holds it up, wags it in the air by his face. "Who is she, and why does she hate you so much?"

I probably shouldn't be as insulted as I am. I blink, force myself to shake it off. "Ruby doesn't hate me."

He flips the phone around, giving me a flash of what he's looking at—the long string of message bubbles from my bossy older sister. Ruby likes to dominate every conversation. "Who is she?"

"Ruby is my sister. And she doesn't hate me."

"Well, she doesn't like you very much, that's for sure." He drops his head and reads from the screen, raising his voice a good octave. "'I know you're so so busy going to book clubs and managing your house staff and all, but stop being such a dick. Last time I checked, I was the single mom with the full-time job, not you, so stop with this princess bullshit and do your part for Dad's party.'" He looks up with a half grin. "She sounds nice."

Nobody has ever accused Ruby of being nice, least of all me, but now it's like all those times when we were kids, when my friends would laugh at her Goodwill fashion finds or her latest Miss Clairol disaster—currently spiky maroon. I have an inexplicable urge to defend my older sister.

As if she knows we're talking about her, another message dings my phone.

He glances at the screen. "She says you better have ordered the damn decorations. What should I tell her, Jade? Did you order the damn decorations?"

The decorations were the source of our latest vicious battle, after I told her to burn the black and gold monstrosities she bought from the dollar store. When the cashier refused to give her a refund, she sent me a Venmo request for twenty-seven dollars. I sent her fifty dollars and three fire emojis, just to piss her off.

My decorations, a dozen classy chalkboard signs and glass bottle garlands I plan to fill with fresh flowers and string with miles of twinkle lights around every tree in Dad's backyard, are downstairs in the basement we just walked through, in one of those big boxes gathering dust.

"Tell her that *she* was supposed to order the decorations. Not me."

One brow disappears behind the mask. "I don't know. I don't think she's going to like that."

He's not wrong. When Ruby gets that message, she's going to lose her mind. But hopefully, once she stops screaming at the phone, once she calms down long enough to *think*, she'll realize something's not right.

"Let me ask you this, what if it was Baxter and Beatrix acting this way? Cussing at each other over text message, egging each other on just for spite? You only get one family, you know. All it takes is for one of you to switch things up and say you're sorry, to change your behavior. My mama used to always tell me, you can't change your sister, but you can change the way you respond to her."

His sudden wisdom takes me by surprise, and though I don't necessarily disagree, this is no time for a lecture. Not when it's coming from an armed man in a ski mask, and definitely not when I'm clutching a screwdriver behind my back, silently debating the most vulnerable spot to sink it in.

His neck.

If I'm lucky the metal tip will slice right through his jugular.

I edge closer. "Maybe, but that doesn't change the fact that we agreed she would do the decorations, and that I would handle the catering."

He shakes his head. "You're awfully stubborn. Has anybody ever told you that?"

I hold my breath. Wait.

The moment turns sharp, measured.

The instant his attention drops to the phone, one word whispers through my brain.

Now.

I body-slam him from the side, sending him stumbling toward the stairs. The phone flies out of his hand and goes spinning down the hall, bouncing off the floorboards like a pinball. His other hand, the one holding the gun, flails for balance.

Look where you're aiming, Cam is always coaching the Bees. *Never close your eyes to the ball.* My ball is that spot at the base of his neck, a velvety patch just above his collar where the skin is marshmallow soft. I glue my gaze there, order my hand to strike there.

I bring my arm down hard, shrieking with fear, feral and black and sticky. At the last second he twists away, using the railing for leverage, hoisting himself up and spinning *away.* The shank misses his neck and slides down his shoulder into his back, slipping right through the fabric and skin and slamming against something hard. Bunched muscle? His shoulder bone? Whatever it is, it's like hitting a rock wall, a sudden stop that jangles all the way up my shoulder.

"You *bitch*," he howls.

He kicks me off him, the screwdriver snagging in his shirt. There's a loud ripping noise, then air. My fingers come away empty, the plastic handle wrenched from my grip. My weapon clatters to the floor by his feet, and he shoves it away with a shoe. It skids down the hall and into the bedroom—too far for me to lunge for it, especially considering the weapon in his other hand.

The gun, aimed at my chest.

"Shiiiiit." I think it. I scream it. Maybe both.

Retaliation comes like a cannon shot, a sudden backhand

to the face. I didn't see it coming, didn't notice the smooth arc of his arm coming at me until it's too late. The heel of his wrist clocks me in the ear, but it's the gun that hits me the hardest. It slams my cheek with a wet crunch, whipping my head backward, blasting stars across my vision, hurling my body into the wall.

I slide down it, and then...nothing. The room swims in and out of focus. There's a strange ringing in my right ear, but no pain. Only a heavy pressure on my cheek, a dull, empty moment where my brain acknowledges the blow, but it doesn't hurt. Not yet.

And then the pain arrives, a shattering explosion on the whole right side of my head. Like a sledgehammer to the cheek, like my face was dipped in lava. Dull and sharp at the same time, fire and ice and a million beestings. It's a sickening agony that short-circuits my brain and lifts me up and out of my body, crowding out every thought except Beatrix, hiding somewhere in this house.

Please, God, don't let this bring her running.

I suck a breath and hold it, listening for a scream, a flurry of footsteps coming my way, but there's nothing. Only silence.

Just in case, I heave myself up off the floor, stumbling to a strategic spot in the middle of the room, gasping in pain while puffing myself up, straightening my back and spreading my legs wide, an easy human target to take a bullet meant for my daughter.

Not happening.

Not today.

"You're going to regret that."

I press a hand to my throbbing cheek and glare, my eyes welling with hot, angry tears.

The only thing I regret, asshole, is that I missed.

CAM

5:51 p.m.

Maxim Petrakis's office is housed on the back end of a strip club, one of the seven he owns in the city, and smack in the middle of a seedy thoroughfare known for its massage parlors and streetwalkers. The parking lot is packed with the pre-dinner crowd, shift workers and folks sneaking in a pit stop on their way home from the office.

Last stop on the desperation highway—for them and for me.

I find a spot at the edge and slide out of the truck into air heavy with noise—the steady bass beating through the club walls, the traffic like crashing ocean waves on the overpass ahead.

I jog across the pavement for a door most patrons wouldn't even notice. Plain, unmarked, unremarkable. A smooth slice of solid steel set flush into the brick, and painted the same bright white. No handle, nothing at all to grab on to—which is probably a good thing, since whoever tries to bust through uninvited is likely to get shot.

A male voice booms from a tiny speaker built into the wall. "Sir, the entrance is on the opposite side of the building."

I tilt my face to the camera hanging from the roofline just above the door. "Cameron Lasky. Mr. Petrakis is expecting—"

There's a buzzing, followed by a sharp click. I lean on the door with a shoulder, and it swings open to reveal a wall of bouncers. Two giant men, both Black, both heavily armed. One of them tells me to spread it, then pats me down with hands the size of my feet.

"I guess it's a good thing I left my gun in the truck, huh?"

Neither bouncer cracks a smile.

They separate, opening the view down a clean, modern hallway. Glass-lined rooms, polished concrete floors, LED lighting. The music is louder here, but not deafening because these rooms are soundproofed, fireproofed, bulletproofed, every other proofed you can think of. Every dollar that gets shoved across the bar or tucked into a stripper's G-string gets counted and double counted here, millions and millions of them per year. Unlike in the restaurant business, Maxim's safes are bursting with cash.

"Third door on the left," one of the bouncers says.

I thank him despite knowing the way—and even if I didn't, the cloud of smoke pouring out of the open door would be a big, fat clue. Maxim Petrakis doesn't give a shit about the state's Smokefree Air Act. He's spent his entire career skirting laws and ignoring regulations, and there's not a politician or policeman in Georgia who can make him stop now. If you don't like your boss puffing on a cigarette all day long, then don't work here. It's as simple as that.

He's wrapping up a call on speakerphone, the only piece of

technology on his glass-topped desk. I give him a bit of space and wait in the doorway.

"That's not what we agreed to, Tony. It's not even close."

As usual, Maxim is impeccably dressed. Custom suit, three-piece and pin-striped. Double-knotted silk tie. Pocket scarf, arranged just so. His hair is still thick and white, combed straight back off his forehead. Say what you will of Maxim's businesses, but he's got the mobster look down pat.

On the other end of the line, Tony launches into what promises to be a longwinded rebuttal, which Maxim cuts off ten seconds in.

"Tomorrow. You have until the end of the day." He punches a button and gives the phone a noisy shove. "Well, well, well. If it ain't the Steak King, as I live and breathe."

Barely. Maxim's lungs sound like a rock tumbler filled with gravel, a noisy in and out that makes my own chest seize in sympathy. Maxim smokes like a chimney. He doesn't exercise or sleep. He eats fried potatoes and red meat drowning in butter sauce, which he washes down with booze. But he's trim and energetic and when he's zipping around town in his convertible Maserati, he looks like a million bucks. Maxim is like one of those deep-water sharks—he'll live to be four hundred.

I lift a hand in greeting. "Maxim. You're looking good. Have you been working out again?"

He laughs, a harsh, phlegmy sound. "Flattery will get you nowhere, kid. Now sit down and tell me some good news. You look like shit, by the way."

I glance behind me for one of the matching white leather chairs stationed across from his desk, and that's when I see him—a guy I didn't notice before, leaning against the far glass wall like a silent sentry. I take in his oily hair, his black leather jacket, and he lifts a pocked chin in greeting.

I turn back, sinking onto the chair. I don't love the idea of an audience, especially considering what I came here to do—beg Maxim for another loan, a whopper, and before I've paid back what I owe him on the last one—but I also don't have a choice. The clock is ticking, each second pounding with urgency in my chest.

"I feel like shit, too, honestly." My leg is going to town under the glass table, and I swing my ankle over the knee and bear down, forcing the thing to stop bouncing. I tell myself to calm down, slow down. Business with Maxim always requires a bit of finessing. "It's been a day."

"I hear Nick pulled through."

Nick—an employee of Maxim's I've met only once, in a dark and abandoned parking lot in Castleberry Hill, who wore an oversize puffy coat and a Braves cap pulled so low, there's no way in hell I could ever pick him out of a lineup. That night I passed him ten thousand in cash, and then I did what Maxim ordered and tried to forget Nick ever existed.

It was a lot easier than I thought it would be.

Now it takes every bit of my will to hold on to my poker face. "I thought you and I were never to speak of that name again."

"This is my house, Cam. Regular rules don't apply here." Maxim flicks his gold lighter at the end of a fresh Marlboro and gives a mighty suck, blowing the smoke from lips like sun-aged leather. "Did everything go as planned?"

The question ignites in my gut, but I manage to nod without pause. "The fire started in the outlet." I don't have to mention which one, or that it was next to the cooking grease. I'm positive Nick reported back to the boss. "Faulty wiring, apparently."

"And the alarm?"

"Malfunctioned."

Maxim lifts a brow. "See? I told you Nick was good. So that's done, then. You can move on."

Move on. If I weren't so totally miserable I would laugh.

Pain seeps across my chest, and as much as I want to ram it with a fist, I can't. Maxim would see, and he'd know there's something I'm not telling him—that Nick's job wasn't all that clean, that despite my performance with Flavio and George the inspectors are already throwing around the word *arson*, which means the insurance payout I'm counting on to dig myself out of this hole isn't looking like the sure thing Nick promised when I forked over that ten thousand.

And then there's Maxim. No way he'll give me another loan, not without the promise of that insurance money, and definitely not on top of the $100,000 I already owe him, plus a three point vig. That's 3 percent interest, tacked on at the end of every week, and onto an amount that is cumulative—meaning it adds up fast. By the time the loan comes due, at the end of the month, it will have more than doubled. Naked ladies and criminal connections are not Maxim's only source of income, or even his primary. Maxim is a loan shark, a highly successful one.

"The insurance adjustor assures me I'll have a check in my hand by Monday morning at the latest. When that happens, your palm will be the first I slap."

I try not to think about what Maxim will do when he finds out I'm lying, but it's impossible. He will send one of those goons guarding the hallway to find me, along with a weapon heavy enough to knock out a kneecap, or a saw that will cut through muscle and bone. A chef missing a finger or two can still cook, but all things considered, I'd really prefer to keep all ten.

Maxim squints into the smoke. "So what's this, then? A social visit?"

The irony punches me in the gut. "Not even close. I'm here because I don't know where else to go. Because I have nowhere else to turn. You're my last hope, Maxim, and I know how weird that sounds but—"

"Spit it out, kid."

"There's a guy at the house with Jade and the kids. He put a gun to her head and he forced his way inside, and then he tied her to a chair and he…" I shake my head, unable to think about what else he's done. "My *family*, Maxim."

I put the accent on *family* because I know Maxim's. I've met his wife, I've cooked for his kids, I know all his grandkids' names and the order in which they were born. Those family values he's always touting? I am praying they translate to mine.

He leans back in his chair, studying me as he takes a deep, long drag that takes all day. Less than an hour until the bullets start flying, and Maxim here is taking his sweet time. The tobacco crackles as it burns its way up the tube.

"That explains why you're so jumpy, at least. How much does he want?"

"Just over seven hundred thousand. I've managed to piece together some cash, but it's not much. I'm still way short."

I sound calm, but on the inside I'm at full-on panic. Maxim is my last resort. If he says no, I'm out of options. I'll lose Jade, the Bees, and it'll be all my fault.

"How much are you short?"

"I need $685,296."

Maxim whistles between his teeth—a sound I don't take as a good sign. It's the most I've ever asked from him, way more than I would normally dare, but the thought of life without Jade, without the sound of little feet tearing up the hardwood floor upstairs as they get ready for school… I can't even process what that would be like, or why up to now I've been okay with missing out on so much of their lives. They're sound asleep by the time I drag my ass home from work, long gone by the time I roll out of bed. I grumble whenever the noise from their morning routine wakes me, but I never get out of bed to give Jade a hand, or kiss everybody before they take off. Why not? What the hell is wrong with me?

He flicks a quarter inch of ash into a silver ashtray. "Let's say I float you this cash. Seven hundred thousand to save your family. How would you pay me back? Your restaurant business isn't exactly booming these days."

"I'll put up all my shops. Every last one of them, including the real estate. I own every building but Bolling Way, and I already told you the insurance money for that comes Monday at the latest. That's only a few days from now. When that happens, every penny I owe you from both loans plus interest will be in your hand by the end of the day. And in the meantime, you can hold the pink slips for all my shops as insurance."

He waves a crepey hand through the air. "What do I want with a couple of overpriced restaurants halfway to Tennessee? I don't go outside the perimeter, you know that. And I told you when you bought that Inman Park property, it's on the wrong side of DeKalb Avenue, which means you can call it Inman Park all you want but really it's Reynoldstown. Bolling Way is the only one of your properties I'd be even remotely interested in, and you don't own it."

"My house, then. A neighbor up the street just sold for two million, with a smaller lot and no pool. Mine's got to be worth more."

"Correct me if I'm wrong here, but didn't you come to me last month for that hundred grand because the bank refused to give you a third mortgage?"

I don't push back, because it's true. There's more debt than equity in our home, way more. If Maxim found out how much, he'd sic his goons on me for even suggesting it.

"You know me, Maxim. I pay my debts on time. And you've seen how hard I work. I work my ass off."

"How hard you work is not the issue, Cam. The issue is the shaky economy on the other side of these walls, and that Bolling Way is the only decent property you got but you don't own it, and that nowhere but in Buckhead are people falling over themselves to pay a hundred bucks for a Lasky dinner when they can toss a decent steak on the grill at home. Tell me, how many times a night do you turn the tables in your other shops?"

I don't answer, because Maxim is not wrong. The only shop pulling in any sort of decent revenue is—*was* Bolling Way. It's what was keeping the others afloat.

"Please, Maxim. I am a desperate, desperate man. I'll pay whatever you want. I will run your kitchens and cook your steaks until the end of time. Just please. I am begging you."

He stubs the cigarette out, then pulls a fresh one from the pack. "I'm a businessman, Cam. You're a businessman. Let me ask you, if you were sitting where I'm sitting right now, would you do it? Would you give yourself the loan?"

No. Hell *no. I'm not stupid. Only desperate.*

I flash a glance at my watch, and my heart wants to crawl out of my chest, *Alien*-style. It's 6:10, and home is still more than a thirty-minute battle through Buckhead traffic.

I swipe a sleeve over my clammy forehead. "What do you want, Maxim? Tell me what you want as collateral, and I'll give it to you. I'll do any…"

My words trail as I get a look at the back of a head, the greasy-haired man leaning around me to swipe the dirty ash-tray from the desk. It's the first time I've seen him from behind, seen that what I first thought was a slicked-back style is really something much more elaborate—a thin patch of scraggly hair combed over a mostly bald crown, then gathered into a wispy bun at the nape of his neck.

A man bun.

He turns to dump the ashtray into a can, and I get a closer look at his face. Deep marks, purple and red scars run across his cheeks and chin and forehead.

"It's *you*. *You're* the asshole who's been following Jade around town. She told me about you."

He grunts, and his expression doesn't change. He just dumps the ashes into the trash can, bonks it against the side a couple of times and sets it back onto Maxim's desk. No reaction. Not even a twitch.

Rage travels through my body like electricity, from my lips and tongue down my spine to the soles of my feet, then surges up and lurches me out of my chair.

"Sit down, Cam," Maxim says, gesturing for me to drop back into my chair. "Nick doesn't work for you anymore, he works for me. He keeps tabs on my investments. That's what I pay him for."

The words are like gasoline on the fire in my veins. Nick, the shady arsonist from the parking lot is also the creepy guy following Jade around town. My skin goes hot then icy, my right hand bunching into a tight fist. I am one second away from losing it when another realization hits.

"Oh my God. It's *you*." I turn, stare across the desk at Maxim. "*You're* the one holding Jade and the kids at gunpoint."

Maxim glances at Nick, just a subtle flick of his eyes, and I know what he's doing. He's calling for backup, those two big bouncers guarding the door are probably already on their way. I'm making more than enough noise.

"You're upset," Maxim says, his tone calm and controlled, "and I would be, too, in your shoes, which is why I'm going to pretend you didn't say any of that." He squints, pointing at me with his lit cigarette. "But from here on out you'd do well to watch your words, do you understand what I'm telling you? Most people don't survive insults like the ones you just hurled."

My shoulders slump. My lungs empty and the room goes slippery, tinged with smoke and the stink of my own sweat. That's it. I'm done. Uncle.

"Just kill me, Maxim. Put a bullet in my head and me out of my misery." Me for my family. It's a rotten trade, but Maxim will see it as a noble one, and at least then this whole nightmare will be over. "Just please. *Please* don't touch my family."

A scuffling noise comes from behind me, two large bodies moving into the room, and I brace for what's next—a tackle from behind, a blow to the skull or fist to the kidney—but Maxim stops them with a hand. "Sit down, kid."

My legs give out, and I collapse onto the chair.

"Here." Maxim pushes the cigarettes and lighter across the desk, and what the hell? I shake one from the pack and fire it up. "You and I have known each other a long time, Cam. We have history. And I shouldn't have to tell you this, but whoever's in your house right now is not one of my people. That's not the way I do business. This has nothing to do with me. You have my word."

For the first time since college, I suck a lungful of cigarette, and it's like riding a bike. My skin goes tingly, my brain blissed out on nicotine. "Then who?"

Maxim shrugs. "I don't know, but you could start by looking at who thinks you owe them seven hundred thousand and some change. The answer is in the number."

I nod. "Yeah, but there's more than one possibility, if you know what I mean."

"You've burned some bridges, huh?" He leans back in his chair, shaking his head. "What did I tell you about loose ends, kid? You've got to tie them up, otherwise they come back later to bite you."

Maxim doesn't mean this literally. He means bury the bodies under three feet of concrete, which is how he wraps up his loose ends. And though I may occasionally use Maxim's money to bridge the tight spots in my business, I don't operate the way he does. I'm a chef with money problems, not a mobster.

But I also run a crew of oddballs and misfits, most of whom could stand to brush up on their anger management skills. Sometimes I'm the one stepping in to defuse the situation, other times I'm on the receiving end of the punches.

But at the end of the day, a restaurant is a business. I'm the one out here taking the risks, doing the backroom deals with guys like Maxim in order to stay afloat. I'll choose my family over any one of those knuckleheads every time. There are going to be some burned bridges.

"As much as I'd love to deliberate which maniac is in my house right now, Maxim, I don't have time. I have exactly—" I glance at my watch and the room goes upside down "—forty-eight minutes to get my ass home with a bag of cash. If you don't loan me that money, I won't... I can't... I don't think I can save them."

He stares across the desk at me. Rock-hard. Giving me nothing. No pity, no sympathy and, most importantly, no olive branch. Not even a teeny tiny twig. Every last ounce of hope I was holding on to with both hands fades away like a cheap buzz.

I toss the cigarette in the ashtray and drop my head in my shaking hands, pressing down hard with my palms until my skull creaks. I wish I could go back and rewind this shitty, shitty day, and undo every one of my decisions. All of them.

No, I wish I could rewind all the way to 2008, to my first time sitting at this very desk, when Maxim told me I was foolish to open a restaurant in the middle of a recession, and

I did it anyway. I wish I'd been content with being somebody else's chef, to whipping up fancy steak dinners on somebody else's balance sheet so I could take paid vacations and the occasional long weekend and not stare at the ceiling until deep in the night, wondering how the hell I was going to make payroll. I wouldn't be Atlanta's Steak King, but come tomorrow I would still have a family.

But I was too cocky, too damn eager to prove I was a better businessman than my father. I had to own my own shop, and I opened my doors when restaurants all over the country were shutting theirs. Maybe that's my problem, that success the first time around ruined me. I'd already weathered what everybody was calling a once-in-a-lifetime recession. When I ran up against another wall, I just figured I'd scale it all over again. I figured I could overcome anything.

George was right. I really am a dick.

Even worse: I am my father.

I reach for Maxim's phone, dragging the machine around to my side of the desk, plucking the receiver from the tray.

Maxim frowns. "Who are you calling?"

"The police. If I tell them to sneak in without sirens, maybe they won't get anybody killed." I tap in the numbers and my sinuses burn, that achy feeling right before the waterworks. This is it. It's time. I don't have any options left.

The line rings once, then goes dead. Maxim's yellow-tinged finger is stomped on the button, holding it down.

"Cam." He shakes his head. "This is not a job for the police. Trust me on this."

"Then what? How?"

Maxim leans back in his chair, looking over my head at the others, the two big bouncers and the man-bunned Nick, then back to me. "I have a few ideas."

THE INTERVIEW

Juanita: I'm sorry. I know we've covered this already, but I'm still stuck on the fact that you didn't call the police. Especially once you realized you couldn't gather the ransom. You knew you were out of options, you just told me you didn't have the money to save them, and still you decided not to call the police.

Cam: Is there a question in there somewhere?

Juanita: Yes.

Cam: [silence]

Juanita: Don't you want to answer it?

Cam: No.

Juanita: No, you didn't call the police, or no, you don't want to answer? Which one?

Cam: Both. Next question.

Juanita: Fine. You testified that you managed to stitch together just over $49,000 from numerous accounts, that you placed the cash for the ransom in a box on the floorboard of your truck, and then…what? Where is that money now?

Cam: Maybe you haven't heard, but I recently filed for bankruptcy. My property was seized and is being sold off to pay back investors and debtors. Whatever cash I had on hand, whatever else I owned of value…it's all gone. My possessions were picked clean.

Juanita: Yes, but that $49,000, there's no record of it in any of your bankruptcy documents. I know I'm not the only one who's wondering, where did that money go? Who has it now?

Cam: [smiles] I don't know, Juanita. But if you find out, I'd sure like to know.

JADE

6:12 p.m.

The man shoves me into the kitchen, where he points me to the bar stools.

"Sit." He punctuates the order by thrusting the gun at my face.

I hoist myself onto a stool.

"Stay."

I don't move.

Good dog.

He moves around the counter into the kitchen, settling the gun onto the island. "Now, let's try this again. Where is Beatrix?"

With any luck, she's in one of those boxes downstairs, or in a dark corner of the attic, or shimmying down a drainpipe and bolting for the neighbors.

"I don't know."

The man rolls his eyes, grabbing a kitchen towel and yanking open the freezer. While he fills the towel with ice cubes, I take in the damage I did with Cam's screwdriver through the twelve-inch tear in his shirt. Underneath, almost as long, a seeping cut is slashed through the pasty skin between his collarbones, like a bloody ditch sliced through raw chicken. It leaks a red curtain down his back. Beneath it, all the way down to his waistline, the fabric is stuck to his skin.

My skin tingles with a triumphant shiver. I didn't kill him, but I made him bleed. I maimed him. That's going to leave a nasty scar.

"If you know where she's hiding, you might as well just tell me now. Because I'm going to find her."

"I already told you. I *don't know.*"

He ties the four ends of the towel around the ice, picks up his gun and carries both across the kitchen. He stares at me, and my heart gives an ominous thud. "Here." He stretches out an arm, the ice rattling in his hand. "This will slow down the swelling."

I take the makeshift compress and hold it to my cheek, hissing when it hits the skin.

"Is it broken, you think?"

I don't respond. I've never broken a cheekbone before so I have no idea, and even if I did, I don't know what the appropriate answer is here. Does he *want* it to be broken? Better to say nothing at all.

"Where *haven't* we looked?"

"Upstairs. It's the only place left."

And it's possible. Maybe she snuck back up while we were searching the basement. Maybe she was going for the upstairs windows because she knows they're the only ones in the house without sensors, so opening one wouldn't have tripped the alarm. If she climbed out the playroom window, she could have crawled out onto a patch of roof that's only gently pitched, the overhang right above the patio. From there, a drop to the terrace tiles below wouldn't have broken any bones. Probably.

Or no—Beatrix is smarter than that. Maybe she escaped when Tanya dropped by, and the alarm was unarmed. She could have slipped out the door in the master, or the back door by the garage. Either one would have dumped her in the backyard, with only a six-foot fence between her and freedom.

Without thinking, I lean over the back of my chair for a better look out the back window. The ice shifts against my cheek.

"What are you looking at?" He raises the gun, following my gaze out the window, pointing it at empty air. "I don't see anything. Is somebody out there?"

I turn back, press my lips together and stare at the counter. No telling what he'd do if he thinks Beatrix might have escaped this place. I just pray she made it outside without breaking a bone. I pray she got out and ran like hell.

A chirp, one I don't recognize, sounds from deep inside the man's pocket. He digs out a battered Android and swipes at the screen with a thumb.

Frowns.

I study his face for clues, but that damn mask is like a shroud. He stares at the floor, his mouth a straight line, and I have no idea what he's thinking. Worry? Anger? His expression gives nothing away.

Pride swells in my chest. My daughter has clearly caught this guy off guard. First escaping her bindings and now disappearing without a trace. Brave little Beatrix getting under this man's skin.

He taps at the screen and presses it to his ear. "Hey...Yeah, I know. We're looking for her now."

There's a long stretch of silence, and my mind whirs, searching for meaning. He's talking about Beatrix, he must be, which means the person on the other end of the phone knows about the home invasion.

How? And who? A conspirator of some kind?

I stare across the kitchen at his phone, straining to hear, to understand.

"No, she's got to be here somewhere. Give me a minute and I'll find her." A pause. "Yes, I know what time it is, but the longer I stand here, talking to you, the longer I'm not looking for her."

I sit positively still, my mind buzzing. What is happening here?

He sighs. "Just tell me how it's going there. What's the latest?"

I take in his cryptic words, imagining some stranger stalking Cam around town the way the man-bunned man did me, taking note of his bag of cash, watching it grow fatter and fatter after each visit to a restaurant safe or the bank, reporting back on his progress. I think of all the preparation a home invasion plot like this would take, all the scouting and scheming. This operation would have demanded weeks of planning, sketching out every possibility, thinking through every potential consequence. And even the best quarterbacks have a deep bench of players and coaches to support them. Whoever's on the other end of that phone call must be one of them.

"Lemme talk to her." The man glances up, frowning when our eyes meet.

My gaze flits away.

"Hey, pumpkin, how you doing?"

Five little words, yet filled with so much meaning. Caring. Concern. Whoever this pumpkin is, he or she is loved.

"I know. Try to get some sleep, okay? I'll be home soon, and I promise to come—" He pauses to listen. "I'm at work, why?" Another pause. "Because I stepped outside to call you. The kitchen was too loud."

The word *kitchen* rings like a gong through my head, and I look up. Our eyes meet again, and he holds a finger to his lips. *Shh.*

"Good. Now get your booty back to the couch, and put your auntie back on the phone, will you?"

The compress has started to drip icy rivers down my neck, and I pull it away from my face. The skin underneath is on fire, part smashed cheekbone, part freezer burn.

"Make sure she takes a nap," he says, his voice going hard again, "but before that do another check of her levels. If they've dipped even the slightest bit then call our cousin, get her to come over. She'll know what to do. In the meantime, watch her like a hawk, and keep me posted. I don't like the sound of this."

Another long pause as I wonder who this cousin is, what problem she's coming over to solve. Surely it can't be worse than the problem currently brewing in this house.

He frowns at the floor, and a shivery finger of dread runs down my spine. Whoever's on the other end of that phone call, their message is not good. I rewind the conversation in my mind, stitching together the parts of it I've heard. Levels of something undefined. A cousin who better come over in a hurry. It's like putting together a puzzle with only half the pieces…unless the other half is Cam. What if this cousin is the one tagging Cam?

Still, it doesn't make sense. Why would she need to come over—and come over where? Here?

The questions flip through my mind in time with the throbbing in my cheek. I sit like a statue, watching and listening for clues.

The man reaches up as if to run a hand through the hair at

his temple, then remembers the mask. His arm falls back to his side. "No. Absolutely not. That will shoot us right back to the bottom, maybe even erase us entirely. Best thing to do is just sit tight and wait this out. And keep an eye on the numbers."

First levels, now numbers—but of what? A bank account? I can't put the pieces together in a way that makes any sort of sense.

I think of Baxter across the street, and I wonder what's taking so long. It's been what—a half hour since I watched him walk down the driveway? Plenty of time for him to ring the warning bell. So what's the holdup, then? Did Tanya not believe him? Or maybe she did and they're coming in silent.

I wince in frustration, and my cheek throbs in response. It aches like there's a knife stuck through it. Every movement is agony.

"Yes, I'm sure. The alarm is armed, and we checked all the doors. Every window but the upstairs ones have sensors. She could have gotten out there maybe, but she'd break her neck trying."

If I didn't know before, I'm certain now. Whoever is on the other end of that phone call knows why this man is here. They know about the ransom plot. They are a coconspirator. I make a mental note, add it to my growing list of clues, along with the one I just saw—that almost-swipe through his hair just now? It means he has some.

"Jade."

I look up, but I take my time.

"Does Beatrix know how to work the panic button?"

It's a possibility I haven't thought of, mostly because I've never once explained to her the workings of the alarm. For Beatrix, the alarm has always been an annoyance, one last delay before getting in or out the door. Even if she knew where the panic buttons were, she probably wouldn't have known to hold it in for three full seconds.

I shake my head. "I don't think so."

"You don't think so. What does that mean? Yes or no?"

"It means no."

"You're sure." Not phrased as a question.

And even though I'm not sure—Beatrix is a smart kid, and she hears a lot more than Cam and I give her credit for—I nod. "Yes, I'm sure."

He speaks into the phone. "I've jammed it, but monitor the scanners just in case. The second somebody's headed this way, I need to know about it."

He's jammed our alarm—is that even possible?

He leans a hip against the counter and fingers his gun, watching me across the kitchen island.

"Keep me posted, will you? I want an update every fifteen minutes or so. I agree it's worrisome, but she's done this before, remember? Just hang in there a little longer. We can't pull the plug on this thing, not even as a last resort. This *is* our last resort, remember?"

I stare at the counter, processing everything I just heard. So far he hasn't said the first word about money—unless that was what he meant with the numbers he mentioned. Maybe post payment, he will take the cash and return to his lists and levels and whatever else this one-sided conversation has been about and disappear from our lives forever. I imagine Beatrix crawling out of her hiding place and rushing into my arms, the two of us racing across the street for Baxter. The police wrapping us in silver foil blankets and peppering me with questions while I hug my children and cry joyful, relieved tears. Maybe this day *can* have a happy ending.

"I know, which is why I've got to find this kid and get everybody back upstairs, pronto. Text me in fifteen, okay? And hang in there. In another hour this will all be over."

At his words, the hairs on the back of my neck prickle with awareness. It's that feeling you get right before the phone rings with bad news, that out-of-the-blue premonition two seconds before your tires hit the patch of black ice. I look up and his gaze meets mine, and that's when I know. Every last bit of hope I allowed myself to feel drains away like muddy rainwater.

What he means is, this will all be over for *us*.

JADE

6:17 p.m.

He slides his cell into the cargo pocket of his pants, his voice jolting me back into the moment. "All right, Jade. No more fooling around. Where's the kid?"

Curled into a ball in some cabinet, wedged between the boxes downstairs, pressed flat between a piece of furniture and a wall. Or maybe sitting on a chair at a neighbor's house, a cup of something hot and sweet in her hands and a blanket draped over her shoulders, recounting her harrowing tale to the police so a sniper can train their gun through a window and shoot this masked-man in his face. Yes, let's pray it's the last one.

He drops his head back and howls at the ceiling: "Beatriiiiiiiix." All hard consonants and dragged-out vowels, fueled by fury. If Cam or I called for Beatrix that way, she'd pee her pants.

I stare with wide eyes at the man, the way his fingers are

creeping across the marble toward the gun. Tension buzzes in the air like static, and I hold my breath, but I don't dare look away.

I listen for movement, the patter of footsteps or the creak of a door, but there's nothing. No sounds, other than cool air blowing through the vents.

"Where is she?"

I drop the towel filled with ice in the sink. Screw this guy. Screw his apology ice pack.

"I don't know."

"Jade. I am not joking here. We're running out of time." He slides the gun from the counter, one smooth move from the marble to his glove to my face. There's a good ten feet between the bullet and my skull and the space is dwindling.

Time for what?

I stare down the muzzle of the gun, and my chest swells and stills.

He aims at a spot directly between my eyes. "Let's try this again. Where. Is. Beatrix?"

I hold up both hands—a sign of defeat, a useless shield— and squeeze my eyes tight. "I don't know. I swear I don't. Please don't shoot."

Something cool presses against my forehead, the hard metal pressing into my skin.

"Beatrix!" His shout is a loud roar.

I flinch hard enough to fall off my chair. The movement and the terror are messing with my equilibrium, and the world turns upside down. I open my eyes, just a slit, enough to catch my balance. The gun is still there, pressed against my forehead, but the man has his head turned, screaming over his shoulder into the living room and beyond.

"You get your sneaky little butt out here right now, missy, otherwise I'm putting a bullet in your mother's skull. You have ten seconds to decide, not a second more, so you better get here fast."

He pauses to listen, but there's nothing but dead air and the sound of light panting—mine.

"Ten…nine…eight."

I think of Baxter across the street, how I didn't get a chance to say goodbye. I think of Beatrix having to live with the knowledge she got her mother killed. I think of Cam, and the older version of him I'll never get to see.

Please, God, *please* let Beatrix be miles and miles away by now.

The pressure on my forehead releases, leaving behind a dull, empty throbbing. I open my eyes and he's walking away, that angry gash already drying up on his back. He stops at the doorway to the living room and shouts into the house.

"Seven…six…five… Four more and then Mommy's dead."

Deep breaths. In. Out. Deep breaths.

"Four…three…"

Tears tap my lap, evaporating into the dry-fit fabric on my leggings. I stare at the man's back, a tall shadow in the doorway to the living room, and sweat drips down my spine. I consider calling out to Beatrix—*Don't take the bait. Stay hidden. I love you*—but the words jam in my throat. I swallow a lump, thick and soggy like a wet towel.

"Two…say goodbye to your mom forever…"

I squeeze my eyes, and my thoughts wander, disconnected and drifting along all the unfinished items on my to-do list. The kids' school projects, in a box downstairs. Thousands of their pictures, forever lost on my phone. The career I'll never get to pick back up, all the design jobs I'll never get to do. That stupid argument with my sister, the dumb decorations gathering dust downstairs. I remember our last screaming match, unchangeable history, every ugly word.

"Last chance, kiddo."

Oh God, Cam. I'm sorry.

I couldn't save them.

The man hauls a breath for the final count, then—

"WAIT."

It comes from somewhere deep in the house, a high and panicked shout muffled by wood and stone and drywall. A floorboard creaks above my head.

"Wait. Don't shoot. I'm *coming.*"

I want to scream and wail and weep—with relief, with dread. Beatrix didn't crawl out an upstairs window. She didn't run to a neighbor's house. There's no sniper outside the windows. Nobody's coming to save us but Cam.

The man glances over his shoulder at me, his teeth flashing. "Lucky you. Looks like you get to live a little while longer."

Forty minutes, according to the microwave clock. Forty minutes for Cam to get here with the money.

And then what? What happens then?

The stairs creak with a body's weight, Beatrix emerging from wherever she's been, giving herself up to save me. The weight of her sacrifice steals my breath, and I make a silent vow that it won't be in vain. My daughter will live to see tomorrow even if I don't.

All I need to do is keep her alive for another forty minutes.

SEBASTIAN

6:20 p.m.

I see that ridiculous hair first, tight ringlets peeking out from the wall by the stairs, and the gun goes hot in my hand. My finger snakes around the trigger, and I'm squeezing down before I can stop myself. The hammer cocks back, a heartbeat away from firing.

"Get your butt down here." My words are a snarl through clenched teeth, and hell yeah, it's meant to scare the bejesus out of her. If this girl screwed everything up, I swear I'm going to strangle her.

"Leave her alone," Jade says from her spot at the bar. Her ass is still parked on the stool, but the rest of her looks ready to spring. Both hands are planted on the marble, and she leans into it hard, like she's about to pole-vault over it. Like she wants to jump into the line of fire.

I aim the Beretta at her head. "Don't move. The second

your feet touch the floor, I won't think twice. I will take you down, and I'm a good shot so don't even try."

Her cheek is a mess, swollen and stained purple. Fractured, I'm guessing, and a twinge of regret hits me between the ribs before the pain in my back wipes it clean. I've never hit a woman before, and swear to God, I didn't want to hit Jade. I definitely didn't mean to hit her that hard, but you try facing a screwdriver coming for your jugular and see how you respond. I did what I had to do.

And what I have to do now is deal with Beatrix.

She slinks across the living room floor in her bare feet—and the kid was smart to lose her sneakers. Easier to control how your feet land when you're not wearing any, and even smarter to have made sure they were hidden so as not to drop us any clues. Maybe that's the problem here, that this kid is too damn smart.

"Want to tell me how you got out of the duct tape?"

Beatrix shakes her head, and the movement squeezes off a tear—and judging by her red eyes and wet cheeks it's not the first. "Not really."

"I was doing you a favor up there, so you know. I put on the TV. I made sure you were comfortable. I even offered you a snack that you flat out refused. I mean, I don't know what else I could have done to make this experience any easier for you and your brother. Do you?"

Her glaze flits away and her fingers go to town, tapping out a silent rhythm on her thigh.

"What the hell is that?" I gesture at her dancing hand with my chin. "Do you have a tic or something?"

Her fingers freeze, and she crosses her arms, pressing both palms in her armpits. "It's notes."

"Notes to what?"

"Bach's B minor partita. You wouldn't understand. It's classical."

Partita—the same term Jade used downstairs. But it's Beatrix's other words I'm focused on. The ones that insinuated I'm stupid.

"Just because I don't listen to classical music doesn't mean I don't know what a partita is. Of course I know what a partita is. You look like the flute type."

She makes a face like I just offered her a bowl of shit soup. "The partita for flute is in A minor, not B. I play the violin."

That expression, her snide tone. It's a reaction I've seen a million times, as familiar as a favorite old coat. It's exactly how Gigi would have responded at that age.

The nostalgia lasts only a second or two before dissolving into something sharp and hot. I breathe through it, a series of quick and shallow breaths.

"Stop looking at me like that."

"Like what?"

"Like I don't have a gun aimed at your head. Like you have a death wish."

The little shit actually rolls her eyes, and this kid. This spunky little kid. From the second we walked in the house, she's been a thorn in my side. Staring me down. Daring me to punish her.

"I'm serious, kid. Look away, or this gun is the last thing you'll see."

"Beatrix, for God's sake, *stop*," Jade says, and to her credit, she hasn't moved. But she's put some space between her chair and the bar and positioned herself at the edge of the seat.

But it does the trick. Beatrix swings her gaze to her mom. "What."

Not a question, and even though she clearly doesn't expect an answer, I give her one. "Don't be a hero." I flick the gun back and forth between the two. "Don't either of you do anything you'll regret."

I'm talking to both of them, but my words are especially for Jade, whose expression is wild. Wide eyes glistening with a combination of fury and horror. Second cheek flushing purple to match the first. Her life or Beatrix's? I can tell she's already made the choice.

By now Beatrix is close enough for me to grab her by the shirt. One good tug and I've dragged her into the kitchen.

"That was a really stupid trick you pulled. Really reckless. You almost got your mother killed. You know that, right? She almost got a bullet in her brain because of *you*. Now say you're sorry."

I wait for some kind of reaction, a flicker of regret or a mumbled apology, but the kid gives me nothing. She doesn't even blink.

A fire sparks in my chest, and I clamp on to her shoulders and give her a mighty shake. A bone-rattling, skin-quaking, teeth-jangling shake. I'm still fisting the gun, and the weapon presses hard into her shoulder, against bone, and it's got to hurt. She flops around like a bobblehead, but I can't pick up the slightest trace of regret in her eyes. No pain, either, not even a twitch.

Only hatred.

Yeah, kid. Sure as shit is the feeling mutual.

"STOP," Jade screams, springing off her chair, and she's fast, I'll give her that. She's lunged around the bar and into the kitchen before I can let go of her kid, planting herself directly behind me. "Stop! Take your hands off her!"

I let the kid go because one more shake and Jade would have jumped on my back, and beyond the fact that it's still on fire from the screwdriver, I need to defuse the situation. I need to get everybody back upstairs and into the theater. Today is too important. I don't have time for this.

I shove Beatrix in her mama's direction, and now, finally, she makes a sound, a long, high squeal of relief. Jade sweeps Beatrix into her arms, murmuring words I can't quite hear, squeezing her against her chest and patting down her hair. I give them five seconds. This little reunion would almost be touching if we weren't running so short on time.

"Okay. So here's how it's gonna go. The three of us are going to march our asses back upstairs, where *you*—" I flick the gun at the girl's head "—get yours strapped to a chair. And don't expect any softballs from me this time. No cartoons. No reclining the seats until they're the perfect angle. And no lightening up on the tape because it smelled weird or it yanked on your skin. Do you understand what I'm telling you here? There'll be no getting loose this time. Now let's *go*."

I round them up with the Beretta, and order them to walk up the stairs.

Jade clutches her daughter by her shoulders, and she keeps her head high as she leads her across the living room. I don't miss the look of longing she casts as she passes the front door, searching for someone—maybe Baxter—out on the street, praying for a happy accident or kismet, a person down there, a savior, who will look up at just the right moment. I keep the gun trained on her back and watch her for a reaction. But either there's nobody out there or she's a damn fine actress.

And I already know that she's not.

"Stop," I say when she reaches the stairs, then peer around the corner. I catch the tail end of a car whizzing by, but otherwise the street is empty. I jog across the living room floor.

Upstairs in the playroom, I flip off the TV, dumping the remote in a bowl on the table. "Back on the chair, missy."

Four attached recliners in a curved row, covered in a buttery brown leather I mangled when I ripped the tape off Baxter. Beatrix's getup is still intact, long lengths of tape a little looser in the middle, where she somehow managed to wriggle out.

This time, they're going tighter. This time, I'll make sure she's good and anchored down.

Beatrix doesn't move.

"Didn't you hear me? I said, back on a chair."

She sinks into the one behind her, one of the middle ones.

"Not that one." I gesture with the Beretta to the opposite end of the couch. "I want you down there on the other end. As far away as possible from the door."

She looks to her mother for confirmation, for help.

"But why?" Jade's gaze flits between me and her daughter. "This is the one she usually sits in. What does it matter?"

"It matters because I said so. Now *move*."

Still Beatrix doesn't budge. And Jade just stands there clutching her daughter's hand, watching me with bloodshot eyes above a shattered cheekbone. "Why are you doing this?"

"You know why. You're the one who gave Cam his marching orders, remember? Though I will say, it's taking him longer than I expected. If he doesn't get that money over here in, oh—" I glance at my wrist, where an ancient Timex ticks away the seconds under two layers of black fabric "—exactly thirty-seven minutes, none of you are going to like what happens next."

She blanches, brown hair floating around her face, and even with that cheek, she really is beautiful. And that stunt with the screwdriver downstairs, the way she's constantly throwing herself in front of her kids. She's a real daredevil, this one. I can see why Cam chose her.

I imagine him racing around town in that stupid truck of his, those ridiculous rims spinning on jacked-up, oversize tires. I hope he's losing his mind with worry and desperation. I hope each second that ticks by pierces him like a bullet in the gut, that he's realizing, this very second, the hopelessness of his mission. I wish I could be there for when the realization hits him—he can't save the people he loves most in this world—when the guilt and desperation and helplessness sit on his chest with the weight of an elephant. I sure would enjoy seeing that.

"What I mean is, why *us*? Out of all the houses on the street, why ours? And why do you need such a specific amount? Why by seven? I don't understand."

Finally. Three hours into this train wreck, and Jade is finally asking all the right questions. I wonder what took her so long. Did she just now work up the gumption? Did she finally piece together that nothing about today is random? I'm guessing a lot came from the clues she overheard in the kitchen, but still. I was expecting these questions hours ago.

"What do you think?"

"I don't know. That's why I'm asking."

"But you must have some kind of theory, or maybe a couple, and I want to know what they are. Why do you think I chose this happy little home? What do you think is happening here?"

"I think you're a parent." She looks as surprised as I am that she said those words out loud, then her expression doubles down. "Or maybe not a parent, but I think there's someone who relies on you to care for them, someone you love very much."

"Because of the phone call?"

Jade nods.

I think back through the conversation downstairs, but I was careful to be vague. I didn't say a word that could lead back to Gigi. I'm positive I didn't mention her by name.

"I didn't say anything about a kid."

"No, but you called somebody pumpkin, and you seemed…"

"What?"

She shrugs. "Worried."

I shake my head. "Stop trying to change the subject. This has nothing to do with me, and everything to do with Cam."

With him having to live out the rest of his miserable days with what he's done. With knowing that whatever happens today, however this ends, it's all his fault. With knowing he was helpless to prevent tragedy.

"What, did he fire you once upon a time? Did he run you out of business? Is this about revenge?"

"This isn't about revenge," I say, though that's not totally true. It's in part about revenge, but mostly it's about getting what I deserve. The money Cam cheated me out of two years ago plus interest, the resulting hole in my income that meant I lost my home and my savings and health care, all the medical treatments that I couldn't pay as a result. For the way Gigi got weaker, scrawnier, sicker. Just thinking about it burns like the skin on my back, where Jade split me open like a hog. "This is about *justice*. About me getting what I deserve. What I am *owed*."

"Owed to you by Cam."

By Cam, by God, by the universe. Take your pick. Nothing about these past two years has felt fair. I'm not leaving here today without taking back what's rightfully mine.

And taking down Cam's family is a nice bonus.

Jade reads my silence as an affirmative. "If you tell me what Cam did, I can help put things right. Cam's not a bad guy. He listens to me."

Her words are like kerosene on the fire roaring in my belly.

First, that her husband is not a bad guy, which means she's either ignorant or willfully blind. Cam is selfish and greedy and will mow down anybody in his way. He *is* a bad guy. He's a guy who looks out only for himself.

And second, that she still hasn't figured out who I am. The same person she shook hands with all those years ago. The same one who only a few months ago, stood here in this very same room and told her my whole, sad story. My money worries, my pain, the constant nightmares a parent gets at watching their child slip away. Jade plopped into one of these leather recliners, wrapped a hand around one of mine, and squeezed out some crocodile tears and a false promise. She's no better than Cam.

So yeah. Too little, far too late for these kinds of platitudes. Like she could turn this train around. Like fixing things could ever be as easy as calling Cam.

"The only way you can help is by making sure that money gets here on time—and he doesn't have much left. What do you think's taking him so long?"

"Traffic. Distance between the safes. Banking rules. A million things."

"Or maybe he's having trouble scrounging up the cash."

"Cam owns five successful restaurants. He runs tens of thousands of dollars over his bank accounts every night, and that's on top of the pile that's already sitting there, money he uses to keep those places running. He decides where every cent of that money goes. If he wanted to get his hands on that cash, he could. There's more than enough. The only problem is going to be time."

Interesting. I stare at Jade for a couple of beats, waiting for her to break character, but her conviction doesn't fade. Maybe she really doesn't know.

I toss her a roll of duct tape I dig from my backpack on a far chair. "Enough stalling. Tie her up, and make sure you do a good job. I'll be checking your work."

She catches the tape, then stands frozen. "What makes you think Cam would have trouble gathering the money? Why would you think that?"

I slide my cell from my pocket and scroll through the texts. Still no word.

"If you know something," Jade says, "you should tell me. I promise you, I can help. I *want* to help."

I roll my eyes. "Do you now?"

I drop the cell back into my pocket and sink onto the last chair, the one with the ruined leather armrests. Jade's voice, her expression—they're a swirling mess of doubt and desperation. My questions have gotten to her, planted a seed of suspicion that if she'd been paying any sort of attention, would have come up ages ago. Clearly this is a woman who only sees what she wants to see.

And now I've given her just enough to get the wheels turning. She might have believed Cam was telling her everything about his business before this day started, but she doesn't anymore. If nothing else, I've accomplished that much, nicked a chink in her belief in her husband.

She stands there, holding the roll of tape like a forgotten cup of coffee, and watches me, frowning. I wait for her to mention the marks in the leather under my fingers, how the tape peeled the top layer of the recliner away like a cheese grater. But then again, furniture is the least of her worries.

"Maybe we should get Cam on the phone again," she says instead. "If you call him on my cell, I guarantee you he'll answer. We could ask him how much longer before he gets here."

"Good idea, but attach the girl to the chair first."

I urge her into motion with the Beretta and, reluctantly, she tugs Beatrix down the line of recliners. She guides her into one at the far end, kneeling on the carpet by her feet.

"You've been such a brave girl," she murmurs, snagging her fingers in her hair. "But let's just do as he says this time, okay? Your father will be home soon, and then this will all be over."

The kid leans forward and whispers something into Jade's

ear. Jade frowns, then whispers something back. I watch the side of her mouth, the way her lips carve out one lone word.

Who. Or maybe *hoot.* Or it could also be *shoot.* Shoot a gun?

"Hey." Both heads whip in my direction, both expressions guilty as hell. I flit the Beretta between them. "What are y'all whispering about?"

"Beatrix says she's hungry. It's past her dinnertime."

"And what did *you* say?"

"I told her to wait."

Wait. It's possible that's what she said. From the side, *who* would look like *wait.* Especially with that swollen cheek.

I lean back on the buttery leather, gesturing to the roll in her hand. "Less talking. More taping. And hurry. It's almost go time."

J A D E

6:25 p.m.

"Sit down."

I collapse onto the coffee table across from Beatrix, an emotional tug-of-war in my chest, vacillating between gratitude and confusion. I wasn't expecting to stay here in the media room. I figured he'd march me across the hall and reattach me to the blue chair, but he didn't. He's letting me stick close to my daughter, at least for now, and I'm not about to argue.

He digs my iPhone from a cargo pocket, sinking back into the leather of the last recliner, the one Baxter was on. He unlocks the screen then pauses, his finger floating above the glass.

"Okay, here's how it's going to go. When Cam answers, you're to ask where he is, how much of the money he's got on his person and how long before he gets here. These are the only things you get to say to him, do you understand me? If he asks about the kids or anything else, direct him back to answers for those three questions. Got it?"

I nod, then shake my head. "Is Beatrix allowed to talk to him?"

He smiles. "Oh yeah. She can talk to him. In fact, missy, maybe you can tell him about how you almost got your mama killed. Special treats for anyone who can squeeze out some tears. Ready?"

Without waiting for our answer, he taps Call, then puts the phone on speaker. I stare at the phone, my heartbeat knocking against my ribs. Cam picks up on the first ring.

"Hello, Jade?"

Click. The man hangs up.

I stare at him, my mouth hanging open.

The man gives me a demented grin. "Just messing with you. Let's do it again."

He goes through the steps again, tapping the buttons on the screen. This time, the phone doesn't even ring before Cam's voice bursts through the speakers.

"Jade, are you there?"

His tone, desperate and plaintive, hits me like a sucker punch, an immediate and forceful blow that forces all the air from my lungs. Last night when he crawled into bed, I fussed at him for waking me up. Cam wanted to spoon, I wanted to sleep, and now I hate myself for it. Why couldn't I have rolled over and told him how much I'd missed him? Why couldn't I have *shown* him?

"I love you, Cam." The words come out before I can stop them, and I know this wasn't part of the script and I'll probably get another broken bone or maybe worse for it, but I am beyond caring. I couldn't stop these words even if I wanted to. These are words that have to be said. "I have since that time you came over in the middle of the night and planted all those purple tulips under my window. We'd been dating for what—three weeks?"

Twenty-three days. And on the morning of the twenty-fourth, when I pulled up the shades and saw hundreds of my favorite flowers swaying in the breeze, my heart flipped over in my chest. I didn't tell him for another month, but I fell in love with Cam, right then and there.

"Babe. Don't… Jesus, please don't talk like that. Where are you? Are you okay? Are the kids?"

"You had me at tulips, Cam. I was a goner. I *still* am. I want you to know that what you and I have, it's for real. The best thing I ever did was walk in your restaurant that day." My face scrunches with tears, and a sharp and searing pain explodes in my cheek—a physical reminder of what's coming after we wrap up this call. The man's expression says it will be so much worse.

"Jade, I… I love you, too, but you're scaring me. Tell me what's happening there."

I sniff, my gaze wandering to my daughter. A solemn-faced Beatrix, who's trying her damnedest not to cry. "We're in the playroom. Beatrix is duct-taped to the chair."

"And Bax?"

"He's with Tanya. She dropped by earlier and took him for pizza." I think about telling him to call over there to check in, but I don't. Every mention of Baxter is a reminder to the masked man that our son is safe across the street, and I'd rather keep his focus right here, in this room. Instead, I say, "Are you almost here?"

"I'm driving as fast as I can. Beatrix, baby, you there? I want to hear your voice, too."

Beatrix heaves a petulant sigh. "I'm fine. He hurt Mommy, though." She glares at the phone as she says it, and I know what she's thinking. She's pissed at being played like a puppet.

"What did he do to Mommy?"

"He hit her on the cheek." Beatrix glares from her recliner

at the masked man, who gives an enthusiastic thumbs-up. "It's swollen and really, really purple."

A long patch of motor and air. I picture Cam in his truck, white-knuckling the steering wheel, the three loud thumps that sound through the phone, Cam's fist hitting something solid.

"Tell him I'm on my way. Say I'll be there as soon as I can, okay? For sure by seven."

Beatrix rolls her eyes. "You don't have to tell him, because he's sitting right here."

"Sir, whoever you are, I want you to know that I meant what I said just now. I'm fighting traffic, but I'll be there by seven. And I have the money."

The man needles me with a finger to the shoulder, and I ask, "All of it?"

"Yes. All of it. I have $734,296 in a bag, headed your way."

I almost faint with relief. Cam's announcement feels like a shimmering oasis in a desert. I hear his words, I process them, but I don't dare believe. Cam has the money. He'll be here by the deadline.

The man nudges me again, and I search for meaning behind the mask. His earlier words echo through my mind like fragments of a nightmare I really wish I could forget. *Ask where he is, how much of that money he's got on him and how long before he gets here. These are the only things you get to say.*

I frown.

He mouths a word that makes my blood turn cold. I know as soon as I say it, as soon as Cam gives me the answer, this conversation will be over. A masked finger is already hovering over the screen. I am not ready for this call to end.

"Hey, Cam?"

"I'm here, babe. I love you and I'm here."

My heartbeat kicks up in my chest again, battering my ribs

like a trapped animal. "When you get to the house, come up to the playroom. The alarm is on so make sure you come through the front doors, and turn it off before you come to the playroom. We'll be upstairs, waiting for you in the playroom."

Playroom. Playroom. *Playroom.* If I say it often enough, if I lean into the word hard enough, maybe something will click in Cam's head. A memory of the cameras, all three of them, recording everything we say and do here. Beatrix's escape. The yards and yards of duct tape. This very conversation. I need Cam to know what he's up against, give him the only advantage we have left.

"Alarm. Playroom. Got it," he says, but does he? Nervous energy crackles in my bones because I don't think he does.

Come on, babe, remember. *Pull up the app on your phone and look.*

I get another finger in my shoulder, another prod urging me to say the word he mouths for a second time. If it's so important, why doesn't he just ask it himself?

And then something else occurs to me: this is twice now he's gone silent while Cam is on the line. Why? Is he worried Cam will recognize his voice?

"Hey, Cam?"

"Still here."

"I'm supposed to remind you, no police, okay? I need to know you didn't call them."

I don't miss the gun of an engine, the way his voice dips with both warning and promise, how his answer isn't really an answer at all: "Hang tight, Jade. Be there as soon as I can."

"I can't believe it. He's got the money." The man's voice is incredulous. He hoists himself off the recliner, grinning down from behind the mask. "That worthless piece of shit husband of yours has actually got the money. He actually did the impossible."

I press my lips together and say nothing. *Not so worthless now, is he?*

Outside the playroom windows, darkness is falling fast thanks to the thick cloud cover. Automatically, my gaze wanders to the clock on a far shelf, a fussy mantel model that looks out of place with the rest of the mid-century decor, its hands permanently stuck on ten past five. A tiny eye embedded in the base of the hour hand watches our every move.

I don't dare glance at the other two cameras, a wall speaker with a sweeping view of the couch, and the dummy fire alarm above my head. Between the three of them, every inch of this room is covered by top-of-the-line, high-definition cameras with motion sensors and enhanced night vision, every movement and sound recorded and stored on the cloud for thirty days.

Whatever happens in this room, there will be proof. Indisputable, undeniable evidence. Three digital witnesses documenting every move.

He slides my phone back into his pocket and exchanges it for the Android, tapping a finger to the screen, pressing it to his ear. "You're not going to believe this but—" A pause, and his grin widens. "See? I told you this was going to work. You thought I was wrong but we actually pulled it off. *Dammit*, we're good."

The same person he was talking to downstairs, I'm guessing. The coconspirator from the kitchen, the one checking the levels. Distracting enough for me to check in with my daughter.

I shift to the recliners, perching at the edge of the seat next to Beatrix. "You okay?"

She shakes her head. "How much longer? I really don't like this."

On the other side of the coffee table, the man's phone call continues. "How are the numbers?"

"I know, baby." I wrap a hand around the back of her head, leaning in to press a kiss to her temple. "Thanks for being my bravest girl. You're the cleverest, most determined kid I know."

Beatrix frowns. "What about Baxter?" My daughter is not the only person she holds to high standards. She's always demanded perfection from everyone else, too, the responsible firstborn, the big sister taking up for her younger brother. She's a kid who takes her job very seriously.

"He's the sweetest and funniest. Of all the babies in the world, I got the two of you, and that makes me the luckiest, proudest mom ever."

I'm fighting tears I hide with a nuzzle to Beatrix's shoulder, looking up as the man says, "Shouldn't be long now. Any chatter on the scanner?"

Beatrix stares at him, too, grabbing on to the cuff of my sleeve, gripping the fabric in a tight fist. She waits until he turns away to lean close and whisper, "She took my signs."

It's the same words she said to me earlier, when I was taping her hands to the chair. *She took my signs*, she said angrily, urgently, and I still don't understand what she means. When I asked her *who* took them, our whispering caught the man's attention. He demanded to know what we were talking about. When I lied—*wait*, I said, rather than *who*—he ordered us to be quiet.

Now, though, he's staring out the window down the roofline and into the backyard. Too giddy with success and whatever this person is saying to hear me whisper the question again to Beatrix, "Who did?"

She shifts her weight, her gaze flitting behind us into the hallway. "Mrs. Lloyd."

No. That doesn't make sense. Mrs. Lloyd is Tanya. The nosy neighbor from across the street.

I still don't understand. Tanya took Beatrix's signs?

I glance at the man standing like a statue with the phone pressed to his ear. The outline of his gun presses up from one of his pockets. "How's she doing?" Whomever *she* is, the answer is not good. It drops the smile right off his face. "That's awful low. Is she acting okay? What did our cousin say?"

I wrap my arm around Beatrix and lean in for a hug, whispering, "What signs?"

She presses her lips into my hair, her breath hot on my ear. "I made signs asking for help and taped them to the window on the front door, but they're gone. I think Mrs. Lloyd took them."

Her message straightens my spine, and I unwind my arm and settle into the seat. Beatrix made signs for the door—which explains the mess on Cam's desk. The markers, the paper she must have pulled from the printer, the tape she dug out of a drawer. I imagine her hasty scrawl, a quick and efficient SOS taped to the front windows.

Clever, *clever* girl.

And now she's suggesting Tanya took them. I try to come up with some other explanation, but I can't. Tanya is the only person other than us to be in the house this afternoon, and the timing is right. There's no other possibility.

I have so many questions. Tons of them.

But one word rises to the top like curdled cream: *Why?*

Why would she march over here with her key, peel the signs from the glass and not say anything about it to me? Why would she spout off some bullshit story about a silent auction and not give me some kind of signal—a wink, a nod or a cocked brow? Why not agree to take Baxter right away when I begged her to; even more, why not volunteer to bring him across the road to safety? Why didn't she see Beatrix's SOS and call 9-1-1 right away? Why has no one come to save us? Why, why, why?

And then I think of something else, and the visual of her walking to the door flashes behind my eyes. The way her ponytail swished and the sweater stretched across her hips, how it was hitched up on one side like there was something in her back pocket—which I now know there was.

Beatrix's signs.

The man turns away from the window, his gaze panning over my daughter and me, and my heart leaps up my throat. He caught us whispering again. My mind races, searching for another bullshit excuse when he looks away.

"Uh-huh," he says, still frowning into the phone.

I take in the squint of his eyes, the thinning of his lips. Whatever the person on the other end of the line is saying, it's not good news.

"All we have to do is keep her steady until tomorrow morning," he says, aiming his frown at me. He gives me his back, turning to the window. "Tomorrow morning we'll get everybody on board, and then we can finally move forward. Until then, all you've got to do is keep her stable."

Whoever's on the other end of that call cranks up the volume, yelling loud enough that he peels the phone from his ear. I can't make out the words, but the voice is female, and her anger, her indignation comes across loud and clear.

"Okay, okay…calm down, will you? You know I didn't mean it like that. I get that you're worried, but so am I. I'm just as worried as you are."

Worry—that *is* the emotion I spotted on his face, a worry I'm all too familiar with. The kind only another parent can have for his child.

That's when all the pieces fall together in a perfectly clear line: I was right before; this man is a father. This person he keeps referring to is his daughter. His *sick* daughter.

I think back to the half of the conversation I overheard in the kitchen downstairs, and it all makes sense. Levels, numbers, all of them worrisome. Cancer? Something deadly, certainly.

So the money is for what—an operation? A life-saving treatment? It's possible he doesn't have insurance, or maybe it's just that his insurance won't pay because it's a last-ditch effort, an expensive Hail Mary pass her doctors won't sign off on.

But still.

What kind of parent would value his sick daughter's life over the lives of my two healthy children? Who would hold a family hostage, threatening them with words and blows and a waved-around gun, in order to pry money out of their father? He thrust a loaded gun in our faces. He used it to pistol-whip me hard enough to crack a bone. Yes, I realize this man is desperate, but desperate enough to trade three, maybe four lives to save his ailing daughter's? What kind of monster would do that?

He turns away from the window, his gaze landing on mine. "I've got to go. Cam's on his way, and I need to get everyone ready."

CAM

6:30 p.m.

I'm doing seventy up a residential street when it comes to me in a flash: the playroom.

Twice now I've talked to Jade, and twice she tried to trip my memory. She worked it into every conversation, multiple times. *Playroom playroom playroom.* But I was too busy spiraling in my own panic, my brain too distracted to catch her meaning.

I slam the brakes and yank on the wheel, careening the truck over some poor sucker's freshly mowed lawn. The tires skid sideways across the soft ground, grass and gravel pinging against the side of the cab.

A hank of grease-slick hair escapes from Nick's man bun, and he yelps, grabbing on to the roof handle. His shoulder slams into the window. "What happened? Did you hit a dog or something?"

"No, but—" I scramble for my cell, charging in the cup

holder. "We have eyes in the room. I can't believe I didn't think of this earlier, but we can watch on the nanny cams. They're sitting in front of the cameras *right now*."

"So pull them up, then."

I give him a look—*duh*—then turn my attention to the phone.

The nanny cams are on the last page, helpfully labeled "iSpy." Jade installed the app the day the cameras were screwed into the wall, and I haven't looked at it since. Too creepy, and unnecessary since we can't afford a nanny. The only person who ever stays with the kids overnight is my mother, and no way in hell am I going to spy on my mom. Ever.

I tap the app, and it opens onto a log-in screen. Two blank boxes for username and password, neither of which I remember. At the bottom of the screen is a key, and I hit it to search my saved passwords, but it's not there. When Jade logged in that first time, for some reason my phone didn't save it.

"Shit."

Nick flips down the visor to check his hair in the mirror. He shoves the strands back in place, poking the ends under the elastic with a finger. "What's wrong?"

"I don't remember my log-in." I try my email and the password Jade uses for everything, BeaBax321#, but it doesn't work. I try the same password with her email, but I get the same result: a shivering screen, a rejection message. I'm locked out. "Dammit."

"Let's just go. We'll see what's going on when we get there." Nick pops the visor closed, then gestures to the two-lane road we were just flying down. A long line of traffic snakes in both directions, headlights blinking in a soft drizzle. The clock on the dash turns my body cold: 6:34.

I plug my email in the screen and tap Forgot Password, then toss my cell to Nick. "Watch my inbox, will you? I should be getting a new password any second." I steer the truck off the grass and poke the bumper back into traffic.

Nick here is a gift from Maxim, as are the two bouncers in the black SUV that had been following us until I hit the brakes, former military trained in all sorts of scary ops who rarely leave his side. Maxim loaned them to me with a toothy grin.

And then he shoved the biggest gift, the *best* one, into my hands. A moving box crammed to the top with crumpled bills. *You wouldn't believe the amount of counterfeit bills that pass through a strip club.* Twenties and hundreds, mostly, most of them passable as real. *Go get 'em, kid.*

Not the $734,296 this guy demanded, not even close. But along with my $49,000 hopefully enough bills to provide a distraction. It's now stuffed in the nylon Nike bag under Nick's feet.

He points me down a mostly empty side street. "Take a right."

"I know the way. You just watch for the email."

A minute passes, then another, while I weave my way through the streets as fast as I dare. On a normal day, at a normal hour, it's a twenty-minute trek from here to my driveway, but this is rush hour, and it's raining again—two surefire ways to make Atlanta traffic grind to a stop.

My phone pings with an incoming email, but with the acoustics of the truck and the tension in the air, it hits me like an explosion. "Is it—"

"Yep."

I snatch my phone from his fingers, prop it against the top of the steering wheel, and do my best to drive without crashing into the car in front of me. My hands are shaking so hard they're vibrating, and it takes me a couple of tries to hit the link, but then my phone shoots me to a web page where I type in the new password, then back to the app and I'm in.

The first camera is from the smoke alarm, a bird's-eye view of the room. Between glances at the road, I spot Beatrix's mess of white-blond hair, and the sight of her is a gut punch. Jade is seated on the recliner next to her, alert but calm, her spine straight on the chair. I think of Bax, gorging on pizza at Tanya's across the street—safe, thank God—and for once I don't want to punch her.

I search the edges of the screen, but all I see are shadows.

I swipe to the next camera and get a head-on visual from the speaker on the wall. A full view of the recliners, Beatrix and Jade, a male-sized body cloaked in black by the windows. Relief starts with a tingle at the top of my head, then courses through me in a warm and glorious rush because they're okay. They're still alive.

And Jade...

Even with that bruised and swollen cheek, Jade is glorious. Hair wild, eyes wilder, her back straight with righteous purpose. Her hands are solid fists on her lap, and her chest is heaving. This is warrior Jade, protective and mama lioness Jade, this is Jade at her most fierce and feral. I've only ever seen her like this once, after Baxter's kindergarten teacher teasingly suggested we find him a talent so he wouldn't always live in his big sister's shadow. I stare at the screen, and in all the eleven-plus years I've known her, never have I loved her more.

Her mouth is moving, flinging angry words. I keep the car on the road and fumble for the volume button.

"...because that is not okay. I get that your daughter's sick, but in what universe does that make any of this okay? You are trading the lives of three strangers for hers, and that's not right." Jade's seething voice shatters the silence in the cab.

"Shut up." The voice comes from somewhere off camera,

low and male and gruff. "You don't know what you're talking about. This is none of your business."

"It *is* my business. The second you came into my garage and held me and my children at gunpoint, you *made* it my business. And you've already admitted Cam somehow owes you this money. It doesn't get any more my business than that. This is my family. You're holding our lives ransom for your daughter's."

The same male voice answers, and it pings something deep in my brain. "You have no idea what I'm going through. None."

"Tell me, then. *Tell me* what I'm missing. Because whatever Cam took from you, it can't be worth a human life."

On the passenger's seat, Nick gives an impressed grunt. "Your wife's a little pistol."

A deep voice booms from the tiny speaker. "I said, shut *up*. Shut up before I shove a gun in your mouth and make you."

Jesus, Jade. Stand down for Christ's sake.

I swipe to the third camera and there he is. Black mask. Black shirt and pants. Black gloves.

Black gun, and he's aiming it at Jade.

"Beretta," Nick says with a derisive snort. "Figures."

I don't know what he means, but I also don't care. My wife is standing up to a masked man with a gun, staring him down. Like the pistol he's waving around has somehow lost its menace, like it's a plastic prop. He thrusts it at her, and Jade doesn't even flinch.

I, however, am losing my shit. The sight of the gun explodes in my chest. I settle the phone on a thigh and slam the gas pedal to the floor, lurching us forward as far as we can go. On the other side of the windshield, traffic reaches into the semidarkness.

"How 'bout I hold the phone while you drive?" Nick says, stretching a hand. "Might be safer that way."

The asshole's voice fills the cab. "All you gotta do is sit there and shut up. Why can't you just do that? Less than thirty minutes until Cam gets here, and then I'll be out of your hair. This will all be over. I'll leave and you'll never hear from me again."

"This won't be over, are you kidding me?" Jade says, and she's shouting. "My children are going to have nightmares for years. You get that, right? They are going to need therapy. *I'm* going to need therapy. You terrorized and threatened us for hours. You broke my cheek!"

"I'm going to kill him," I mutter, white-knuckling the wheel. Up ahead, where the road ends in a T intersection, the light flips to yellow. "When we get there, I'm going to freaking murder this guy."

Nick shifts nervously on the passenger's seat, jutting his chin to the light. "You're, uh, not gonna make that."

I floor the gas, watching the masked man step forward on the screen. "Have you seen my back? You're lucky this wasn't any worse."

A hundred feet, maybe less, and only one car in front of me. So far neither of us has hit the brakes. "Come on, come on."

Nick grabs on to the handle above his window. "Seriously, man. You're cutting it too close. The light's about to—"

"Shut *up*."

On my iPhone screen, the man is still talking, his voice loud in the car: "...didn't mean to hit you that hard, but may I remind you that you started it by coming at me with a screwdriver. I was just defending myself. You don't know me, Jade, but I don't put up with that kind of aggression. I fight back."

"Yeah, well, ditto," Jade says, and I feel equal parts fear and pride.

The light changes to red, and the driver in front of me hits his brakes. I jerk the wheel to the left and swerve around the slowing car into the oncoming lane, right as another car, a red Mini, turns right into my lane.

Our eyes meet. His are big and round, a terrified teenager going up against a jacked-up truck in a doomed game of chicken. He lays on the horn, then ducks out first. He yanks the wheel and barrels into a ditch.

The lane clears. Nick curses. I blow through the light and take a hard left, a ninety-degree turn that lifts two tires from the pavement.

"Holy shit," Nick mumbles as I work to straighten out the wheel. "You really do have a death wish, don't you?"

What I have is exactly twenty-four minutes to get home.

I fumble for my phone, but it's gone, flung from my lap into that dead space between the seat and the center console, the black hole where crumbs and crumpled receipts go to die. I keep my eyes on the road and dig my hand in, but I don't get very far. My hand is too big, the slot too tight.

Nick bats my hand away. "You drive. I'll dig out the phone."

Meanwhile, Jade and the guy are still talking.

"If Cam were here, he'd tell you this day was coming. I swore I would take back what he took from me, plus attorney fees and interest. I *told* him I'm not some wimpy asshole he can push around. That money is rightfully mine."

I freeze, my fists clenching the wheel because a memory is taking shape in my head. Last year, January, in the courthouse parking deck. I was headed to my truck when he stepped out from behind a stairwell, thirty minutes after the gavel had come down on my side. I won. He lost. A Fulton County Superior Court judge agreed I didn't owe him a penny.

Is that what this is about? The Oakhurst shop that fell through?

"Motherfucker." I bounce on the leather bucket seat, my

muscles jolting with pent-up energy. "That motherfucking fucker."

Nick drags the phone onto the middle console, and I grab it and hang a sharp right onto a side street, skidding to a stop. I squint at the image of this asshole's covered face, zooming in until it fills my screen.

Nick leans over the console, craning his neck. "What? Do you know this guy or something?"

"Oh yeah." I stare at the masked man and the fuzzy edges of his face, and suddenly all the puzzle pieces fall into place. Storming my house, holding my family hostage, clocking my wife in the face. "You better believe I know who this asshole is."

I also know what today is about—and it's not money.

This isn't about money at all.

THE INTERVIEW

Juanita: What is your relationship with Maxim Petrakis?

Cam: Who?

Juanita: Maxim Petrakis. He's the owner of a number of strip clubs in town, a man who moonlights as a loan shark and criminal matchmaker. The Greek mob version of Match.com, though you won't find that job description on his website, by the way. That's just the word on the street. According to the police, his only transgression is speeding.

Cam: Never heard of him.

Juanita: There's a picture of the two of you looking pretty chummy on the celebrity wall at Club at Chops. Slicked-back silver hair, impeccable dresser, big smoker.

Cam: Now that you mention it, I think I may have cooked for him a couple of times.

Juanita: But you've never borrowed money from him.

Cam: I'm pretty sure loan-sharking is illegal, Juanita.

Juanita: So that's a no?

Cam: [smiles]

Juanita: Two people said they saw you jogging across the parking lot of his Cheshire Bridge club on August 6. One claims it was late afternoon, the other says it was more like dinnertime. That puts you there an hour, maybe more before you were supposed to deliver three-quarters of a million dollars to your Buckhead home.

Cam: We've already established I was desperate.

Juanita: Desperate enough to borrow three quarters of a million from a known loan shark?

Cam: Sure. I would have robbed a bank if I'd thought about it while they were still open.

Juanita: So you *were* there.

Cam: I was a lot of places. The whole afternoon is a blur.

Juanita: [sighing] Did you or did you not go to Maxim Petrakis's strip club on the afternoon of August 6 and ask him for a loan?

Cam: I can promise you this, I don't owe Maxim Petrakis a penny.

JADE

6:36 p.m.

The Android chirps from somewhere deep in the man's pocket, and my frustration feels limitless. An interruption, and right when we were getting somewhere. I bear down on the ground below my feet and concentrate on the two words he just used: *attorney fees.* I latch on to them like a pit bull.

"So you and Cam were litigating something—what?"

My voice wobbles with a hammer throbbing in my cheek, with fear of the force of his backhand. I glance at Beatrix, watching silently from her recliner next to mine, her hands sticking out from the duct-tape bonds in tight, hard fists.

The man watches me from the other side of the coffee table.

"You'd think I would have learned. After everything that I'd heard from his former chefs and partners, I should have known Cam would pull some kind of dirty tricks. I should have known he'd find the biggest shark in town and sic him on my lawyer. He crushed us, found somebody who could win on might rather than merit." The stupid phone chirps again, and he reaches down to unbutton the flap on his cargo pants, his eyes flashing. "And it wasn't just me he took down. He took down my whole family."

My mind flips through what I can remember of Cam's legal issues. The problem is there have been so many. Beyond the basic hazards in serving the public—falls, broken glass, burns and cuts and food poisoning—there are a million things that can go wrong. Labor laws, noncompetes, immigration issues, liquor licensing, noise and traffic. Most of them frivolous enough he doesn't bother to share, or if he does, it's only to vent and complain. I hear him out, but I rarely remember the specifics.

"Did you go to trial?" I ask, because those are the only disputes I know something about, and miraculously, there have been only two. The first was ages ago, a leasing dispute when Cam opened his second shop, which became the impetus for his strategy of owning the real estate for his restaurants whenever possible.

The other was almost two years ago. A location on the outskirts of Atlanta that fell through at the last minute, a disgruntled almost-partner Cam dismissed as sour grapes. He sued, Cam won. The end.

Or so we thought.

"Hell yes, we went to trial. There is something seriously wrong with the legal system in this country when the only way to win is by having the deepest pockets. My attorney went up against a whole team of Cam's hotshots, who buried her in paperwork and nonsense. They froze my bank accounts, put a lien on my house and intimidated my family with an armed private investigator who followed us all over town. They played every dirty trick in the book, and it worked. I'd lost before I even stepped foot in the courtroom."

The phone rings again, and he pulls it from his pocket, but he doesn't look. Not yet.

I keep his attention on me. "So that's why us. That's why this house."

This—all of this—it's about Cam. About resentment and animosity. The kids and me, we're just pawns.

The phone rings for a fourth time but my questions have him too riled up. He doesn't so much as glance down at the screen.

"Do you know what happens when your bank account is frozen? You can't pay your bills, that's what. You learn real quick how to space them out, to borrow money from the mortgage in order to pay the electric bill, until your bank tries to take back the house, so you swipe the phone money to pay the mortgage. My point is, that shit catches up with you eventually. They come after you then. Your house, your cars, your assets. They take everything, and they don't stop until the only thing you've got left to your name is the clothes on your back and a credit score that'll get you laughed out of every bank. They even took my daughter's medical vest. They took her oxygen tank!"

"That doesn't seem right."

"Oh, you think?" He makes a sound, a kind of angry bark. "It's evil is what it is. She needs those things to breathe. When I threatened to go to the police, they replaced it with an old piece of shit machine that weighs a ton, not caring that carrying anything over a pound gets her winded. You tell me how that's fair."

"It's not. You're right to be angry."

The man seems surprised by my answer. He frowns, matching my gaze with his glare, while the phone rings one last time before flipping to voice mail.

"Damn straight I'm right. And don't even get me started

on insurance. It doesn't get much more preexisting than cystic fibrosis, which means when we were forced to switch, none of the good ones would touch us, and the ones we could afford don't cover half the therapies she needs to survive. Those companies make it so complicated you give up. Throw your hands up in despair. Do you know what the out-of-pocket costs are, even with decent insurance? Do you?"

"No, but I'm guessing it's a lot," I say, but this is where my mind is traveling: down the stairs and out the front door and down the hill and across the road, to the painted brick home across the street. Tanya Lloyd's house. To those stories she's always sharing of her poor, beloved niece, the one with cystic fibrosis. The one Tanya is organizing a fundraiser for, the one she just asked me to donate my time and talent to, the one who desperately needs the money to pay for the lung transplant that is this girl's last hope.

"The FDA came out with this groundbreaking CF drug last year—a game changer, they're calling it. Do you know what it costs? More than $300,000 a year. If you're lucky, you've got insurance to cover most of that and a big, fat pot of savings to fill the gap, but what about the rest of us? We're just supposed to sit around and watch our kids dig their own graves?"

What are the odds? Of all the little girls suffering from CF in this city, what are the odds Tanya's niece could be the same girl as this man's daughter? A million to one, probably.

A coincidence? Maybe.

Except I no longer believe in coincidences. Not anymore. As of today there are no more coincidences.

Especially not since I now know Tanya took Beatrix's signs. No wonder the police haven't come. Tanya tore down my brilliant daughter's SOS signs before anyone could see, right before she walked out the door with Baxter.

The room spins. My lungs lock up. My skin goes hot and my blood icy cold.

Tanya has Baxter.

"And while I'm at it, here's another disgusting fact for you. Canadians with CF live ten whole years longer than Americans. Why is that, do you reckon?"

He seems to expect an answer, so I press my hand to my churning stomach and give him one. "I'm betting it has something to do with insurance."

"Damn straight it does. Americans love to criticize Canada's state-run health-care system, but the only thing ours is serving are the bottom lines for the drug and insurance companies. A bunch of crooks and thieves. They don't give the first shit about the number of bodies they have to trample over in order to get to their private planes."

I try to talk myself out of it, scanning my memory for any other connections we might have shared. Stories of her sisters' husbands—Dave who works in HR, Robby the banker. Her ex, Thomas, whom I've never met, a litigator who traded her in for a much younger, much blonder woman named Tiffani, who Tanya is certain was once a stripper. Her niece's father, who is not a brother but a cousin—a *cousin*—who lives... where? Who does what? I have no idea.

Funny how in her endless babble Tanya refers to everyone she's ever met by name, childhood friends and college pals, the neighbors and their kids, even the neighbors' dogs and the cashiers up at Kroger. And yet she's never once called her cousin by his. Come to think of it, I don't know her niece's name, either. Tanya's only ever referred to her as "my sweet, sick niece."

My heart stops. My mind screams.

No. Dear God, no.

The man clutches the phone in a fist, stepping closer. "I've spent every last penny I have to make sure my little girl stays alive. Medicines and copays and therapies, all of which my crappy insurance refuses to cover. I'm here to tell you that American insurance companies are the devil. Their existence has nothing to do with health. It's about getting rich, pure and simple."

"You told her you were in a kitchen. When we were downstairs, I mean, the first time you talked to her. You made it sound like you were at work."

"Well, I lied. I haven't worked a job in months. When could I when I'm the only parent she's got? I spend every minute of the day and night taking care of her."

The man studies me. Frowns. "What's wrong?"

Is this a trick question? I open my mouth to answer, but the only sound is a clicking of my tongue against the roof of my mouth.

"Why are you all sweaty?" His eyes go squinty, taking me in. "You can stop pretending you give a shit. Your sympathy act doesn't have me fooled, you know."

Project calm. Pretend you don't know. It's the only way to make it out alive.

I force myself to breathe. "It's not an act. I'm a parent, too. My children have spent more time than I'd like to think about today being threatened with a gun or a knife, and now my oldest is taped to a chair. I know what it's like to feel helpless."

"I'm helpless because of Cam. Cam did this, not me. This is all his fault."

I press my lips together and say nothing. This man's money problems are shitty, yes. The consequences for his sick daughter are definitely tragic. Cam may have had a hand in knocking over that first domino, but I still don't see how any of this is his fault.

I glance at my watch: twenty more minutes. I think of Baxter across the road; my son is in the hands of the enemy. He's in the enemy's house. Getting to him is everything, the sun and the stars and the moon. Twenty minutes is an eternity.

I sit up straight and try to breathe and think.

Keep him talking. Survive for twenty more minutes. It's the only way.

"Where is your daughter now?" I say.

"Don't worry, she's not alone. Someone's looking out for her."

The coconspirator auntie on the other end of the phone.

I recall his worry about the levels and numbers, that vest and oxygen tank he mentioned just now. Tanya told me all about the vest, an inflatable machine that vibrates and loosens the mucus so the patient can cough it up. It's like physical therapy for the chest. Her niece wears it twice a day.

"How is she?"

His face fills with worry. "She needs a lung transplant. Real soon."

"I—" *I know,* I was about to say, two little words that would tip him off. *I know who you are. I know your third coconspirator.*

She has my baby boy.

"You what?" he says.

"I'm sorry."

His phone chirps again, the screen glowing against his masked fingers. Now, finally, he checks the screen. Smiles. Turns it around so I can see.

My heart alights, beating so suddenly that it's almost painful.

Cam.

The man swipes a thumb across the screen and presses it to his ear. "Cam. To what do I owe the pleasure?"

At her father's name, Beatrix jerks on her seat, her expression so hopeful it cracks open my heart. My children, both of them, love their mama. I know they do. Whenever they scrape a knee or have a nightmare, when they need a kiss or a cuddle, they come crying to me. But Cam always gets the best of them—the moments when they want to laugh or play or just sit quietly and talk. When they curl up beside him on the couch on the weekend even though they don't give a flying fig about football. There's no one they worship more than their father.

And now Beatrix wants nothing more than to believe that her father is about to storm the doors and save her. Save *us*.

Honestly, kid: ditto.

"Hang on, hang on. Let me put this on speakerphone so everybody can hear." The man pulls the phone away and taps the screen, then holds it in a palm. "Okay, big man. How about you say that again."

"You asshole! Listen to me, hear these words I'm about to say to you. You can hit me. You can break my bones and point a gun at my head. You can pull the trigger and blow out my brains, but you do NOT TOUCH MY WIFE." The last bit comes out in an enraged shout, a deafening roar that rattles the windows and my bones.

The silence that descends is sticky, pulling like tar.

The man gestures to the phone in his hand. "Go ahead, Jade. This one's all yours."

"I'm fine, Cam. Honestly."

"Babe, do not listen to this guy. He is lying to you, I swear. None of that stuff he told you was true. I didn't take anything from—"

"Uh-uh-uh," the man interrupts, his mouth millimeters from the microphone. "Yet again, you think everything is about you, but I'm here to tell you, Cam. This is about *me*. About all the myriad ways my life is screwed up because of you. And I hate to tell you, but now your daughter knows, too. She knows the kind of shitty man her father is."

"This has nothing to do with them, Sebastian. This is between you and me. Let my family go."

Sebastian. That's his name, the almost-partner, the lawsuit instigator. *Sebastian.*

He holds the phone inches away from his face. "See, that's where you're wrong. When you reneged on our deal, you took away my ability to protect my family, which means this? This right here, right now? It's also about yours."

"So, what—an eye for an eye? Is that what this is?"

"Maybe. Maybe it's karma."

"Oh come on. That's bullshit and you know it. You're not the only one who lost money on Oakhurst. I lost out in that deal, too, remember?"

"Let me tell you the difference, *Cam.*" Sebastian makes a face when he says the name, spits it through an ugly curled lip. "You lost what's for you pocket change while I lost *everything.* I lost my savings, my livelihood, my house, my wife, the shirt off my back and my daughter's. I had to declare bankruptcy, and you know what happens to your chronically sick kid when you do that? You get to swap out your health insurance with Medicaid. How do you tell your little girl that they won't approve the lung transplant that's supposed to save her life because you can't afford the medication she needs to make those new lungs stick? This money you're bringing me, it's what you took from me plus interest, plus all the medical costs, which thanks to you, my shitty insurance doesn't cover."

"That…that's absurd. What do you think the hospital is going to say when you hand them a bag of cash? You don't think they'll start asking questions?"

"They can ask as many questions as they want, but at least my baby will get her new lungs."

"Sebastian, they're going to catch you. You know that, right?"

"Shut up."

"I'm trying to *help* you."

"Oh, like you helped me before?" he scoffs, and his tone darkens with disgust, with fury. "Sorry, Cam, but that shit don't fly. Your promises hold no credibility with me anymore. Zero. Not after what you did last time I came to you with a problem. Tell everybody here what you said."

There's a long stretch of patchy air, and then: "I'm not... I don't remember what I said."

But it's a lie. Cam *does* remember, I can tell from the pause, the way his voice went wobbly. He knows *exactly* what Sebastian is talking about. He just doesn't want to say it with me and Beatrix listening.

"Look, I'll call the contractor and explain," Cam says, dropping back into businessman mode. Problem solver, go-getter, get-'er-done achiever. "I'll tell him this whole thing was my fault. I'll get him a check first thing tomorrow morning. I'll deliver it to him personally."

"Don't bother, he already got his cut from my bankruptcy attorney, and it was a hell of a lot less than the hundred grand you and I were supposed to pay him. But let's get back to the subject at hand. We still haven't heard the last words you said to me."

Sebastian's brows disappear behind the mask, expectant, and he's got my full attention. My eyes stay trained on the phone, and I lean forward on the recliner, waiting, barely breathing. I hear Beatrix licking her lips, the creak as she shifts on the leather chair. Otherwise the room is silent.

"I..." Cam pauses to puff a frustrated breath, to clear his throat. "You have to understand. Two of my shops were bleeding cash. I had to pump every cent I owned into keeping them afloat. And it was *your* name on the deed, *your* name on the contract. I wasn't legally bound to pay either of you a penny."

"Let's ask Jade what she thinks, shall we?" Sebastian stretches his arm, holding the phone between us like an offering. "Let's say a man shakes on a business deal and assumes his partner is operating with the same honor, so he dives into an expensive renovation, fronting the costs out of his own pocket. Only the partner isn't honorable, and he's a no-show when it comes time to sign the partnership agreement, leaving the man with a half-finished building and a stack of unpaid bills. Shouldn't that partner have to share the burden of the costs?"

Cam's voice fills the room. "Not according to the law, he—"

"Shut up, Cam. I'm not talking to you. Jade?"

I inhale. Nod. "Yes. Yes, I think he should."

I know this is what Sebastian wants to hear, but it's also the truth. If that's indeed what Cam did, walking away after promises were made and costs accrued, abandoning ship might be legally sound, but morally? Ethically? There's a reason I haven't heard any of this from Cam.

"See? Jade agrees. She thinks you're in the wrong, too. So what do you think she'll say when she hears about the rest—"

"Sebastian, I don't—"

"—how I came to you on my knees and with tears in my eyes, begging you to honor the verbal agreement because for my daughter it was a matter of life or death. Do you remember what you said to me then?"

Silence.

Sebastian steps closer, stopping directly under one of the nanny cams nestled in what looks like a fire alarm. He looks at me, but his words are for Cam. "I'm going to need an answer. What did you tell me?"

"I…" A pause. A frustrated groan. "I said it wasn't my problem."

"Not *it*. She. You said *she* wasn't your problem. My daughter, dying in her bed because I couldn't afford her medicine, was not your problem."

My stomach turns. Cam's words hit me hard, and I think I might vomit. I tell myself it's not true, that Sebastian is stretching the truth. Cam is a man who takes care of his mother. Who passes dollar bills out the window to the homeless people begging at stoplights. Who volunteers at soup kitchens and donates his extra food to the food bank. Not someone who would tell another father—a potential business partner—his sick and dying daughter wasn't his problem.

With a victorious grin, Sebastian flips his cell around, holds it high in the air like a trophy. "Say it again so everybody hears. Louder, this time." On either side of the fake fire alarm, twin ceiling fans cast eerie shadows on his mask and clothes, as menacing as any monster.

"I said she wasn't my problem."

"Right. Just like how what happens next to your wife and daughter isn't mine."

"Please, Sebastian." Cam's voice is pleading, thick with fear. "Just…let Jade and Beatrix go, and I will make sure your daughter gets her lungs, I swear to you. I'll pay for them myself if I have to, and we won't involve the police. You don't have to go to jail for this. We can work this out. *Please*."

Sebastian pulls the phone right up to his mouth and shouts, "Too late. Now get your ass home with my money or your kid dies and then your wife dies and you will sit there helpless knowing there's nothing you could do about it. You won't be able to stop the people you love from dying, and you'll have to live the rest of your miserable life knowing their deaths are all your fault. Then you'll finally understand what you did to me. You'll feel the pain I felt."

Beatrix's face screws into a purple coil, and I scoot closer, wrapping a hand around her ankle.

"I feel your pain now," Cam says, his voice low, calmer now. He's holding it together, but just barely. "Just hold on. Don't do anything you'll regret. I'll be there in eighteen minutes, and then I swear to you we'll fix this. I want to fix this."

Sebastian checks the time on his cell. "In fifteen they'll all be dead."

"Come *on*, Sebastian. I *know* you. You may hate me for what I did, but you're not evil enough to kill innocent people. You're smart, you're caring and you're a great father. No father deserves the kind of worries you're carrying around, but you're not that guy. I know you don't want to do this."

"Oh yeah?" He steps closer, his eyes flashing when they land on mine. "If you know so much about me, smart guy, then you know I have nothing left to lose."

JADE

6:45 p.m.

Fifteen minutes.

Fifteen minutes until Cam gets here and I can run across the street for Baxter. I don't think about everything I just heard, about the lawsuit and Cam's callous dismissal of a girl's illness, or the fact that Cam said it would be eighteen minutes and in all the years I've known him he has never once been on time. And it's raining again. Atlanta's rush hour is still in full swing. There are so many possible complications, but I tell myself he will get here on time. I can't think of what will happen if he's too late.

The words chant like a mantra through my head.

Fifteen minutes, fifteen minutes, fifteen minutes.

Sebastian pushes off the windowsill and grabs his backpack off the floor. He shoves a hand in deep and roots around, but not before dumping the gun and both cell phones onto the side table next to Beatrix. I would protest—*Too close, what kind of idiot puts a loaded gun within arm's reach of a child?*—if her arms weren't strapped to the chair.

"All right. Game time. Let's go."

I stare at him in horror because I'm pretty sure what's about to happen. Still, I have to ask, "Go where?"

"On the chair." He pulls his hand out of the bag and gestures to the recliner at the far end, as far away as possible from Beatrix. "That one."

I shake my head. "I want to stay next to Beatrix."

He digs through the bag again, his hand emerging with a fresh roll of duct tape. "This is not up for discussion. I'm not asking you which chair you want to sit in. I'm telling you which one, and it's the last one." He drops the bag on the carpet by the side table.

Questions fly through my mind. What's going to happen once I'm tied down? How do I save my daughter when I'm strapped to a chair? I try to think of some way to frame the questions so Beatrix doesn't understand, but the idea of being tied down and helpless to protect her has me too panicked to think straight.

Fifteen minutes. It feels like an eternity. There's no way I can stall for that long.

He finds the edge of the tape and tears off a long strip. It rips off the roll with a harsh clatter.

"Mom—" Beatrix begins, but I stop her with a look.

"Please," I say to Sebastian. "If you let me stay here, I'll make sure she stays quiet and does as you say. We both will."

He shakes his head, and my throat dries up like sandpaper. It's a setup. Sebastian is a parent, which means he knows the agony I am feeling at the thought of being separated from my child. At being helpless to save her. He has to know what this is doing to me.

Sebastian lifts a brow—a silent *Well?*—and Cam was wrong

about this man. He is *not* a good guy. Anyone who separates a mother from her child, who ties her to a chair and turns her defenseless is evil. Never, not once ever in my entire life, have I wanted to kill someone like I want to kill this man. He is a *monster*.

I look at my daughter, silent and strapped to the couch, and her expression makes my stomach hurt. "No. I won't do it. You can't make me."

"*Mom.*" Beatrix widens her eyes, round and insistent. "Just go, okay? It's *fine.*"

A hand reaches into my chest, seizes my heart in a fist and squeezes it in two. Beatrix is always doing this—acting mature beyond her years, assuming responsibility for matters a little girl shouldn't have to assume responsibility for. An inflexible, type A perfectionist who carries the weight of the world on her shoulders. Now she sees my distress and wants to comfort *me*.

"It's *not* fine." I shake my head, and tears tumble down my face. I will not sit apart from her. I won't.

"Come on, Jade, ticktock. Get moving, or I'll drag you there myself."

Thirteen minutes. All I have to do is hold on for thirteen more minutes.

My mind shuffles through the items around me, inventorying the ones that are heavy enough, sharp enough, solid enough. The fern in a ceramic pot, the footed bowl on the coffee table, the antique marble bust, the PlayStation guitar on the stand in the corner. These are the things that could bash in a head, but I'd never make it to any of them in time, not without getting shot in the back. He's too strong for me to fight, too fast for me to outrun.

I grab on to the recliner, digging in with my entire backside until every part of me is flush to the chair. If he wants me on the other one, he'll have to unglue me from this one first.

Sebastian cocks his head. "Hey, what do you think Cam meant when he said don't listen to me?"

It takes a second or two for my mind to catch up to his sudden change of subject, and then another few seconds for the meaning to come to me in a slow drip. Cam told me not to listen to Sebastian. He said he was lying, that none of the stuff he told me was true.

Which also means that Cam heard our conversation. He remembered the nanny cams, he was listening and watching. He heard everything.

"What?"

"Cam, when he called just now. He said, Jade, don't listen to him, referring to me. It was one of the first things he said after I put him on speakerphone. What do you think he meant by it?"

"I don't..." My voice breaks, and I swallow. Force myself to breathe. "I don't know. He probably figured you'd been telling me all sorts of awful things about him. Which is true, by the way. You have been."

"Possible, but it seemed like he had ears in the room or something. Almost as if he's been watching us the entire time. What, does he have ESP?"

I think of my phone on the side table next to the gun, the colorful cartoon image of a baby's face among the apps on the third page, above the word *iSpy*. Two little swipes of his finger, a couple of taps to the screen, and Sebastian would be staring at himself on the screen. He'd see me clinging to the recliner next to my strapped-down daughter. He'd hear my lame-ass lie, coming at him in stereo: "That's impossible."

Sebastian gives me a one-shouldered shrug. "Maybe, but Cam still knew. I mean okay, sure. Let's say he had a hunch

I'd gotten in your ear, but he sounded so certain about it. Not even the slightest hesitation or a question mark, just pure conviction right out of the gate. Doesn't that seem kinda funny to you?"

"Not even a little bit."

He regards me, silent, as the lights flicker on in the backyard outside, a golden glow that filters up to the window. They work on a timer, which means it's dangerously close to seven.

"Right, right." Sebastian's shoulders relax under the black fabric of his shirt, and mine do, too. He goes back to his tape, and I blow out a silent breath while at the same time, my fingers tighten on the cushion.

He transfers the strip from his fingers to the side table, the stubborn tape not wanting to let go of his gloves. As soon as he frees one finger, the tape sticks to another, and he tucks the roll under a bicep so he can use both hands. When he's free, he whirls to face me.

"But what if it was? I mean, you wouldn't be the first parent to stick some spyware in a teddy bear so you know when the babysitter has fallen asleep on the job. What do they call those things? Nanny cams." He looks around demonstratively, taking in the decor, his gaze finally landing on Baxter's stuffed gorilla, sticking out from under the coffee table. He reaches down, wrangles it off the floor.

If Baxter were here, he'd be going ballistic. Gibson doesn't like to be squeezed.

Sebastian holds the animal in front of his face. "Hey there, gorilla. You got any nanny cams in that big fat belly of yours?" He gives it a good shake, then tosses it to the floor.

I stare at Gibson, wedged between the table and the carpet by my feet, and try to breathe.

Sebastian steps to the center of the room, rotating in a slow circle. "Though, if I were going to install nanny cams in my house, I sure as heck wouldn't put them in something as cliché as a stuffed animal. I'd be a little more creative, maybe hide them in a plant—" he steps to the coffee table and rifles through the fern directly in front of me, shrugging when he finds nothing but fronds and dirt "—or a picture frame. Books. You've got a bunch of books over there on the shelves. Any of them contain cameras you forgot to tell me about?"

I shake my head, but I'm not very convincing. The strips of tape dangling from the console, the insistence I move to the far chair. He's all but forgotten that plan now, but I can't shake the feeling that something's off. That this is all an act.

It's certainly possible he's seen the nanny cams on my phone. He's had plenty of time to look, moments when I was tied to the blue chair and wouldn't have seen him nosing through my phone. *This is a test*, he said the first time he asked me about the cameras. This could be one big ruse to watch me paint myself in a corner.

One by one, he inspects the possibilities in the room. He runs a gloved finger down the book spines, bends to study the bowls and vases on the console, pulls the paintings away from the walls and peers behind the frames. He takes his time, moving around the room so slowly, so leisurely, I begin to think he's running down the clock, dragging the drama out on purpose.

He parks his feet in front of the shelves, standing dangerously close to where two cameras are hidden—one in a speaker high on the wall and the other in the ugly mantel clock. Above my head, about five feet to my left, the third camera provides a birds-eye view from what looks exactly like a fire alarm.

Nobody will ever know the difference, the installer assured me as he screwed it into the plaster. *Not unless they sell fire alarms for a living.*

Now Sebastian extends a long finger at the ceiling, and my

heart stops. "What about that thing?" He points to the motion sensor, its light flickering red in a corner of the ceiling.

It takes me a second or two to find my voice. "Just another Santa cam."

He grins. "Maybe that's where Cam got his information, then. What do you think, Beatrix? Does your dad have a hotline to Santa?"

Beatrix doesn't respond.

The second he turns back to the shelves, I decide, is the best time to strike, and with the marble bust. The gun is too far but the bust is right there, on the table between us, and it's plenty heavy, the base square and sharp enough to crack a skull. A good whack would take any man down, but there's ten feet, maybe less, between us. I'd have to be fast, my attack stealthy and silent. I don't know if I can clear the space fast enough.

"You know, if I were going to hide a nanny cam in this room, I'd put it in something nobody ever really notices. One of the ceiling speakers, for example." He tips his head and studies them, his gaze bouncing between the four mesh circles flush to the plaster. "Those look legit. If there's a camera in there, all I gotta say is bravo. That fire alarm, however..."

He comes closer, climbing up on the coffee table to get a better look.

My blood runs cold, an icy chill that starts at the back of my neck and creeps down my back like an invisible finger.

Sebastian reaches up, knocks the alarm with a gloved knuckle. "There are better models on the market, you know. This one looks cheap, and you know what's weird? It doesn't match any of the others you've got in the house. The one out in the hallway, for example, is a whole different brand. How do you explain that?"

He knows.

The words boom in my head like from a megaphone, loud

and terrifying. This little tour around the room, the battle between the chairs…it's all part of his evil game. I was delusional to think he wouldn't know about the cameras. Maybe he's known about them all along.

How many more minutes until Cam gets here—Ten? Eight? An eternity, when every second feels volatile.

"And why ten past five?" he says, gesturing to the dummy clock. He hops off the table and crosses the room to the shelves, comparing the time to a cheap watch underneath a sleeve. The time is off by almost two hours. "Why not ten past three, or four, or six? Why five?"

Because it's the no-snack zone. It's what I told the installer when he asked the same thing. A time of day the kids know not to bother me for a rumbling belly. The answer will always be no.

I say nothing.

"Hey, you know what else is weird? When the kids and I were watching cartoons earlier, I noticed one of the wall speakers wasn't working." He points with a long arm. "Must have a short or something."

My whole body is shaking now, and I am thinking through my next move. Sebastian is far enough away, his back half turned. I could probably make it to the hall, but not without Beatrix, and I would never leave her here. My only move, the only thing I can come up with, is one of defense—to drape my body over hers, sacrifice myself by covering her body with mine, taking her bullet.

Sebastian's grin is slow and sinister, like he read my mind. "Such a shame. I thought you were smarter than this."

Are we still talking about the cameras? The kids? Cam? I have no idea, and I'm pretty sure I'm not supposed to. This whole conversation feels staged, another one of his sneaky attempts to control and manipulate. These threats he's lobbing, they're vague on purpose. Meant to throw me off.

And it's working.

My cheeks are hot, burning like smoldering coals.

"We've met, you know. More than once."

This surprises me, and it doesn't. He was in business with Cam, which means at some point our paths would have crossed. Cam parades me by all his staff, especially management and investors, but the problem is there are so many. I'm not like Tanya. It's impossible for me to remember them all.

"Sorry, but I—"

"And you know what you said, every single time?"

I shake my head.

"You stuck out a hand and said, 'Hi, I'm Jade Lasky. So nice to meet you.' Don't you just hate that? When people you've met and talked to multiple times treat you like a total stranger? When they think so little of another human being that they can't be bothered to remember your face or name?"

Prosopagnosia. It's a neurological disorder that makes people unable to distinguish between faces. I know because Cam is always teasing me that I have it.

In my defense, I meet a *lot* of people. People who see me at the restaurants or with Cam at parties, who buddy up to us and act like we're old friends, but none of it is real. They don't know me, not really, and I sure as hell don't know them. It's part of being a celebrity chef's wife; I'm lit up with the glow of his stardom.

"I can't see your face," I point out instead.

He comes closer, marching across the carpet and around the table until he's close, standing right in front of me. I try to move back, but there's nowhere for me to go. My calves are already pressed against the soft leather of the couch. I stare into his eyes and search for something I recognize, something unique in the shape or size or color, but there's nothing. Hazel and almond-shaped, like half the people on the planet.

"You really don't know?" He licks his lips. Smiles. "Are you sure about that, Jade? Like, really, really sure?"

The room falls silent, everyone waiting for my answer. Pain shoots through my cheek and I wince, blinking against it. I look him in his unremarkable eyes and force myself to steady my breathing.

"No, but if you take off that mask, I might."

His pupils go dark, like a tiny man inside his eyeballs flicked off the lights. From ho-hum hazel to stormy black, just like that.

It's the last thing I notice before he pulls off the mask.

JADE

6:52 p.m.

It takes me a minute to place him.

Partly because he's lost weight since the last time I saw him, a good twenty pounds melted off his limbs and torso and hollowing out his cheeks. His hair is different, too. Shorter. Lighter, almost completely gray.

The other part is because it's been a few months. I haven't seen him since the spring.

"I remember you. Except your name wasn't Sebastian. It was something else."

Though admittedly, that doesn't explain the other times.

I close my eyes and try to reconstruct the meetings in my mind, but the only one I can come up with with any sort of certainty was this past April. Him, waving at me through the windows as he climbed the front steps. Me, opening the door to invite him in. He introduced himself, but not as Sebastian, as—

"*Bas.* You joked that your wife refused to call you that, that she preferred the name 'Bossy.' I laughed and said she sounded like a smart woman." I pause, the obvious question rising in my head. "Which one is it?"

"The only one who calls me Bas is my mother, God rest her soul."

"Do you even have a wife?"

He shrugs. "I guess, though I haven't seen or heard from her in years. She could be dead for all I know."

I don't respond, mostly because I still don't know what to believe. There have been so many lies, and if she's been gone that long, I don't see how their estrangement could possibly be Cam's fault. The stories flicker through my head like a disjointed dream, random bits of information he hurled at me over the course of a couple hours. That he grew up in New Orleans, that he moved here after Katrina, that he married his high school sweetheart. The one thing I haven't forgotten is that this guy was a talker.

Only one detail matches up to the bits and pieces I've heard from him today: "You told me about your daughter. You didn't tell me what was wrong with her, but you said she was sick. That she was dying."

My words hit him like a slap. He winces, then nods.

A rising high school junior and budding artist, a genius with charcoal and pastels. A sensitive girl with a pretty name. "Gigi."

"That's right." He looks impressed. "She was named after my grandmother."

And then, another memory, one that arrives with a sickening spasm. "I promised to help, didn't I?"

Actually, it's worse than that. I made a promise to connect him with one of Cam's regular clients, a board member at Piedmont Hospital. I wrote down Sebastian's number and asked for a couple of days to connect the two.

And then?

And then I got busy. Running errands and picking up school uniforms at the mall. Meeting friends for lunches and coffees. Carting the kids to violin and soccer and the movies, cooking healthy dinners for my family. I went back to my busy, cushy life, and I didn't even think about Sebastian and his poor, sweet, sick daughter until many weeks later, when I pulled a wad of lint from the pocket of freshly laundered jeans and connected it to my broken promise.

But it wasn't too late. I could have tracked Sebastian down. I could have picked up the phone and called that board member. I could have done *something*.

And yet, I didn't.

I swallow down a surge of self-loathing. "Jesus… No wonder you hate me and Cam so much."

Sebastian barks a laugh. "You think?"

"I'm so sorry, Sebastian. I wish I had an excuse, but the truth is, I don't. All those things I told myself at the time, all the reasons I justified not following through…of course they're all bullshit. I mean, of *course* I could have followed through. I *should* have. But the more time passed, the more I just figured…" I look up at him and I search for the right thing to say, even though I know there's not a word that exists to make this right.

"You figured what? Spit it out. What did you figure?"

I wince, closing my eyes. "I figured it wouldn't matter, since our paths would probably never cross again anyway."

"Even though they'd already crossed a handful of times." He grimaces, shakes his head. "But of course, you didn't remember that, either, did you? I was just a stranger with a sorry face and a sad story."

"I *know*. And I hate myself for it. If I could go back and change things, I would in a second. The board member's name is Gordon Howard. He's in my phone. Let's call him together, right now."

"And say what, exactly?"

"That your daughter is sick. That you need help navigating her options. You didn't tell me what she had, but tonight I heard you mention cystic fibrosis. You said she needed a lung transplant."

He nods. "Her doctors say they have four, maybe five months left in them, and that's assuming she doesn't pick up B. cepacia, which for someone with CF is pretty much a death sentence. She needs that transplant."

If I wasn't convinced before that Gigi is Tanya's niece, I am now. How many sixteen-year-old girls in Atlanta are facing this exact situation? We must be talking about the same person. We *must* be.

"And the most screwed-up part is that the insurance will cover the lungs. But only if I can guarantee I have the money for all the therapy and antirejection drugs she'll need to have after."

I say to Sebastian what I told Tanya when she told me the same story. "I'm so fucking sorry."

Beatrix sucks in a breath at the curse word, but she's heard worse, a *lot* worse from her father, and if there was ever a situation that warranted the f-bomb, this is it. A girl's life cut short before it's really begun, on the verge of womanhood, because her father can't afford the medication to make her lungs stick.

"Tell me about it," Sebastian says. "And those drugs are just the beginning. There's testing and rehab, and do you know they even want to charge me for flying the lungs in to the hospital? Why is that something I should have to pay for?

If you can't afford to live in this country, they're more than happy to just let you die."

"But Cam's right, though. This is not the way to go about getting money for her operation."

My comment seems to anger him. He puffs up his chest and balls his fists, glaring across the coffee table at me. "You think I wouldn't give her my lungs if I could? You think I wouldn't rip open my own chest and yank them out myself if I thought it would save her from wasting away? Knowing I'm a match is the worst kind of torture because it doesn't do either of us any good. I still can't help her. She's still going to die without that operation."

Despite everything, the gun, and the threats, and my son in the enemy's house across the street, and my daughter strapped to the chair, sympathy rises in my chest for this man. For a sick girl I've never met.

"I'm sorry. That must be so hard."

I mean every word, too, just like I meant them the first time I said them—in this very same room even, after I brought him coffee and a muffin so he could take a break from installing the nanny cams. Sebastian—Bas—came highly recommended by none other than Tanya across the street. The neighbor who's always picking up our mail. Bills, junk, bank account statements. What we've always assumed was a friendly gesture was her way of keeping tabs.

But the more pressing point is, Sebastian knows about the cameras. He's known it all along.

Not only that.

He spent an entire day up here, banging around the playroom, drilling holes in the ceiling and walls, pointing out the best placement for maximum visibility, upselling me on products that were top-of-the-line, quizzing me on my security system because "maybe it's time for an upgrade." He even installed the nanny cam app on my phone, then dragged it onto the third page, so it would be with all the other house stuff.

And today, he *chose* this room. He brought us here on purpose. Strapping the kids to the couch, questioning me about Cam, ordering me around. Even where he's standing now, one foot planted on the corner of the rug, his body pointed into the room, puts his uncovered face in all three shots. Everything about this seems intentional.

He wants Cam to see. He wants him to watch what's about to happen on his little screen while he's rushing to get here with the ransom.

"But that won't help you with your hospital bill. A pile of cash that big will be a red flag. You'll get caught. What happens when the police show up at your door? They'll confiscate the money, and then where will you be? Who will help Gigi then?"

"She'll be fine. At home with a new set of lungs."

"But *how*? You just told me her insurance won't pay for the transplant unless you can pay for the antirejection drugs."

"It's taken care of. I've taken care of it. And we're getting off track. Let's not forget that I wouldn't be standing here if Cam had kept up his end of the deal. He *owes* me this money."

Frustration rises, hot and choking in my chest. "You'll get arrested! There's got to be a better way."

Sebastian's brows shift into a sharp V. "You don't think I've tried everything? I've written letters, I've filed a million appeals, I even showed up at Channel 7 and begged that reporter Juanita Moore to do one of those investigative deep dives. She said the story wasn't 'fresh' enough to be interesting to the public. I'm out of options. This right here is the very last one, and I'm prepared to see it to the end in order to save my baby girl. You'd do the same if you were in my position."

I look at Beatrix, then think of Baxter across the street,

and my eyes water. I'd tear my lungs out for them, rip out my still-beating heart. "You're right. I would. In a heartbeat."

"So get in the chair."

I shake my head, planting myself deeper into the one next to Beatrix. "Let me help. Let me call Gordon. Maybe he can help you and Gigi."

My offer straightens his spine with anger, with indignation. "It's too late! This isn't some silly story where you can slap on a happy ending. This is my life, and you can't even imagine the shit I have to go through. Have you ever stuck your card in an ATM and have it *not* spit out cash?"

Not since college, I think dully, but it seems like an answer I shouldn't admit out loud.

I think about where he left the gun, on the table to my right, but there's no way I could get there first. Not with Beatrix in the way, with Sebastian's body parked a good three feet closer. Better to keep quiet and wait.

Sebastian's scowl says he knows the answer. "That's what I thought. So you keep on living your American dream up here in country club fairy-tale land, but enjoy it while it lasts because life can turn on a dime. Believe me when I say there's no safety net to catch you when you fall. For people like me, life is not something to enjoy but to survive. Your American dream is my nightmare."

"It's true, I can't possibly understand what you're going through, and I can't be your safety net, but I can help you get one. Think what you want about Cam and me, but we have influence. People listen to us. If we call up the news stations and make a stink about what is happening to you and your daughter, we can change your situation. We can start a Go-FundMe and make sure everyone who comes through the restaurants knows about it. We can help."

"A GoFundMe, like we haven't tried that," he scoffs, rolling his eyes. "Last time I looked there were six of those things, and *maybe* we scrounged up enough money to pay for three months of treatment, and then what? On the fourth month her body rejects the lungs, and it's a death worse than what she's going through now."

"There has to be something I can do."

Sebastian shakes his head, gestures to the empty chairs on either side of me. "You can stop acting like you give a shit and get in the damn chair. Cam will be here any minute."

The panicky feeling returns, a vibration in my bones, a hot itch just under my skin. "Sebastian, please. *Please* let me help you."

I stare up at him, and it's so obvious to me now, the violent loathing in his eyes. The ugly anger, a hatred that all afternoon I thought was meant for me, but it's not really. It's for Cam. And the second he gets here, the instant he barrels up those stairs and into this room, the bullets will start flying.

And Sebastian won't be aiming for Cam.

He'll aim at me. At Beatrix.

An eye for an eye. Our daughter for his.

Today—all of it—it's about getting even.

CAM

6:54 p.m.

"Where'd your colleagues go?" I squint into the rearview mirror, hoping to pick out the two big bouncers in the car on my bumper, but the rain is really coming down now. There's nothing but glare in the glass. "Is that them behind us? I can't tell."

Nick twists around on the passenger's seat, checking the back window. "Not unless they suddenly turned eighty and white. They passed us ages ago." He wriggles his cell from a pocket on his leather jacket. "Lemme see where they're at."

While he makes the call, I stare into the line of traffic snaking up Peachtree Dunwoody and my heartbeat goes berserk. Two lanes of bumper-to-bumper traffic going well under the speed limit, with nothing on either side but bushes and ditches. I'm stuck, nowhere to go but forward.

Come on, come on...

Nick pulls his cell away from his ear. "Darius says they're

almost there. He also says we've got a problem. That video footage you're watching? He's watching it, too. Apparently, those nanny cams of yours are streaming on YouTube, maybe some other places, too."

I think about what this means—that someone hacked into the video feed, that others might be watching as well—but my mind moves like sludge. I can't do the math, can't ferret out if this is a good thing or bad. What I know for sure is that I need to get to the house and fast.

"Darius wants to know our ETA."

I glance at the clock. I have six minutes left, when I'm more like seven or eight from home. I shouldn't have pulled over to check my phone. I should have handed it to Nick, let him do it, but I was too stubborn, too much of a damn control freak. George and the others are right; I really am my own worst enemy.

"Tell them we're going to be cutting it close, that they should wait for us in the backyard. He's in the media room, so tell them to watch the window above the patio. And for God's sake, no bullets. My wife and daughter are in there, too, and I can't risk it, not even if it looks like a clean shot."

I check the footage on my phone, balanced in a palm at the top of the steering wheel. I've been flipping between the three cameras, watching Jade park herself on the chair next to Beatrix and coax a conversation out of an unmasked Sebastian. Stalling.

"Let me help," she says. "I want to help you and Gigi."

Nick hangs up, shoves the phone back in a pocket. "This traffic is really jacking with our plan."

I stare at the sea of brake lights and try not to puke because he's right. This traffic is a problem, and so is the fact that Darius and Vance are about to beat us there. They need me to go in first, to turn off the alarm and unlock the back door, then flush Sebastian out of the playroom with the promise of money in the truck. As soon as I've lured him away from Jade and Beatrix, the bouncers and Nick will take Sebastian down, right before they disappear into the night.

But the timing is tight. I drift to the right, nudging the truck into the nonexistent shoulder, then jerk the tires back onto the road just in time. The bumper misses a stone mailbox by a hair.

"Isn't there a shortcut?" Nick says. "Try a side street or something. There's got to be another way in."

"Shut up and let me drive."

I ride a Buick's bumper and swipe between cameras on my phone, checking in on every angle. I stop on the bird's-eye view of the room and see Beatrix is getting restless in her chair. Her right hand is tugging at the bindings.

Nick grunts. "Maybe the others should go ahead and—"

"*No*. Not unless I give them the sign. Not until things go south."

"Pretty sure things went south hours ago."

I don't respond, even though Nick is right. Again.

I white-knuckle the wheel and look past the Buick to a turnoff up ahead, marked with a stone pillar and a bright green street sign. Fifty yards. Only fifty yards of this deadlock to go.

I flick my lights and press forward until I'm flush to the Buick's bumper, keeping one eye on the camera feed. Sebastian is getting worked up, his whole body becoming energized. His face gleams, and he starts moving about the room, bouncing between the three cameras, giving them full-on shots of his face.

He says my name, and my lungs go hard as concrete.

"He told me it was a no-brainer. He said his other shops were spitting out profits in the first year. He guaranteed we'd have our money back, that we'd double it in no time. He knew I was counting on my investment to pay for Gigi's medical costs, and he swore he wouldn't let this project fail. And then you know what happened? He let it fail. He walked away and left me holding the bill."

I glance over at Nick. "I never said any of that. He knew about the risks. He's lying."

Nick grunts, a detached sound that says he couldn't care less either way.

"Seriously, man. That's not how it happened."

I don't know why I'm being so defensive, why I care that this man-bunned, leather-clad arsonist who's been following my wife believes me, but there it is. I am ashamed of my behavior. I don't want anybody to know what I did.

"What, a kidnapper lie?" Nick swings an ankle over a knee. "Shocking."

When Sebastian floated the idea of us becoming partners, offering up the building he'd inherited from his grandmother in return for a stake in the restaurant, I warned him there were risks. But in the same breath, I also told him not to worry.

Oakhurst was to be my sixth shop in a city that couldn't get enough of me. All we had to do was fix the place up, fire up the grill and open the doors, and people would come running. I didn't use the words *no-brainer*, but I might as well have. I certainly gave him that impression.

And then Fred couldn't fill the tables in the West Side shop—first on weekdays, then weekends. Staff was walking out, abandoning ship for restaurants that could keep them flush with tips. I had no other choice but to fire Fred and step in, but it took a few months to get back up to speed. No way I had the bandwidth for a sixth shop.

George's parting word whispers in my ear: *karma.*

Of *course* I knew when Sebastian offered to front the renovation costs before either of us had signed on the dotted line, I should have told him to hold off. Every time he'd call with an excited update on the latest investment, new windows and a new roof and floors, a new layer of asphalt on the lot or the top-of-the-line appliances he paid for out of his own pocket, I knew I should have put on the brakes. I watched it all happen, and I never once told him to stop.

His face when I bailed. God, I will never forget it, or the words he said to me over and over. *I need this, Cam. I need this or my daughter will die.*

I told myself he was exaggerating, that universal health care would pay for whatever treatment his sick daughter needed. I figured another chef would be enticed by the promise of a Lasky-grade kitchen and snap up my sloppy seconds. I was wrong on both accounts, and the truth is, I didn't much care. I was too damn busy trying to keep my own ass afloat.

But I said it. God help me, I told him his dying daughter wasn't my problem. And now Jade knows, and Bea knows, and they probably blame me for all of it, and they're right to.

"Cam."

Jade's voice is loud and urgent, bleating in my iPhone's speaker. My gaze snaps to the screen.

Jade is standing now, staring into the camera—the speaker on the wall. Her head is tipped back, the couch spread like wings coming off her shoulders, Beatrix on the far end. Jade's eyes are big and wide.

"Cam, don't come here. As soon as you do—"

"Shut up." Sebastian's body steps into the shot, moving fast, a blurry black blotch on my iPhone screen. "Don't listen to her, Cam."

He shoves her out of the shot.

"Don't come inside!" she shouts. "He's going to kill us either way!"

I swipe to another screen, searching for the bird's-eye feed.

Sebastian lunges, and my screen becomes a jumble of sound, of bodies. I stare at it, gripping it hard enough to snap the thing in two, trying to hold it together, trying to *see*, but my world has gone foggy with fury. Jade screams, then Beatrix. Nick dives for the wheel, jerking the truck's tires back on the road, and orders me to let up on the gas.

I lift my foot and scream into the cab, *"What is happening?"*

I see Jade, sprawled across two empty chairs, her feet tangled with a squirming Beatrix's. Jade scrambles to sit up, to protect our daughter, who is calm in a way that pierces my heart. With an unbothered expression, Beatrix leans over the armrest and reaches for her mother's hand.

Sebastian stalks up to the speaker, talks right into it.

"Listen to me, Cam. If you ever want to see your family again, I'd advise you not to listen to your wife. Get over here, now. Bring me my money. You have three minutes."

His lip is curled up on one side, his face red and ugly, splotchy in the high-definition, full-color camera, but it's not his face I'm looking at.

It's Beatrix's.

Over Sebastian's shoulder I take in my daughter's cool stare, her clamped down jaw, the look of calm determination. It's a look anybody else might mistake for boredom, but not me. I know Beatrix too well. This is the expression she gets when she's steeling herself, gathering up all her courage, right before she walks onto an orchestra stage.

With both hands, she shoves her body to the edge of the oversize chair and pushes to a shaky stand. Feet planted to the carpet in front of her chair. She looks at her mother on the chair next to her. At Sebastian, still spitting mad, screaming into the speaker. At the side table, and a black smudge that looks just like—

"No."

With helpless horror, I watch my daughter pick up the gun.

THE INTERVIEW

Juanita: In the months since the home invasion, your daughter, Beatrix, has become an internet sensation. That still shot from the nanny cam footage of her sneaking out of the playroom made the cover of the *New York Times*, and there are Facebook groups and fan pages and hundreds of GIFs and memes dedicated to her bravery and daring. There are Hollywood producers competing to tell her story, even talk of putting her face on a cereal box. That must feel…

Cam: Strange. Surreal. Bizarre. All of the above.

Juanita: I'd imagine it's also a big invasion of privacy.

Cam: I'll say. You people are pretty relentless.

Juanita: I agree the media can be tenacious, but that's because this story is one that holds widespread appeal. A celebrity chef, a brave little girl who also happens to be a violin virtuoso, a masked and armed man who targeted you and your family, a shooting captured on camera—

Cam: A villain who's only out for money.

Juanita: Are we talking about him or you?

Cam: [shrugs] Up to your viewers to decide, though pretty sure I know which side of the equation they'll fall on.

Juanita: That moment when Beatrix picked up the gun, you were watching on your cell phone. You saw your daughter pick up a deadly weapon, and there was literally nothing you could do to stop it. I can't imagine what that must have been like.

Cam: [long pause] My heart, it just…stopped. Like, no pulse, no blood pumping at all. My muscles locked up, and it's a miracle I didn't hit a tree because I couldn't tear my eyes off the phone. I didn't look at the road. All I could see was my baby on that little screen, holding a gun, waving it around. And I was completely helpless to stop her.

Juanita: Because you were still miles away. Stuck in traffic.

Cam: [wipes eyes] Nothing could have prepared me for that kind of terror. *Nothing*.

Juanita: So what did you do?

Cam: I drove like hell. I prayed to a God I've spent most of my life either ignoring or mocking, a God I have zero business asking any favors. I swore that if He or She would just spare my family, just… [shakes head]

Juanita: Do you need to take a break?

Cam: No. I'm all right.

Juanita: Take all the time you need.

Cam: I swore if God would spare them, keep them alive and in one piece, then I would never ask for anything ever again. And all those things I used to care about, the restaurants and the real estate and the houses and cars, I'd give it all up. Because here's what happens when your family's lives are at stake. There's this…white-light moment of clarity, a lightning-bolt realization that you're an idiot and all that shit you've spent so much time and effort accumulating is worthless. The banks can have everything. I don't want any of those things anymore. Without Jade and the Bees, it's worthless. *I'm* worthless.

Juanita: August 6 was your wake-up call?

Cam: [nods] I'm just sorry it happened too late.

JADE

6:57 p.m.

I'm so busy watching Sebastian that I don't notice it at first.

The way Beatrix's arm reached across the armrest and into my chair just now, like her wrist wasn't connected to the leather. The object she pressed in my hand.

Long. Hard. Warm from body heat.

Automatically, I close my fingers around it, concealing the thing in a fist.

But I don't look. And I don't consider how it could be possible. Not yet.

I'm too distracted by Sebastian's shouting into the wall speaker, a long tirade about how Cam better get here and get here in a hurry. How he shouldn't listen to me.

Three minutes until seven, the blink of an eye and an endless eternity at the same time. Sebastian is furious, this situation so volatile. Anything can happen in three minutes.

And then realization hits.

The warm, hard, sticky thing in my palm.

I unfurl my fingers just enough to peek inside.

It's Cam's pocketknife, the one he's had since college, a scratched and beat-up thing that once belonged to his grandfather. Cam keeps it more for sentimental value than for its usefulness, storing it under a stack of wrinkled business cards in an antique box in his study. As far as I know, he's never showed it to the kids.

But Beatrix knew where to look.

Not only that.

In the middle of a life-or-death emergency, when she had only a few seconds to scout out a hiding place, Beatrix went for a weapon. She found the pocketknife in Cam's hiding place. This is the reason we don't have a gun.

My smart girl kept her wits about her. While the three of us were downstairs searching the basement, Beatrix was in Cam's study, gathering weapons and making signs. She's my four-foot, curly-haired, levelheaded hero.

I close my fingers around the knife and twist around on my chair.

Beatrix's seat is empty. She stands in front of it, bare toes digging into the carpet. Her hands hang loose by her sides, free from their bindings.

Behind her, the duct tape lies wrinkled and deflated on the leather. Sawed completely through, four messy slices in the metallic silver, by the pocketknife in my hand. It must have taken her forever, and all that time I didn't see. None of us heard a sound.

Especially not Sebastian, watching from the other side of the coffee table. He has both hands raised, fingers spread wide, palms pushing against the air. "Don't even think about it."

My gaze returns to Beatrix's hands, but I only see one of

them. Her left hand, hanging empty by her side. The other is concealed by her body.

And yet I already know what's in it.

I see it from Sebastian's suddenly blanched skin, the way his eyes go twitchy. I see it in the set of Beatrix's mouth, her rod-straight back and trembling shoulders. From the way my mind stops screaming long enough to hear what's happening out-side, the soft but steady sound, whistling like a distant wind.

I know what's in Beatrix's hand long before she lifts her arms and I see the gun. She grips it in two white-knuckled hands.

And that whistling outside? It's not wind.

It's sirens.

Sebastian's earlier words echo through my brain: *At the first sign of sirens, the bullets start flying. First the kids, then you.*

And now it's *Beatrix* holding the gun, *her* finger curled around the trigger.

Sebastian doesn't move.

The moment slips into crystalline focus.

"Move back," Beatrix says. "Get up against the wall. Do it."

She's like a stick-figure drawing of someone holding a gun, all sharp angles and straight lines, her arms extended from her body in a perfect triangle. It's the amateur stance of someone who learned her gun skills from comic books and cartoons, who's never held a gun, never even had an interest in a toy one.

My chest swells with terror, and I shift to the other side of the chair. "Beatrix, sweetie, give me the gun."

She shakes her head, hard and sharp, a rapid back-and-forth that shivers her curls. "I mean it, mister. Back up." Her muscles are taut, her finger twitching where it's bent over the trigger.

Sebastian takes a tiny backward step. "Be careful with that thing. This isn't some plaything, you know, that gun is deadly.

One wrong move and you could shoot yourself in the foot or worse. What if you shoot your mama?"

"I'm not aiming at my mom. I'm aiming at you."

"Come on, kid. You really don't want to do this."

"Yes, I do. I really, *really* want to shoot you." Beatrix's voice breaks on the word *shoot*, and she thrusts the gun for emphasis. "Now move *back*. I mean it. Go!"

Sebastian takes another ministep. "So that's it, then, you're going to shoot me. Better make it good. Better not miss."

Beatrix closes one eye. Her muscles never so much as quiver when she holds the violin, but now her aim is all over the place. She's close enough, though, that even a wide shot could be deadly. The femur, a collarbone, a direct hit to the head.

I hold out a trembling hand. "Beatrix, I mean it. Give me the gun."

Another shake of the head. "Not until he moves back. He's still too close. Move *more*."

"Or maybe you should just wait until the cops get here. Let them handle things." Sebastian tips his head to the window, to the sound of sirens. The wailing feels like a hallucination, like if I cover my ears they'll disappear, fading away into silence. I picture police cars hurtling through the streets behind our house, colorful lights cutting through the dusk and rain like swirling lanterns. In another few minutes, they'll be squealing up the drive.

"Stop talking. And move back more." Beatrix enunciates each word slowly, deliberately. "Please don't make me say it again."

It's a phrase I say to the kids often, and in exactly that same tone, and my words coming out of my daughter's mouth wrap around my heart and squeeze. It never works on them, either.

Sebastian's soles stay planted to the floor.

I slide onto my knees on the carpet. I'm afraid any sudden

movement will set Beatrix off. Slowly, steadily, I stretch my hand farther.

"He's right, baby. You're so brave, but let me handle this, okay? Give Mommy the gun."

Except for two candy-red spots high on her cheeks, Beatrix's face is shockingly pale, white and translucent like melted candle wax, like a body dredged from the depths. The effect is terrifying, especially when coupled with her voice, high with icy anger.

"*No*. Not until he gets back to the wall. All the way. Mommy, make him move."

The sirens are getting steadier now, undulating waves through the air on the back side of the house, which means they've made the turn into the neighborhood.

"Sweetie, give me the gun."

Beatrix's body is wound tight, her shoulder muscles bunched under her pink polka-dot shirt.

Sebastian's gaze flicks to mine, his eyes going wide, like *do something*. "Put the gun down, missy."

"I'm not your missy."

I move on my knees, edging closer to curl my hand around Beatrix's, take control of the gun and shoot Sebastian in the head. And just to be sure, I'll shoot him in the heart, too. *Bang bang*. Dead.

And then I will carry this gun out the door and across the road and point it at Tanya until she gives me back my son. I will tear her limbs from her body if I have to.

Sebastian points a gloved finger to the ceiling. "Hear that? They'll be here any minute."

I keep my eyes on Sebastian, the gun a black blur in my periphery. "It's true, sweetie. The police are on their way. They're coming to save us. Let them handle this, please. Give the gun to me."

I reach for the gun, at the same time Beatrix steps to the side, and my hand swipes air. I don't try again because I know that expression, the way her eyes and jaw are locked down tight. There's no way she's putting that weapon down, not even for me. Not even for the police.

Beatrix's finger tightens around the trigger.

Sebastian's gaze zeroes in on the gun. "Hey, watch it there. That gun has a heavy recoil. You might want to loosen up on that trigger."

Beatrix lifts the gun higher, aiming it at Sebastian's chest. Dead center.

"Okay, fine, you got me, but don't do anything you're going to regret. Once you pull that trigger, there's no going back. You can't take back a bullet."

My daughter squeezes her eyes and the trigger.

JADE

7:02 p.m.

Unlike my daughter's, my eyes are wide-open. I see the flash of the gun as the bullet takes flight, the way the recoil is a sledgehammer to Beatrix's shoulder, how it pops her clear off her feet, bounces her body off the recliner and sends her sprawling.

I see the bullet smack Sebastian high on a shoulder, the spatter of blood where it enters his skin, the way it punches his torso into the wall. I see the smear he leaves on the eggshell paint as he slides down to the ground, the way his lips curl upward into a smile.

"I told you somebody'd get shot at the first sign of sirens. Didn't I tell you that?"

My ears are still ringing from the gunshot, but I hear his breathy laughter loud and clear. Another stupid, demented joke. Despite the bullet, despite the blood turning his shirt shiny, he's pleased with himself.

His gaze wanders to Beatrix, still half-flopped on the floor, to the gun lying next to her on the carpet. Her face is still fish-belly white, but those two spots on her cheeks are so red they're almost purple. "I gotta give you props, kid. You've been an excellent adversary. A real pain in my ass, but an excellent adversary. I didn't even see you cut yourself loose. What'd you use—a knife? Scissors?"

Cam's pocketknife pulses in my hand.

Beatrix fumbles for the gun, but I lunge and beat her there, plucking it from the floor, swinging it back to Sebastian. I've shot a gun only a few times in my life, and if Cam were here he'd tell you I'm the worst shot he's ever seen. But with less than ten feet between me and my target, I'm certain I could do some damage. Head, torso, heart. I'll keep shooting until I hit something lethal.

But Sebastian hasn't moved. He just sits there, slumped against the wall, legs bent like an awkward grasshopper. His knees jut upward, bony caps pointed to the sky.

He presses a palm to his shoulder, wincing. "Do me a favor and make it a kill shot this time, would you? Put me out of my misery." With a groan, he stretches his legs flat onto the floor. "I can't be a hundred percent sure, but I'm guessing the only people who will shed a tear for me are the ones watching from those cameras."

I frown, gaze flitting to the dummy speaker above his head. "What people?"

"Oh, did I forget to tell you? Those camera feeds don't just stream to your phone. They stream to mine, too, and a couple of other people's. Oh, and maybe a laptop or two that may or may not be pushing the footage onto the internet. I guess I forgot to mention it."

Beatrix scoots closer to where I am on my knees. With my

free arm, I shove her behind me. "Mommy, what cameras?" she says in my ear.

Sebastian gestures to them—the clock, the speaker, the plastic fire alarm. "One, two, three. Wave for the camera, kid."

All this time, he's had access to the cameras. All these months, he's been watching me, my children, our family, like some creepy, clandestine version of Big Brother.

I stare at him in shock, in horror. "You've been *spying* on us?"

"Don't look so disgusted. I closed my eyes to your and Cam's, uh, alone time. I didn't watch because hell, good on you. Married all these years and still getting it on, bravo for you two lovebirds. But I'm no Peeping Tom. That's not what any of this is about."

"What's it about, then?"

"I just told you. Those three cameras have been uploading today's action—and hoo boy, has there been some action— to the internet."

"Why, so there's video of you killing us?"

The bastard rolls his eyes. "Hello. Who's the one holding the weapon?"

"You still have a switchblade."

"I also have a bullet in my shoulder, which hurts like a mother, by the way. And judging from the volume of those sirens outside, cops are about to bust through the front door and storm up here in—" he points a gloved finger to the ceiling, listening "—what do you think—two, three minutes tops? That doesn't give us much time."

"Time for *what*?"

"Time for your darling husband to get here with my money. Time for me to take it and disappear into the night."

"That doesn't make any sense! You just told me there are people watching, which means they'll know who you are.

Cam and I know who you are. All of us can pick you out of a lineup."

He winces. "Yeah, I'm not going to lie, the pulling-off-the-mask bit wasn't exactly part of the plan, but we've already determined I am a desperate, desperate man. I can't let my baby girl die, Jade. Her death is not an option."

A tiny pang beats behind my breastbone.

Understanding.

Sympathy.

As much as I hate Sebastian, as much as I hate what he's done to me and my family, I feel sorry for the father who's about to lose his daughter. I feel sorrow for Gigi's illness, for having to live however many days she's got left with the knowledge of what her father did—for *her*.

Focus, Jade. This man doesn't deserve your compassion.

I spot a roll of duct tape on the floor by the windows.

"Get up." Without taking my aim off him, I push to a stand and shuffle Beatrix and me that way. "Stand up and move to the chair. *Slowly*."

"I hear it's hard to get blood out of such fine Italian leather. That doesn't seem like a very good plan."

"Get *up*." I kick the roll closer with a foot, then poke the gun in his direction, aiming it at his face. "I mean it, Sebastian. Get on the chair."

"No."

"What do you mean, no? I'm the one holding the gun, remember? Now's not the time to negotiate."

He gives a blithe shrug. "So shoot me."

"What about your daughter? How is me shooting you going to get her new lungs?"

"Nothing is a guarantee, Jade. I've thought through every possibility of how to save my girl, and none of them is a sure bet."

"What about your cousin Tanya? Couldn't she help?"

A momentary flash of surprise—that I've done the math, that I've connected the dots—before his brows dip back into a frown. "That asshole ex of hers, Thomas, he's a litigator. Her divorce agreement barely covers enough to feed and clothe the kids and mortgage payments, on a house he still owns. Tanya doesn't have any money. She's as broke as you and Cam."

"What are you talking about? Cam's not broke. He owns five restaurants. Successful ones."

"Oh come on. You don't still believe in that fairy tale, do you? His investors own the restaurants. He owes them more than he can pay."

"But Cam just told you he has the money. He'll be here with it any minute."

"Sure, but we've already established your husband is a liar."

"He wouldn't lie about something that important."

"Oh no? Did he tell you he pulled out of the Oakhurst deal because he's broke? No—not just broke. Your husband is in hock up to his eyeballs."

I shake my head, a jerky back-and-forth that's overly force-ful. "That's…that's not true."

It *might* be true. Cam just told Sebastian that his shops were bleeding cash, and I'd have to be blind not to have noticed how about a year ago, Cam started wincing at the first ques-tion about work. How overnight, he sprouted frown lines and gray hair, how once frequent invitations from his inves-tors suddenly dried up.

But come on. Money problems? Not with this house, two kids in private school, a daughter under the tutelage of the most sought-after violin teacher in the city. Not with what we spend on cars and clothes and vacations. This past March, when I lost the tennis bracelet and matching earrings Cam gave me one Christmas, he gave me a new set without complaint. Why would he do that if he's short on cash?

Sebastian draws an *X* with a finger on his chest. "Swear to God. Not unless Cam's suddenly won the lottery and even then, the buzzards would have picked his winnings clean. His creditors aren't the type to play around."

Still, it makes no sense. If Sebastian knew there was no possibility of him walking out of here with the cash he needed for his daughter, why put us through all of this? Why risk his own life, his *freedom*, for a mission impossible?

I don't understand any of it.

A pounding shakes the level beneath us, a boom of a boot against wood, and I know instinctively it's not Cam. Cam has a key. He wouldn't need to bust through his own front door.

The police.

Their sirens swirl loud and steady in the falling dusk just outside, and my gaze goes to the front of the house, to the stretch of solid wall bordering the hallway, through the wood and plaster and stone, down the hill to the painted brick two-story home across the street.

Baxter.

His name whispers through my brain, a siren's song tugging me to him, a gravitational pull between me and my son. I don't care about Sebastian, bleeding onto my wall. I don't care about tying him down or shooting him in the face or taking out both his kneecaps. I don't even care if he gets away. I can only think of one thing.

I drop the tape to the floor and grab my daughter's hand.

JADE

7:09 p.m.

Beatrix and I race down the stairs to the main floor, cloaked in shadow because nobody thought to turn on the lights.

It's a way I know by heart, and I'm navigating the dim space when I run smack into a body, a head-on collision with the human wall at the bottom of the stairs.

Two massive men, big and solid like bouncers, their bodies blocking the way like giant boulders. I ricochet off their thick chests, and then I clutch Beatrix to me and scream.

"Don't shoot," one of them says, holding up his hands. "We're the good guys."

"Friends of Cam," the other adds.

Cam. At the name, my heart and lungs unclench, but not my finger on the trigger. I don't know all of Cam's friends, but I definitely don't know these men. I might still need the gun.

"Where is he? Where's Cam?"

"He's meeting us at the car."

There's a breath or two where I almost believe them, these two strange men who are motioning for me to follow them into the night just because they claim to be friends of Cam. Behind them, at the back of the house, the floor looks like a sky of stars, glass shards glittering in the glow of the outside lights.

It's not the front doors they just busted through. It's the back.

And why the back? The police are almost here, and they'll be coming through the front. Why not throw open the doors and meet them outside?

I'm also wondering what happened to the alarm, why it's not wailing. Or maybe it is, and I'm just not hearing it over all the other noise—the crunch of glass, the approaching police, the blood pounding like Niagara Falls in my ears.

Beatrix twists around, her expression strangely calm as she stares out the front windows. The lawn is lit up like a laser show, swooping white arcs in a disco of red and blue. Police cars careening up the drive.

The two men bolt for the back.

"Let's go," one of them calls over his shoulder. "We gotta hustle."

"Tell Cam we're going for Baxter."

I turn into a sudden light, white and blinding. Two giant spotlights pressed into the front-door glass, twin suns that ignite our skin, surrounding us with light brighter than day. Beatrix shades her eyes with an arm, but I just close mine. My hands are filled with the gun and a fistful of my daughter, and no way in hell I'm letting either of them go, even though I am all too aware of the danger. A loaded weapon, an obvious threat. I hold it in a loose fist by my side.

Shouts bombard us through the doors.

Open the door!

Police!

GUN.

Freeze don't move don't move.

The windows on the front door explode, a hailstorm of glass shattering on the foyer tiles, skipping across the marble to the hardwood. I open my eyes at a sound I know instinctively, a hand reaching inside to flip the dead bolt. Big black silhouettes stomp inside, crowding around us, barking questions. One of them pries the gun from my fingers.

Ma'am, are you okay?

Is your daughter hurt?

Is either one of you injured?

I reach for the first officer I see. "My son. He's in the house across the street. He's in danger."

JADE

Beatrix and I stand on Tanya's front lawn, shoulder to shoulder with a female cop whose orders were to tackle me if I moved. I wanted to go in, of course I did. I told them I knew the layout of the house, could point out the rooms where Baxter might be, but the cops wouldn't hear of it, so here I stand, stiff with terror, staring at Tanya's front door and praying.

That Baxter is inside.

That he's alive.

That Tanya hasn't hurt a hair on his body.

"What's taking so long?" Beatrix says. "Why can't they find him?"

I clutch her hand and try not to scream. I don't think Tanya would hurt Bax or kidnap him, but what do I know? I've been wrong, so wrong about her. I stare at the house and think surely it can't be much longer.

A dog barks in the not-so-far distance, the deep, animated

chuffs of a very large, very angry animal, and I picture Sebastian running up on it in a neighbor's backyard. I'm sure he's made a run for it by now, and I can't drum up an ounce of concern that he might have escaped the police. They'll catch up to him soon enough, and right now I can only think of one thing. I stare at the jagged line of Tanya's rooftop rising into the darkening sky, and my heart twists into a painful knot.

"Jade." The voice comes from behind us, and I whirl around to spot Cam dodging police cars as he sprints down the hill.

"Daddy!" Beatrix wrenches her hand from mine and takes off across the grass, racing to meet her father halfway. Their feet hit the asphalt of Club Drive at the same time, and she takes a flying leap that lands her in Cam's arms. They close around her in an instant.

"Oh my God. Oh my *God*. You're okay." Cam cradles Beatrix to his chest, and I go mushy with relief, with joy. "Thank God, you're okay."

"I shot him, Daddy. I shot the bad man."

"I know, baby cakes, and it almost gave me a heart attack. Please don't ever do that again. My old heart can't take it." His gaze searches out mine like a heat-seeking missile. "Let's go see Mommy."

But I'm already almost there, jogging across the lawn, calling to him across the driveway. "I gave him to Tanya, Cam. I didn't know."

"Didn't know what?" He stops at the edge of the grass, taking me in, his brow crumpling. "Oh, babe, your face. I'm so sorry he did that to you." He reaches out a hand, stops just short of touching my broken cheek with his palm. "I'm sorry for a lot of things."

I shake my head, tears smearing my vision because now is not the time for apologies. I need Cam to hear me. I need him to understand.

I clamp my fingers around his forearm, the one wrapped around Beatrix's back, and give it a good shake. "Tanya is Sebastian's cousin. She has Baxter."

Understanding flashes on Cam's face, and from deep in the house come shouts. A child's scream. A deeper voice barking orders. With a jolt, he shoves Beatrix in my arms and takes off at full sprint for the door.

The police officer isn't fast enough to stop him, but she stops me, pulling me back by an arm.

Her grip is like a vise on my wrist. "Wait. Wait until it's safe."

But when will that be?

I clutch Beatrix tight and think of my sweet, funny baby boy, picturing him safe on Tanya's couch, blissed out with a belly full of pizza. I think of what I'll do if that's the case, all the sacrifices I will make to repay the universe. I'll see to it that that vile man's daughter gets her lungs. I'll donate my house, my jewels, my car if I have to. I'll do *anything*.

"If you really want to quit violin, you can, you know." I press a kiss into my daughter's hair. "I'm sorry I pushed you so hard."

All my prodding for Beatrix to log her practice hours, my tiger-mom tendencies and inflated expectations for her future, my pushing her into auditions or the spotlight whenever my friends came around. I told myself it was because as her parent, I was responsible for ensuring she honors this magnificent gift she's been given by God, by the universe. But maybe her perfectionist tendencies come from me, in an effort to please *me*.

Which can mean only one thing.

Beatrix is not the one who needs to change.

I am.

I make a silent vow: no more dragging her across town to lessons three times a week. No more hiding the remote because it's practice time or dismissing her tears because she's sacrificing yet another social event for the violin. No more bandaging calluses and bloody fingers—not unless she chooses to put them there herself. From now on, whenever Beatrix tells me she wants to quit, I will shower her with kisses and tell her it's up to her. I will hand her the controls, allow her to dictate the contents of her own life. My daughter can be anything she wants to be. Who am I to decide?

Slowly, she shakes her head against my shoulder.

"Seriously, Bea. You can play piano or softball or take art lessons, or you can lie on the couch and do nothing at all. This is *your* life, not mine. You get to decide how to fill it."

"But I don't want to quit. Not until I get the Locatelli, and even then." She shakes her head again, and her voice is quiet but resolute. "I don't want to quit."

"Then why did you say you wanted to?"

She leans back just enough to give me a sheepish grin. "My legs were tired. At least with the piano you get to sit down."

Miss Juliet's schoolmarm voice barks in my mind. *Back straight. Spine aligned. Head up. Violin begins with good posture, always.* Most parents want their children to grow up. Cam and I should have spent more time coaxing Beatrix to grow down.

I drop a kiss on her nose. "You are my hero, do you know that? What you did this afternoon was so brave, and I am so unbelievably proud to be your mother."

She wraps her arms around my neck and squeezes, her curls tickling my ear. "Did Daddy really do that to the bad man's daughter?"

My mind stutters back to Cam's coerced confession, the heartlessness and money problems Sebastian dragged into the daylight, offenses that sometime in the past ten minutes I've already forgiven. There's nothing like watching your firstborn daughter wielding a gun to illuminate the things that matter. Cam. The Bees. I can get past anything but losing one of them.

"I don't know, baby. Maybe. But none of it matters without Bax. Let's get him back first, and then we'll think about how we fix our family."

And I will fix this family. No matter what happens next, Cam and I will claw back the power Sebastian took from us when he stepped out of the shadows and forced his way into our home. Some things are impossible to put behind you, but this will not be one of them. If it's the last thing I do, I will fix us.

Suddenly, there's commotion at the front door. A cluster of bodies emerging, big and small. Tanya's kids, the Montgomery twins from down the street, Cam with a Baxter-sized body balanced on an arm. My heart stops, and I squint into the darkness, unable to move.

And then a small voice, soft and scratchy and as familiar as my own pulse, the most beautiful sound in the world: "Whoa. How come there are so many cops?"

SEBASTIAN

Ten Minutes Earlier

No money. A bullet in my shoulder. The whole house shaking from the cops busting in downstairs. This wasn't exactly how I planned for things to go.

And all because of that sneaky little Beatrix, wriggling out of her bindings not once, but two times. She looked so cute when I fixed them a snack. An adorable little Houdini in a pink polka-dot shirt. It's why I underestimated her, because she reminded me so much of my Gigi.

I shove my aching body to a stand, wincing at the sharp stab in my shoulder. Beatrix's bullet ripped through muscles and tendons, I can tell, maybe nipped at a bone, but at least it missed my heart, and it shot all the way through. I know from the heavy wetness on the back of my shirt, the red smear I leave on the wall. The drips that fall from my elbow to the fancy carpet as I limp to the side table and my phone.

The screen is lit up with a million messages—no surprise

there. Tanya and my sister, Hannah, blowing up my phone, the back-to-back calls and messages practically vibrating it off the table where I dumped it next to the gun. I ignore their messages and fire off a text to Hannah.

Send the link to tonight's video to Juanita Moore, her card is on the fridge. Do it now, quick, before the cops arrive. People are either going to hate me for what I did, or they'll understand. I'm counting on you to make sure enough fall in the second category to help Gigi. Love on her for me, sis. Take care of my baby girl. I love you.

I turn the phone off and toss it to the floor.

Dethroning Atlanta's Steak King. I can't deny it is sweet, sweet revenge. With any luck the whole world will see how their favorite celebrity chef screwed a poor, single father out of the money he needed for his dying daughter. Now every-body will know that's the kind of person Cam is, a man who values money and power above all else. Talk about going out in a blaze of glory.

It's funny. When Tanya called to say that none other than Cam Lasky had moved in across the street, I couldn't believe my stupid luck. Keep your friends close and your enemies closer, isn't that what they say? I told her to play dumb. I told her to ingratiate herself with his pretty wife, to make herself necessary in their lives, to keep her mouth closed while my brain stitched together this plan.

The other big surprise? That Cam was strapped for cash. He didn't tell me that part when he pulled out of our deal, just that he had "other business matters that needed his full attention." I didn't find out he was dead broke until I sued him for damages, for funds his attorneys told mine he didn't have. By then my money was long gone, cash I'd set aside for Gigi's care but Cam assured me was a safe investment in him.

I turn to the dummy speaker, step right up to it and smile.

"This isn't the way I wanted today to end, baby girl, I want you to know that. Maybe one day, after you get your lungs and a baby boy or girl of your own, you'll find some understanding in that big heart of yours. But before you do any of that, take a little peek under the bread in the freezer, will you? I love you, Gigi. So much. Never forget that."

I blow a kiss at the camera and turn away.

I didn't come all this way without a backup plan, and a backup to the backup to the backup. Like I'm always telling Gigi, she's getting those lungs if it's the last thing I do. It's time to pull the parachute cord.

I figured if anybody could pull together the ransom money, it would be Cam. Even deep in debt, that man knows every martini-swilling, tweed-wearing, steak-overpaying asshole in town. Surely he could sweet-talk some of them into loaning him some cash.

And who knows? Maybe he did, and maybe he didn't. I won't believe it until I see that promised bag of cash, until I can count out the bills.

Jade was a surprise, though—not the money-loving Buckhead Betty I originally thought. The way she kept throwing herself in front of her kids. That move downstairs with the screwdriver, how she was constantly risking her life in order to save theirs. That kind of love is a beautiful, beautiful thing.

I think of my Gigi at home, coughing up mucus into a cup. No more pain. No more money problems. No more constant worry about her fate.

Heavy boots clomp on the stairs, and I press myself to the wall, pulling out the switchblade in my pocket, flicking it open and holding it high in my good fist. The blade reflects a glint of white ceiling light that blinds me to everything else. The pain in my shoulder as I lunge for the cluster of cops filing through the door, the shouted warnings right before the blade sinks into someone's skin, shots ringing out like a string of firecrackers. Everything but my baby's sweet smile.

"Hi, Daddy," she says as she reaches for my hand.

My freedom for Gigi's lungs. My life for hers. I'm more than willing to make the trade.

THE INTERVIEW

Juanita: The nanny cam footage went viral the second it hit the internet.

Cam: Yeah, for all their tough talk about cracking down on violent content, the social media platforms sure do a bang-up job, don't they?

Juanita: Most people would agree they failed pretty spectacularly. One tweet led to a couple dozen, which led to hundreds more, crossing over onto Facebook and Instagram and You-Tube. Sebastian and his two accomplices, his sister, Hannah, and your neighbor Tanya Lloyd, certainly didn't anticipate things taking off that fast. The police traced the feed to your home. They got there in the nick of time.

Cam: Well, that's debatable. Jade and Beatrix were already

downstairs when they busted through the door. They'd already gotten away from Sebastian, but the police killed him anyway.

Juanita: Because he attacked one of the officers with a knife. She was in the ICU for days. She almost died.

Cam: Yes, but why couldn't they have just tackled Sebastian to the ground? Did they have to kill him?

Juanita: Yes, because again, he attacked an officer of the law.

Cam: Sure, but he did it because he was out of options. Not just broke but buried in debt, and unable to get treatment for his dying child. So you tell me. What else was he supposed to do?

Juanita: I don't know. Certainly not hold a mother and two small children for ransom. Certainly not break a woman's cheek.

Cam: Still. There's something inherently wrong with a system that would allow a girl to die simply because her father can't afford drugs that every other Western country would have given her for free. Every single societal safeguard that was meant to catch Sebastian failed. Every single one of his options was snatched away.

Juanita: [sitting back in chair] Sebastian held your family at gunpoint. He tied them to a chair and threatened their lives. He physically hurt your wife and traumatized your children, all because he carried so much hatred for you. Because he wanted revenge.

Cam: I know, and I think about those things a lot. There's not a day that goes by that I don't get flashes of Jade's mangled face or Beatrix waving around that gun. I have to relive those awful moments knowing they happened because of me, because of things *I* did. But at the end of the day, I keep coming back to the fact that Sebastian acted not for himself, but for a child. *His* child. The one he loved the same way I love Beatrix and Baxter, with every inch of my heart. I don't know, Juanita, the answers don't feel so black-and-white.

Juanita: You make it sound like you've forgiven him.

Cam: I don't know about forgiveness exactly. Some pity and regret. Actually, scratch that. *Lots* of regret for what I did.

Juanita: But in the end, Sebastian got what he wanted. Gigi Long didn't die. Thanks to those videos, people flooded Go-FundMe campaigns with money. Hospitals and doctors stepped up with free medical care. Gigi got her lungs. Her doctors say she's on track for a full recovery.

Cam: [scoffs] No thanks to Sebastian's life insurance company, who refused to pay her a penny.

Juanita: Because he looked into a camera and announced to the entire world what he was about to do. He told his daughter where to find the insurance papers, and then he threatened police officers knowing they would retaliate. Life insurance policies carry an exclusion for suicide.

Cam: When you push a man to the edge of a cliff, you can't get pissy when he jumps.

Juanita: Are you implying the insurance company made the wrong decision, that they should have honored Sebastian's policy?

Cam: Yes, that's exactly what I'm saying. Suicide by cop is not a thing. Or at least it shouldn't be.

Juanita: Or maybe you just have a bone to pick with insurance companies, seeing as yours didn't pay out, either. Not after you confessed to insurance fraud and—

Cam: *Attempted* insurance fraud. My attorney was able to talk down the charges.

Juanita: Because you also confessed to arson in the first degree. You got six and a half years.

Cam: And I deserved them. But for the record, I confessed to Jade first. I told her everything, and I mean everything, before I went to the police. There are no more secrets between me and Jade. Nothing's stayed buried. She knows every single thing.

Juanita: Does she know what happened to the missing $49,000?

Cam: I already told you. It was in my truck, and then it wasn't.

Juanita: Yes, but if that's really the case, why would she tell me to look into it? What do you think she meant by that?

Cam: I don't know. You'd have to ask Jade.

Juanita: She wouldn't tell me, either. But I did do a little digging. I took another look at the GoFundMe campaigns, and do you know what I found?

Cam: [doesn't respond]

Juanita: I found a donation of $49,514.27 made in late August. Three weeks almost to the day after Sebastian forced his way into your home, after the same amount disappeared from your truck. The donation was anonymous. There was no name attached.

Cam: I know what *anonymous* means, Juanita.

Juanita: I just think it's strange, don't you?

Cam: It is quite the coincidence.

Juanita: A gift like that, though…if people found out you were behind it, that would go a long way to improving your public standing.

Cam: I already told you. Scrubbing my image is not why I'm here.

Juanita: And Jade?

Cam: What about her?

Juanita: Is it possible that maybe she wanted me to discover the donation? So that people might look a little more kindly on you?

Cam: [doesn't respond]

Juanita: Come on, Cam. I thought you were here to set the record straight.

Cam: I am. I did. I confessed my crimes in front of a judge and now your cameras. I'm paying for them with six and a half long years of my life. Years where I'm missing out on violin concertos and soccer games and birthdays and anniversary dinners and a million other important moments.

Juanita: Okay, different question then. Do you think Jade has forgiven you?

Cam: It's a lot to forgive.

Juanita: When I spoke to her last week, I asked her the same question. I asked if she forgave you.

Cam: And?

[Door opens, male voice from off camera]: Sorry, Ms. Moore, but time's up. I'm going to have to ask you to wrap it up.

Juanita: I just have one last question. Please, may I ask it?

Man: Okay, but make it quick.

Juanita: But what about all the people watching? People who've been following your story since the moment it began, the afternoon of August 6. They want to know where things stand between you and Jade. What should I tell them? Are you still a couple?

Man: By my count that's three. [approaches desk] All right, Cam. You know the drill.

Juanita: What do I tell them, Cam?

Cam: Here's an idea. [stands, offers wrists to guard] Tell them to do what they've been doing all along, to use their imagination.

★ ★ ★ ★ ★

ACKNOWLEDGMENTS

My Darling Husband is a work of fiction, but like all fiction, it's a story rooted in truth. I live in Atlanta, a city with its fair share of violent crime. Home invasions occur here often enough it's almost easy to become numb to them…until one day it happened to people I know. Their story began much like Jade's: an armed stranger confronting the mother and children in the garage and forcing his way inside. The ransom he demanded was an odd amount, a number he'd gotten from a bank statement pilfered from their mailbox. That family survived, but their experience got me thinking. What would I have done in that mother's shoes? How far would I go to save my children? My answers formed the basis for Jade's actions in *My Darling Husband*.

Writing her story was a solitary endeavor, but it wouldn't be a book without a team of talented, passionate, dedicated folks to bring it out into the world.

My agent, Nikki Terpilowski, is brilliant at helping me navigate the sometimes choppy waters of this business while always keeping her eye on the horizon. Thanks for being my fiercest advocate and loudest cheerleader. We make a great team.

At Park Row, Laura Brown's editorial guidance was as gentle as it was genius. She's the one who planted the very first seed for this story in my head, then took what I wrote and helped me shape it into a book. I am so grateful for her patience and wisdom, as well as for that of the stellar team at Park Row, including Erika Imranyi, Emer Flounders, Gina Macedo and all the folks working tirelessly behind the scenes. I am so blessed to have found a home there.

So many thanks go to Emily Carpenter for being a fantastic first reader and an even better friend. Emily and our fellow Calamity Dames, Amy Impellizzeri and Kate Moretti, have talked me off many a ledge. I can't wait to hug your necks again. Thanks, too, to Laura Drake, who reads my first crappy attempts and ever so kindly points out where they could use some work, and to Allison Anderson, whose winning bid got her the dubious honor of having a character named after her father, Gordon Howard. Gordon, I hope I did you proud.

And finally, the biggest thanks go to my kids, Evan and Bella, and to my very own darling husband, who in no way resembles Cam Lasky. My world begins and ends with you three.

Also by bestselling author
KIMBERLY BELLE

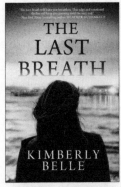

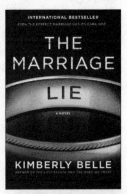

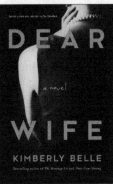

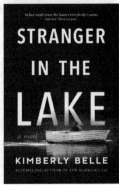

Available now.

Connect with us at:

BookClubbish.com/Newsletter

Instagram.com/BookClubbish

Twitter.com/BookClubbish

Facebook.com/BookClubbish

MIRABooks.com
BookClubbish.com

ParkRowBooks.com
BookClubbish.com

PRKB1156TR